Rise of the Fallen

by
Benjamin Oneal

© 2023 Benjamin Oneal
All Rights Reserved.
No part of this publication may be reproduced, stored in a retrieval system, or transmitted, in any form or by any means, electronic, mechanical, photocopying, recording, or otherwise, without the written permission of the author.
This book is printed on acid-free paper.
First Published by Benjamin Oneal
Anderson, IN
ISBN: 979-8-9858049-3-5
Library of Congress Control Number: 2023902354
This book is a work of fiction. Places, events, and situations in this book are purely fictional and any resemblance to actual persons, living or dead, is coincidental.

I want to thank my wife Huong, for putting up with my long hours at the computer, my children, Lucas, Kimberly, Stacy, and Justin for being often reluctant sounding boards to help me work out problems with my stories, and my three wonderful grandchildren, Aria, Merrick, and Hannah who are responsible for keeping me young.

Special thanks to Autumn J. Conley, who worked her magic, and made me realize how important a good editor can be in bringing a story to life.

Other books by Benjamin Oneal

The Benjamin Kroh Series:
Die Laughing
Die by Proxy
Die by Vengeance
Die by Design

Science Fiction:
The Serpent's Gift

Anthology:
Excretions of an Atypical Mind

The Omega

Gods No More

Benjamin Oneal

Chapter 1

It was the 100th anniversary of the signing of the Galactic Treaty between the New Empire and the Freewill Alliance. Societies throughout the galaxy prepared for the upcoming celebrations. Of course, not all felt the day was meant for jubilee; some were preparing for something quite different. In fact, every being in the galaxy would soon bear witness to the event that would send waves of fear throughout the known universe.

Many citizens had conveniently forgotten the time before the Galactic Treaty, an era when a great darkness ruled the stars. In the years since the treaty was signed, the galaxy had settled into a steady routine of rebuilding, under a freewill doctrine.

The treaty did not ensure peace for all. Life for Archangel Michael on Vapula, a high-security prison planet in the Purgatorian sector, was very difficult indeed. The prison planet was home to only the most dangerous individuals. Michael, along with Gabriel, was doomed to spend the rest of his existence there, struggling to survive. Not a moment passed when scrutinizing eyes were not on them, and they were forbidden with interacting with one another. Each prisoner was required to work ten hours a day, allotted only one hour for exercise, and all remaining hours were spent in the tiny confines of their assigned cell.

Rise of the Fallen

In addition to that, inmates were deprived of the Factor, the life-extending agent discovered by the residents of Eden tens of thousands of years earlier. Since then, the Trees of Life had been introduced to the galaxy and added thousands of years to the life expectancies of those who consumed the wonderful fruit. Only two planets in the galaxy were confirmed to be capable of growing the fruit, Eden and Earth, which made those worlds very important to the galaxy. To be sure, the inmates of Vapula, including Michael and Gabriel, would live significantly shorter lives than others, but, considering the conditions of the prison planet, that might be a blessing.

The environment on Planet Vapula was harsh, to say the least. At the sweltering dawn of each new day, the relative star baked the surface, making the days nearly unbearable. During the summer months, temperatures boiled to as high as 120 degrees, and even darkness offered little relief; nights were hot and muggy, with temperatures never dropping below 90. It was fortunate for the prison population that they mostly remained underground. Their days were filled with hard work in smoldering, steamy conditions, and the foul stench of sweat saturated every breath.

They were tasked with mining impervisium, a very light but strong metal. When combined with aluminum, it created an almost indestructible outer shell for the ships of the new Empire fleet and the Freewill Alliance. Prisoners were only allowed to travel to the surface to unload imports and load the exports, or they could spend their hour of exercise time there when they could withstand the heat. It was a privilege reserved for only the most trusted inmates, and Michael and Gabriel were not among those.

The fallen Archangels tried to make their best of the dire situation. When they were not working, they worked out to energize their bodies and minds. Michael refused to give the guards the pleasure of seeing him falter. Always, he thought of why he was there and all those who had heaped such a cruel fate upon him. While Zabkiel and Sandel were key figures on that list, his central focus was Justin Grant, human excrement that he was. Bitter fantasies about vengeance on Grant was all that had kept Michael going over the last century.

***

Also in the Purgatorian sector, Jesus found his life on Naberus quite different from his life as God on Heaven. Those who once trembled at his feet now saw him as little more than the village idiot. While he had always put on airs that he had great power and ability, it had become quite evident that the only true skill the pretentious, spoiled God possessed was proficiency in being totally taken care of and coddled. He was not equipped for survival on Planet Naberus. Before it was mandated that no harm should come to him, he had suffered abuse almost daily. His tormentors were furious with him, for he had been behind the financial ruin, maiming, and killing of their loved ones. He was the most hated man on Naberus. Only Magdalene and his children showed him anything near leniency, and they didn't even like him that much.

In spite of the strict laws prohibiting his abuse, Jesus was subject to periodic beatings by inmates and prison personnel alike. All of them desired a little payback for the evil he had wrought upon them and their families. He had made countless enemies during his reign as ruler of the Empire, and countless Galactic citizens had died at his hand. Emotions still ran high, even after 100 years. Even those who had chosen to let go of the hatred and go on with their lives were quick to avoid him or treat him as nothing more than the town drunk.

Because he refused to take care of himself, and without the ability to ingest the Factor, his health began to fail. Unlike the other residents of Naberus, who accepted their fate, Jesus neglected his own physical wellbeing, preferring to wallow in self-pity. He lumbered piteously around Bathim, his new hometown, in tattered clothing, still trying to order others to do his bidding. If, perchance, someone gave in to the temptation to throw something at his uncrowned head, which happened at least once a week, he was quick to call for his invisible guards to have the offender eliminated. He always seemed to be in a half-crazed state. He seemed to suffer from delusions of grandeur, acting as if he were still Lord God of the Empire. He loudly made demands and expected everyone to conduct his wishes, oblivious to the fact that they blatantly ignored him.

Most of the inhabitants of Bathim would have opted to see him dead, but they avoided him to prevent themselves from breaking the law by eliminating him like the scourge he was. Even now, Jesus was protected. They knew if they acted on their desire to exterminate him, they and their kin would suffer greatly, possibly even be put to death. So, for a century, they endured the rants and mindless ravings of the pathetic figure they had once called God.

During the latter years, no one paid their former Lord much attention. Even his family did everything they could to distance themselves from the tattered shell once known as God, and no one felt the slightest bit of sympathy or pity for him. In his ubiquitous state of drunkenness, he roamed the streets and continued to waste away. Although there was a home for him, he was more often found in a waking stupor in the back alley of a bar or lying along some busy city street. His physical condition was desperate, and his mind was a wreck. For the last fifty years or so, Jesus had survived only because the prison guards were given strict instructions to keep him alive.

Chapter 2

On the day the galaxy was to celebrate the anniversary of the fall of the old Empire, two fleets of attack ships hovered in deviant space, awaiting orders. When those orders came, simultaneous attacks were executed, with brilliant precision. The first was launched on Planet Vapula, a high-security prison planet for the most dangerous criminals. Although the incarcerated souls were treated with dignity, they were not free to move about; instead, they were housed in various facilities and monitored day and night.

Agents on Vapula were ready, prepared for their comrades to strike. Right on cue, 100 Imperial ships dropped out of deviant space. First, they disabled the guard ships. Next, they concentrated their efforts on the planetary defenses. The ten ships posted around the planet were no match for the overwhelming power they faced. To their credit, the guards did manage to take out seven of the attackers before they were disabled or destroyed. Nonetheless, powerful, targeted shots against the planet defenses destroyed any chance of retaliation.

Next, ten ships landed on the planet to begin their assault on the ground. The prison planet guards were no match for the Imperial troops, and excellent intel had given the invaders a heads-up on the best places to touch down. Soon the Imperial soldiers controlled the command station. Just one hour after they arrived, they reentered deviant space with the two prisoners they had come to rescue, along with hundreds of others who were sympathetic to their cause.

Archangels Michael and Gabriel were now free, but they were both exhibiting the effects of being deprived of the restorative fruit of the Tree of Life. Along with a few wrinkles, Michael had a scar on the left side of his face, a souvenir from an assassination attempt early in his incarceration. As the years passed, others tried to end his life as well, but only the first attempt had caught him by surprise.

Because of the attack, the prison planet was in chaos, and distress signals were sent. The prisoners outnumbered the guards by thousands; the guards knew if help didn't arrive soon, they would eventually fall as casualties of the mutiny. Backup could not reach them for at least seven hours, so they were on their own until then.

***

As the onslaught on Vapula began, a simultaneous rescue mission was carried out on Planet Naberus. Just as it was on Vapula, 100 ships emerged from deviant space over the minimum-security planet Naberus, attacked the guard ships, and disabled ground defenses. Although Naberus was defended and staffed with power equal to that of Vapula, it was only a Level 1 prison. The inmates there were not necessarily dangerous enemies of the new Empire. It was more of a place of exile than a prison, and most who were there were low-level criminals and their families, along with those who simply chose to follow Jesus. The inhabitants lived in houses, towns, and communities and were granted freedom of movement, as long as they checked in once annually. They had formed their own self-governing society in such an orderly fashion that they were now considered citizens of Naberus, rather than prisoners. The soldiers stationed there functioned more like police than wardens or guards.

There were two absolute restrictions for all who lived on Planet Naberus: First, they were forbidden from traveling off the planet and communicating with anyone off world. The most critical rule, however—and one that weighed heavily on many as the years passed—was that they no longer had access to the Factor. That severely limited their lifespans.

They were free to procreate, albeit with a strict limit of two children per family. As the population grew, Naberus prospered. Life on Naberus was so good, that the citizens no longer thought of themselves as prisoners. This was just as well, since Naberus was never meant to remain a prison planet. It was presumed that in the years that followed, ground presence would continue to diminish, until only a few lonely guard ships remained to patrol the planet.

Their ultimate goal was to someday be granted membership in the Freewill Alliance. Unfortunately for some, acceptance would come only after the first adults to arrive had died. Those hopes and dreams were shattered, though, when the warships dropped out of deviant space, and orchestrated a well-planned surprise attack on this otherwise peaceful prison planet.

Just as on Vapula, agents on Naberus knew about the attack and had prepared the way for rescue. All 100 ships were sent there to rescue just one individual, Lord Jesus himself. He was in much worse shape than Michael, for his century of imprisonment had been far more damning. Had he undertaken even the most basic hygiene and self-care, he might have been able to cope, but the years of neglect had taken its toll.

Finding Jesus was not an easy task for the Angelic soldiers. Most nights, he drank beyond excess and fell into a stupor, blacking out wherever he was. The guards could only keep an eye on him by implanting a tracking device in him the day he arrived. The Lord's saviors finally found him hunched over in a debris-filled alley behind a restaurant, blazed out of his mind from binge drinking. He did his best to lift his head and utter a moan as the soldiers approached.

It did not take them long to realize that finding him was the easy part. Jesus emanated the stink of uncleanliness, and his filthy, unwashed skin only accentuated that. In spite of the nauseating smell, they were forced to touch him. All who knew of him were wise enough to stay upwind of him, but those sent there to fetch him didn't have that option. The guards on Naberus forced him to bathe before his quarterly health checks, but that did little to prevent the stench. Since they were given strict instructions to keep him alive, they had to provide him with medical care and currency to live on. Unfortunately, most of his *per diem* was wasted on drugs and alcohol. Despite their best efforts, the dirt and the aroma always returned within a week or two, much to the disgust of those he encountered.

"Bring me a drink, peasants!" Jesus ordered them, blinking in a crazed way as he struggled to focus on the soldiers.

"Okay, let's go."

They were none too gentle as they picked him up and escorted him out of the garbage heap from whence he came. The unfortunate ones tasked with carrying him were desperate to clean themselves and change their clothes before they returned to duty, because the contagious, putrid odor of the man was soon theirs to share.

"How dare you touch me? I am your God!" Jesus drunkenly declared as he clumsily flailed in vain, trying to get away from them, causing them to reluctantly hold him closer.

A second later, he passed out again, so he was entirely unaware of being hauled to the transport. Soon, he would be on the warship in space above the planet. He regained consciousness just before they carried him aboard.

One of the soldiers gave him a glass of water and tried to explain, "We are here to rescue you, Lord Jesus."

"Rescue me?" Jesus asked, then smirked and belch. "I am the almighty God!

"Yes, milord, I know," the soldier said, humoring him. "Michael and Gabriel are waiting for you."

Jesus smiled at the mention of his Archangels.

Before they put him on the transport, the soldier asked the one question he'd been ordered to ask: "What about your family, milord?"

Jesus blinked twice more, then stared blankly at him for a moment, as if he did not understand the simple inquiry. Finally, he croaked, "Bring them to me."

As they waited for his family to be found and brought to

the transport, the soldiers ordered the townspeople to bathe Jesus. Even then, no one stepped forward to do the dirty deed; they were resentful of their so-called God, to say the least. After some were struck down and others were beaten severely for their insubordination, volunteers were plentiful.

It didn't take long for the Disciples to find their Lord's family. Once word got out about the attack and the search for Jesus, his many kin were quick to gather at the home of his mother, Dilyla. All fifty-plus of them were led to the transport. Jesus had no idea his bloodline had flourished on Naberus, and he was unaware that he was a great-great-grandfather already.

By the time the soldiers delivered the whole of his family to the transport, he was thoroughly cleaned and wearing the finest white linens, restored to the pristine appearance he usually displayed during his reign as God. Although the garments hung loosely on his thin, frail body, the new and improved vision of him in all his former glory gave the gathering crowd a sense of dread, especially since the soldiers seemed to harbor an utter devotion to him. Many in the crowd had slighted and physically assaulted Jesus in one way or another during their time on Naberus, and one angst-laden question lingered in their minds: *Will he remember?*

His family, along with throngs of looky-loos, watched the strange events unfold before them. As unnerving as it was for the majority of them, it was also the most interesting thing they had seen in a very long time. Some realized what was happening and begged to be taken away from Naberus. Whatever happened from that moment forward, they knew they were about to see something they would talk about for the rest of their lives.

As they were about to depart, one of Jesus' Disciples asked again, "Milord, what shall become of your family? Shall they accompany us?"

Jesus peered cruelly at his relatives. "They have done nothing for me here, nor have they found room in their hearts for their Lord God," he slurred. He then paused and donned a menacing smile, then pointed at Magdalene. "Bring her to me."

Two soldiers walked into the crowd, grabbed Jesus' wife, and jerked her toward the transport.

"Thank you, my love!" she squealed, beaming a sheepish smile at him. "You will never regret this decision to take me with you," she cooed, trying to present an air of innocent devotion while looking back at her family without a hint of sorrow over leaving them behind. She longed for the power and lavish lifestyle she once had with Jesus, and she didn't care in the least about the fate of her children or grandchildren.

Jesus held on to the Disciples beside him for balance. As Magdalene stood in front of him, ready to begin her new life among the stars, he withdrew a dagger from the waistband of one of the Disciples and brutally stabbed her in the heart.

Everyone screamed in horror as they watched Magdalene fall at his feet. It was a shock to see their mother, grandmother, or great-grandmother stabbed to death before their very eyes. Parents tried to shield their children's eyes from the mayhem, but it happened so quickly and unexpectedly that they didn't have a chance to do so. Jesus had no regard for anyone's feelings, not for those of the strangers in front of him and not for the whimpers of his own grandchildren. As always, he had no regard for anyone but himself.

Jesus looked up at the shocked assembly and smiled. "Do not mourn the evil harlot. She was unfaithful to your Lord God and deserved far worse punishment and pain than the merciful death she just received." With that, he waved at Dilyla.

Jesus' mother absolutely glowed with pride as she watched her son start his journey back to his rightful place as God. *I never liked that awful Magdalene anyway,* she seethed, with a sneer.

Finally, Jesus turned and, with the help of his Disciples, wobbly disappeared into the transport. "Leave them. Just leave them all," he muttered, right before he passed out. Once the transport reached the warship, the unconscious deity was whooshed into more comfortable quarters.

Soon after the 100 Angelic warships entered deviant space, they set a course to rendezvous with the rest of the Disciple fleet.

Chapter 3

Just as the Freewill Alliance warships arrived at the two prison planets in the Purgatorian system, the once-almighty Angelic fleet gathered around Planet Dellos. While it had once numbered in the thousands, the fleet was now a mere fraction of its former glory. Nevertheless, their desire to rule the galaxy remained strong, almost obsessive. The 700 ships converged as plans for the retaking of the galaxy began to take shape on the planet below.

Dellos, a world well outside the boundaries of the New Empire, was an isolated but beautiful planet that had only recently been colonized by humanoid nomads. They had arrived only 200 years prior, after their exodus from their previous world, which had been ravaged by war.

The colony had just reached its 205-year anniversary when the Resurrectionists arrived. Unfortunately for the Dellosians, the planet they fled to turned out to be the perfect hiding place for the Disciples to plan the rescue of their leaders. The poor souls had barely escaped their home planet, only to be systematically eradicated by the Resurrectionists on Dellos. While they fought a good fight, they were ill-equipped to mount a reasonable resistance against the Angelic soldiers. In the end, their efforts amounted to nothing more than an annoyance. At its prime, the colony boasted 7,000 people; far too quickly, this was reduced to less than 1,500, and those few who did survive become slaves on their own world.

As soon as Jesus landed on Dellos, it was declared the property of the Resurrectionists. For all intents and purposes, Lord Jesus had risen from the dead. As soon as he recovered from his century of self-neglect, he would gleefully reclaim his place as rightful leader of the Empire.

Michael and Gabriel met their Lord's transport and walked beside Jesus, as he was carried to the infirmary. Once they reached the facility, all three received doses of the Factor, a luxury they had not enjoyed for a century. That, along with the best medical care the Resurrectionist had to offer, would significantly aid in their recovery.

Unlike Jesus, the Archangels had strived to stay in the best physical condition they could on their prison planet of Vapula. Conditions were harsh there, to put it lightly, and the guards had worked them hard, but through their determination and extreme willpower, they had remained rather fit. For that reason, they were released from rehab in only two weeks.

On the contrary, Jesus' recovery required an extended stay. He spent the next six months regaining his physical health, but his mental state was a different matter. It took almost a year for his doctors to transition him from a raving madman into the proper mindset of a Lord. Daily sessions with the Illuminator helped to ease and repair his mind, and that sent him well on his way to becoming the Jesus he was before he was exiled to Naberus. Of course, he was still a spoiled, power-hungry adolescent, too eager to order the deaths of anyone he felt deserved his wrath. Wise to his whims and his demented schemes, the doctors, nurses, and orderlies were merely switched out rather than being unjustifiably executed.

Chapter 4

Justin Grant, New Earth Chief Counsel, sat at his desk, wringing his hands. News of the prison breaks had smacked him with the force of an uppercut to the jaw. After so many years living in peace, he knew it could only mean one thing: *Evil is loose in the galaxy once again.*

Like so many others, Justin was guilty of living with an out-of-sight-out-of-mind mentality. Naïvely, he had not thought about Jesus, Michael, or Gabriel in a very long time. *Why should I have?* he reasoned, trying to console himself. *We've been free of the evil Empire for 100 years.* While the news of the escape of the evil dictator bothered him greatly, Michael's escape really scared the living shit out of him. Jesus was totally deranged, but the Archangel was a powerful, vengeful, stone-cold psychopath.

Justin stared at the screen in front of him as he video-conferenced with Sandel, leader of the Freewill Alliance, and Zabkiel, God of the New Empire. It was the general consensus that Jesus would not go gently into the good night. Although no one could predict precisely when and how it would occur, there was no doubt in anyone's mind that big trouble was on the way.

"We must step up security in…well, everywhere," Zabkiel offered.

"You are right about that," Sandel agreed.

"We know they will strike, but we've no idea when, where or how. Any thoughts?" Justin nervously asked.

"The most obvious targets are Heaven, Hell, Earth, and Eden. Protecting those must be our top priority. If any of them fall to the Empire, it will be a crushing blow to the galaxy," Sandel offered.

"Right." Justin sighed, then added, "No matter what we plan for, I fear it won't be enough. I don't mind telling you that the implications scare the shit out of me."

"Understood. We know for certain that their fleet consists of at least 400 warships."

"Well, a captured Disciple did reveal the possibility that some enemies of the New Empire and the Alliance are joining forces with the Disciples of Jesus."

"Damn. If that is true, we could have a bigger problem than we realized," Sandel admitted.

"Enemies of the New Empire? Who are we talking about?" Justin asked.

"Well, as you might imagine in regard to such an enormous galaxy, many star systems are not on friendly terms with the Empire or the Alliance. In reality, though, I'm sure not many would be much help to Jesus and his Disciples," Zabkiel explained.

"Who are we most worried about?" Justin asked.

"The Dumah, the Sauroptors, and the Titans, if you ask me." Sandel said confidently.

"Great. A trifecta of the worst of the worst." Zabkiel said clearly incensed.

"War is never pleasant, my friend," Sandel said.

"Right again," Justin conceded before they ended the call.

***

Later that evening, as Justin sat at the dinner table, he told his beloved Salome everything he had learned that day. He certainly did not want to worry her, but he felt she had the right to know. Not only that, but he also hoped to convince her not to travel off world unless it was absolutely necessary. He knew she was often too brave and stubborn for her own good, and he was concerned for her safety.

"I'm sorry, my love, but we are at a critical point on Paradisus and Aurora," Salome informed him. "I need to be there."

"But, Salome—" Justin started.

"But nothing, big boy. As I said, I *need* to be there."

Justin knew her well, and once she had made up her mind, it was futile to try to change it.

She noticed his pouty face, smiled, and offered him the only compromise she could. "I promise to be careful."

Chapter 5

After the Lord Jesus was as close to his former self as possible, it was time to move forward with the attack plan. He sat at the head of the conference table in the most elaborate chair they could find; after all, he was the Lord God. While they brought him up to speed, Jesus felt powerful once again, and it thrilled him to no end to hear everyone acknowledge him as God.

"Michael, when will I have my kingdom back?" he asked matter-of-factly.

"Milord, the New Empire has grown quite strong in the years we have been away. It will not be an easy task," Michael answered.

"But I want my kingdom now!" Jesus said like a petulant child, glaring at him.

"I am afraid that is not possible, milord."

"Why not?" Jesus asked, as if he had just been refused a treasured toy.

"Because we have only 700 ships at our disposal. The New Empire has thousands," Michael said, choosing his words wisely, because he knew Jesus' mind was still fragile.

"Then let's build more ships."

"Milord, it will take too many years to construct the number of vessels required to regain your throne. However, there is...another way." He paused for a moment, fearing his next words might possibly make his Lord go berserk. "If we form alliances with those who dislike the New Empire, we might gain enough power to destroy all our enemies."

Jesus beamed as Michael said, "...power," and "...destroy." With a twinkle in his eye, he said, "Then let us form the needed alliances."

"To that end, milord, we have contacted the Titans and the Dumah, so—"

"What!? Never!" Jesus interrupted.

"But, milord—"

"Michael, you, of all people, should remember the Uranus rebellion. Uranus the first, nearly killed my grandfather Jehovah during that uprising."

"Yes, sire, I recall." Michael's mood soured as he remembered it.

"Then why, in Heaven's name, would you even consider collaboration with such a dangerous enemy?"

"Because, without the help of the Titans and the Dumah, I fear there is no way we can possibly retake Heaven, at least not for hundreds of years, maybe thousands. My heart cries out for you to be on the throne much sooner than that, milord."

The Archangel's remarks hit Jesus where it hurt. The thought of not ruling the galaxy for the next 1,000 years or more sent a shiver through his soul. After a moment, Jesus composed himself and asked, "If—and I mean *if*—I decide to join forces with Cronus, can we trust him?"

"That, I cannot say, dear Lord. From what I gather, he is happy with his piece of the galaxy and only seeks better relations with the Empire. What I can swear to you is that I will kill him myself if I see even a hint that he wishes to betray you."

"Very well. I will meet with him to discuss terms of our alliance. If I decide to join forces with the Titans, do we still need the Dumah?"

"I believe we do, Lord. They are excellent foot soldiers.

They will fight to the death and sacrifice as many of their kind as necessary. They desperately wish to expand their territory, so their only desire is the acquisition of new planets to inhabit. We can offer them that."

Jesus nodded. He knew the Dumah were always loyal to whatever cause they were fighting for. *We can put their suicidal tendencies to work for us,* he thought, knowing that, in the end, there might not be enough survivors to worry about.

"Once we regain control of Heaven and you are on the throne, we can wipe out all the vile creatures that remain. If need be, we can also destroy the Titans." Michael said with a sly smile.

"I like the way you think, Michael," Jesus said, wearing his own sinister grin.

"I have learned from the best, milord," Michael replied, knowing it was always wise to stroke his leader's overinflated ego.

Michael was relieved to see that Jesus had mellowed a little. Still, the temperamental Lord would fall back into his old ways very quickly, so he had to tread lightly every time they spoke. Forward thinking and very strategic in their own right, Archangels Michael and Gabriel had made contact with the Titans and the Dumah during Jesus' recovery from his incarceration on Naberus. They were already prepared, but they knew they had to make Jesus think the brilliant idea was his and that they had his permission to execute their plan.

"I am sure they are ready and willing to meet with you at your request. I cannot imagine a single person in this galaxy, who would not jump at the chance, to be in your presence, my Lord."

"You're right of course. Have you secured a safe rendezvous point?"

"Yes, of course. Planet Omael is far enough away from the Resurrectionists' home world. No one will suspect us to meet there."

"This is *not* my home world," Jesus indignantly corrected. "Heaven is."

"Sire, Dellos is..." Michael began, then quickly realized it was unwise to argue with Jesus. "...only temporary. Once we conquer the galaxy again, Heaven will be your home world, and the Empire will be yours to do with as you see fit."

"Very good point, Michael," Jesus agreed. "How is security on and around Omael?"

"Fifty warships are presently protecting the space around the planet, and an additional 100 or more will accompany you there. Ground forces have secured the meeting place and are keeping it under close surveillance."

"Very good. Then I will see them one week from today. We need time to prepare."

"Consider it done, milord," Michael said, then bowed before he left the room.

Chapter 6

Michael left for Titan space the next morning. Many of his crewmembers were unhappy about their newest assignment. Jesus' Disciples had not forgotten the Titan rebellion, and none of them trusted Cronus. Now, they were forced to escort the Archangel to the home world of the very man who had caused all their pain. The story of the Titans was old and tragic, and the hatred they all shared, was great indeed.

Uranus was the leader of a very powerful family on Heaven during the reign of Jehovah. He had dreams of sitting on the throne and leading the galaxy. After losing his bid to become God, he decided to take it by force. Once Uranus gathered the Angels loyal to his family, he led the coup.

Their first act was to try to kill Jehovah himself. An agent who had risen through the ranks and positioned himself as a royal guard made the assassination attempt as Jehovah slept. Fortunately, Elohim, the Lord's newborn son, cried out as the guard was about to strike. Jehovah stirred from his sleep at his child's cry and held the guard captive until help arrived. The failed killer was taken away, but before they were able to interrogate him, he killed himself.

As they dealt with the spy, a force loyal to Uranus attacked the palace, and explosions were widespread. Laser beams cut through the darkness as soldiers from both sides breathed their last. For three days, the battle raged. Uranus was almost successful, but there was one thing he did not count on: the love of the people for their God Jehovah.

Just as things seemed to turn in Uranus' favor, the citizens of Heaven rallied around their God, along with the remaining soldiers. With makeshift weapons they found in their homes and the few they managed to plunder from the fallen Angels, they pushed back the enemy forces.

Once the coup was finally stopped, it was decided that everyone linked to the rebellion would be banished from Heaven. On the day of banishment, over 4,000 were loaded onto ships and transported to the world now known as Titan. All known members of the Uranus family line and all co-conspirators and their relatives were taken to the new world just outside Empire space.

It was decided that the Titans would be left on their own and contacted only after Uranus passed on. Then, and only then, would the Titans be approached to negotiate a possible trade agreement. As the next few thousand years ebbed on, the Titans became the stuff of legends. Stories of them and their evil deeds evolved into the nightmarish, mostly true tales parents told their children to trick them into being good.

Of all the stories they told, the most frightening involved Cronus sacrificing children in rituals. Some even said he ate his own offspring. Whether or not the nasty narratives were true, little ones believed them. Those children grew up fearing possible alliances. To many of the children, Cronus was the embodiment of evil, and remained so well into their adulthood.

***

"Welcome back, Michael," Cronus said, rising to greet him.

"Cronus, Jesus has agreed to the possible union of our forces. He wants to meet one week from today."

"I knew you'd get him to agree."

"It wasn't easy."

"How is his health?"

"Excellent."

"And his mind?"

"It took a while, but he is almost as mentally nimble as before. Also, I'm not sure if the technicians who worked to restore him had anything to do with it, but he seems to have mellowed a little."

"That is a very good thing. I am not so sure I could tolerate his childish tantrums."

"You must be cautious at the meeting, Cronus. Jesus is delicate and must be handled carefully. Treat him as the God he believes himself to be, and you should fare well."

"Why should I pander to a spoiled child?"

"If you want to continue this alliance, you must do as I say."

"Very well," Cronus said with a sigh. "I will make every effort to accommodate his holiness." He smiled, but there was no humor in it.

"So, the meeting is a go?"

"I believe so. What of the Dumah? Will they be joining us?"

"Yes, as far as I know. Jesus sees the logic in using them. Gabriel is personally inviting them to the meeting. I am sure they will attend, when they hear what we have to offer."

"Vile creatures, those Dumah, but they will fight till the last one dies, as long as their queen commands it. What about the Sauroptors? Are they onboard?"

"They, too, have received promises of expanded territory. Yes, they are ready to join us," Michael assured him. "The day before the meeting, I will communicate the coordinates for the planet where it will take place. Be sure you arrive at exactly the scheduled time. Otherwise, you may be attacked as soon as you enter normal space."

Cronus laughed again. "Yes, I'm well aware that I am not everyone's favorite person. I will arrive promptly."

Chapter 7

While Michael met with Cronus, Gabriel finalized the arrangements with the Dumah. The insect-like species was one of the oldest in the galaxy, but the gap of time that spanned between the Dumah becoming truly sentient and finding the ability to move among the stars was much longer than it was for many others throughout galactic history. They resembled ants, and they all followed the wishes of their queen, even if it meant their deaths. Once, they had moved against the Empire. Jesus' father, Elohim, along with Lucifer, led the fight against them then, and while many Empire ships and Angels were lost, they were ultimately victorious.

When Gabriel and his entourage set down on Insectus—the best possible translation they could find of the Dumah home planet—they were fearful. Gabriel had met with the Dumah twice before, but that made no difference. Insectus was one of the most beautiful blue-green planets in the galaxy, full of lush rainforests and beautiful, blue seas. The average temperature was higher than on most planets, and since there was plenty of plant life, the oxygen level was supreme. Still, Gabriel did not like being there.

The Dumah were quite different from any other lifeforms he had encountered. If nothing else, their caste system made them unique. Every wish of the Dumah queen was carried out by the colony. The drones were much smaller than the rest, and their only function was to fertilize the princess.

Once they performed that task, they soon died. The workers were responsible for cleaning, gathering, building, and piloting the ships that carried them into space. The soldiers were much bigger than their counterparts, with large mandibles that could easily cut a man in half.

The Dumah cared nothing about other lifeforms, and they were happy to eliminate anyone who got in the way of their expansion. The star system they controlled was once full of diverse beings, and the Dumah instinctively knew the importance of maintaining balance in the nature of the worlds they conquered. The lifeforms who did not rise up to challenge the Dumah were left alone, unless they were considered food.

The insect creatures seldom traveled to the surface. They resided in colonies, scurrying through a complex tunnel system that only they could comprehend and navigate. Upon their arrival, Gabriel and his companions were escorted by three Dumah. He assumed two were lowly workers, but the larger one was certainly a soldier. The visiting Archangel felt his insides twist with anxiety, the deeper underground they went. Within seconds, Gabriel was hopelessly lost in the subterranean labyrinth.

Five minutes later, he found himself standing before the Dumah queen. With the help of his universal translator, Gabriel captured most of what she said to him. He made absolutely certain that she understood the time and the coordinates of the upcoming meeting.

"So, you are clear on what we are requesting?" he finished, looking at her curiously.

The thought processes and workings of the Dumah mind were strange indeed. Even the universal translator struggled to make sense of their communications, but, after a moment of staring the Archangel down and making a grotesque clicking noise, the queen gave him her assurance.

"Yes," the translator recited. "What worlds be ours?"

That was followed by more indistinguishable, untranslated clicking.

When Gabriel did not answer immediately, the Queen

seem to reiterate the same indecipherable raspy clicking, and the translator simply asked, "What worlds?"

"Once this is over, there will be hundreds for you to choose from, if not thousands," Gabriel said.

There was more clicking before the translator captured the meaning. "We need more worlds, many worlds," he said.

"If you help us win back the Empire, they will be yours for the taking."

Click...click...rasp...click.

"We be there," the translator finished.

Gabriel was relieved to be on his way back to Dellos. Insectus terrified him, especially the Dumah themselves, and the sooner he could get away from them, the better.

***

Sauroptors were a reptilian species, whose home was the planet Sauros. While they had ancient roots, they had not been around as long as the Dumah. They resembled upright, talking, predatory dinosaurs, and they were savage warriors who lived to conquer. Still, they could not face up to the might of the Empire. That limited their expansion beyond their own star systems, so they were more than happy to join the fight against their oppressors. The representatives of the Resurrectionists contacted their leaders on Dellos and let them know, "The Sauroptors are in, 100 percent."

The Sauroptors originally came from the planet Sauria. A philosophical disagreement forced the Sauroptors to separate from their home world, in allegiance to their desire to conquer. The Saurians were beings of peace. They were not part of the Freewill Alliance, but they did have a limited trade agreement. When the Resurrectionists were seeking allies, they approached Sauria, the home world of the Saurians. Their hope was that they would join their brothers in the fight against the new Empire and the Free Will alliance. The Saurians rejected their request and made it clear that they were not welcome.

In their scans, the Resurrectionists found no signs of ships protecting the planet. For that matter, they spotted no defenses at all. With that in mind, they decided the planet was ripe for the taking. It would be the first real test of their ability to conquer the galaxy. They waited until fifty more ships left deviant space to begin their assault on Sauria.

As their forward guns cut white-hot lines through the darkness of space, aimed at the capital city, their disrupters seemed to be repelled by a force field like none they had ever encountered. After repeated failed attempts, 30 Ressurectionist warships suddenly glowed in a strange shade of blue. Then, just like that, they were gone. The Resurrectionists retreated into deviant space as fast as they could, grateful that their mistake in judgment didn't cost them any more losses.

***

On Planet Omael, one week later, the gathering of the Empire's most dangerous leaders took place. Among them were Cronus, representatives of the Dumah and the Sauroptors, to archangels, and one ex-God.

"Cronus..." Jesus growled, bitterly nostalgic about the time when Uranus, Cronus's father, led a coup against his grandfather. He was still so angry about it that he struggled to say the man's name. "Tell me...What do you hope to gain from this alliance?"

"I only ask for your goodwill, milord. We yearn to be part of your Empire," Cronus said. He was sure he tasted bile in his throat when he referred to Jesus as his Lord.

"And what role do you expect to play in *my* Empire?" Jesus snidely asked.

"Nothing more than I do now, milord. I will continue to rule my worlds, but it will be under the leadership of my God. That said, I will be available if you require my services in support of your galactic Empire at any time."

Jesus looked at Cronus suspiciously for only a moment, till the false praises took hold of his mind. "If that is truly all you require, you will have that and so much more," he said, smiling.

"Thank you, Lord," Cronus said. He bowed slightly but breathed an internal sigh of relief when Jesus moved on.

"And you, Dumah?" Jesus asked. "What do you expect to gain from this alliance?"

One of the Dumah representatives began to hiss and click. "We promised new worlds. Need new worlds."

"If that is what you require, you shall have it," Jesus said with a smile. He wondered if the Dumah were clever enough to realize they were only being used and that they would likely be destroyed once he regained control of the galaxy. Doubting that they could possibly be that intelligent, he finally said, "It seems we have reached an agreement."

Again, the Dumah hissed and clicked.

Finally, Jesus turned to the Sauroptors, a species that actually frightened him. They were large and physically menacing, and the razor-sharp teeth and claws on their hands and feet promised pain. Courtesy of the Illuminator, he had witnessed the lizards tearing through enemies, and he had to stifle the urge to shudder as he thought of it. Finally pulling himself out of the horror, he asked, "And what do you desire?"

Their language consisted of pushing air through a resonance chamber, causing a sort of deep, snoring growl. That, along with a vast array of clicks and hisses, had evolved over millions of years into a very sophisticated form of speech.

Their elegant speech came from the translator, in sharp contrast to their appearance: "We also want more worlds to conquer. This cooperation between the Alliance and the Empire has greatly curtailed our expansion. All we require is access to new areas of the galaxy."

"Very well," Jesus said.

"Please don't mistake our meaning. We do not expect worlds to be given to us. Our desire is to conquer worlds for ourselves."

"Once we regain control of the galaxy, you shall have many new worlds to conquer," Jesus assured the Sauroptors.

The meeting continued for a while longer as all sides detailed what they brought to the alliance and the precise nature of the benefit they represented. Finally, Jesus stood, which was a sign that the meeting was at an end. He opened his arms in a welcoming gesture. "Because of what we have accomplished here today, the new Empire and the Freewill Alliance will fall. The effects of our alliance will soon be felt throughout the galaxy, and soon we will take back what is rightfully mine."

The Sauroptors had one more thing to say, perhaps a bit of a jab at Jesus' attempt to appear superior. "We heard you approached the Saurians and lost a few ships." The two Sauroptor representatives vocalized what could only be assumed to be laughter. "We are the best warriors in the galaxy. Even we would not move against them."

Jesus frowned at the obvious ridicule but outwardly regained his composure. "There is much to think about and plan. Please return to your home worlds, and we will contact you when we are ready to move."

They were still laughing when they left the conference room.

Jesus couldn't believe the impertinence. Furious, he stood, trembling, and turned to Cronus and Michael. "How dare they disrespect me in that manner!? I want them dead... now!"

It was obvious to Michael that Jesus had no more respect for their continued existence than he did for the Dumah, but the Archangel knew there was no way they could defeat the Empire without their help. "Milord, we need them, at least for now," he pleaded.

"I agree. It would be foolish to exclude them from our fight. We cannot go challenge the Empire without them. There will be plenty of time to deal with their insolence later," Cronus assured him, in a more commanding voice than intended.

"Are you suggesting that I deserve to be humiliated, Cronus? Or, perhaps you are just calling me a fool," Jesus growled.

"No, milord! Of course not," Cronus sputtered.

"Just remember, you are here only because I have allowed it. I am your God, and you will treat me as such. I am willing to forgive you for this one error in judgment, since you have been away from Heaven for so long. Consider it a gift, Cronus. Now, you and Michael make sure those creatures make it to their shuttles." With that, still red-faced with wrath, Jesus turned and stormed out of the room.

Cronus squinted, and the hostile expression on his face was homicidal.

Michael caught his arm and held him back. "Let it go, Cronus. It's not worth it," he advised.

"How long do we have to put up with his childish rants?" Cronus asked after Jesus was out of earshot.

"Only until we take Heaven," Michael responded. "Many Disciples have pledged their lives to him, and we need the numbers on our side for now."

"Well, as soon as we are victorious and we stand on Heaven as champions, I will kill him myself," Cronus vowed.

"You intend to murder your own grandson?" Michael asked.

Cronus stared at him in disbelief. "You know?"

"I've known for a while," Michael said. He then repeated, "You would kill your own blood?"

"Don't remind me. If not for his adolescent tantrums, I would be on the throne, and the galaxy would be mine. How could such a beautiful plan be so far off the mark in the end? I placed Dilyla in the perfect position to carry it out, but she lost control too early. I should've corrected the situation then," Cronus lamented. "Now, I am forced to coddle this disease-minded child who sits on a throne that should've been mine long ago!"

Well, that explains a few things. Michael smiled at the thought.

***

Later that evening, as Jesus sat in his chambers, thoughts of the future weighed heavily on his mind. In particular, he could not set aside the disrespect the Sauroptors, and Cronus had displayed against him earlier.

The thought of genocide to eradicate the gross Dumah and the Sauroptors brought another smile to his face. He took secret delight in fantasies of destroying Cronus and the entire Titan home world as his thanks for their help in securing the galaxy once again. "Vengeance is mine, saith the Lord," he mused, then laughed aloud.

Chapter 8

Heaven, Hell, Earth, and Eden employed the most security they possibly could, without leaving the rest of the galaxy entirely unguarded. Over the last 100 years, the New Earth fleet had grown significantly, equipped with state-of-the-art ships. The New Empire, Hell, and New Earth had an open agreement to share all technology, for the betterment of life and defense for all the associated worlds.

Even though the planets of the Long-Life Cooperative were technically part of the Freewill Alliance, that portion of space was protected by New Earth Security, NES. Even though security there was ultimately under Justin Grant's supervision, Stolas Tezalel, once known to Justin as Triple-6Soldier, served as official head of NES. When Justin first met Stolas, he thought very strongly that even though he was from hell, he resembled the Native American actor, Wes Study. When he was young of course. Thanks to the factor, he still did.

Stolas' second-in-command just so happened to be Justin's daughter. There were rumors that Rachel Anh Grant had only been granted the position because of her father, but in reality, she worked her way up through the ranks and earned her place.

"How's it look?" Justin asked.

"We are as ready as we can be, but we could have a

problem," Stolas warned.

"A problem? What kind of problem? Are we protected or not?" Justin asked, a little confused.

"Yes, we are protected, except for—"

"Except for what!?" the panicked Justin interrupted.

"We will be vulnerable if there is an all-out attack," Rachel offered.

"Do you think that's likely?"

"No, but you know what a crazy bastard Jesus is," Stolas said with a frown.

Justin shook his head. "Yes, that's pretty common knowledge."

"It could devastate most of the Disciple fleet, but it might be too much of a temptation for Jesus to avoid, having control of one of the only two planets that can grow the Factor. If he accomplished that, he might be able to position himself again as one of the most powerful people in the galaxy," Rachel added.

In spite of the dire circumstances they faced, Justin couldn't help but feel proud of his daughter and who she had become. He knew her only as Anh, her middle name. It was with great pride that she was named after her grandmother, the first earthling to leave the planet and walk through the stars almost 500 years before. Her Asian features were a spitting image of her grandmother, Anh Marbas, who was originally from Earth. Rachel's grandfather, Jared, met her at a party hosted by Isaac Newton, in 1687.

As they sat in Justin's office, rehashing every scenario they could produce, there was a knock on the door. Justin's niece and personal assistant, Laura, informed him that Zabkiel wanted to talk with him.

Once the room was locked down and shielded, Justin activated the video screen. In the image that appeared there, standing beside Zabkiel, the New Empire leader, was Justin's son, Jared, the ambassador to the New Empire.

"Zabkiel, is everything okay?" Justin asked.

"So far, yes. I just want to catch you up on some things I've learned. I've got Sandel on the other line. Do you mind if I patch him in?"

"What the hell do we need him for?" Justin said with a smirk, just as Sandel's face populated the screen.

"Thanks a lot!" Sandel said, smiling.

"Okay, okay, let's get down to business," Zabkiel admonished.

"Right. Sorry. So...what's going on?" Justin asked.

"We have put the Holy Ghosts to work, looking into the possibility of followers joining Jesus. I think they may have found something, and the news is not good."

"What did they discover?" Justin asked, dreading the answer.

"Well, it seems Archangel Michael was seen in the Titan system." Zabkiel informed them.

"The Titan system?" Justin inquired.

"Yes, the home world of Cronus. Planet Titan was founded by Uranus, after he, his family, and all is co-conspirators were banished from Heaven after their failed coup. I will send you everything we have on Titan and Cronus, as well as other possible cohorts. Suffice it to say, if Cronus plans to join Jesus, it changes the dynamic in a big way. We don't yet know the full strength of the Titan fleet, but it will certainly double what the Disciples have."

"Damn!" Justin sounded frustrated.

"Damn is right." Sandel agreed.

"And there could be others, you say?" Justin asked.

"Did the Ghosts find out anything about the Dumah, Sauroptors, or Turailians?" Sandel asked.

"It is not easy to get close to the Dumah or Sauroptors, as you know, since they are insect and reptilian, respectively. They trust no species but their own. However, that does not mean they won't join a fight against us. It all depends on what they've been promised in exchange for their help." Zabkiel was discouraged.

"On what Jesus is bribing them with, you mean." Sandel added.

"Exactly. On the other hand, the Turailians are more like us. The Ghosts have been watching their home world for quite a while. There is no indication that they have been contacted by anyone connected to Jesus. Then again, it's still too early to say for sure." Zabkiel said.

"We must all keep vigilant watch on the outlying areas of our respective territories, surveilling for any signs of movement. Remember, my friends, our strength is our knowledge. We must share any and all disturbances in our respective sectors, no matter how small, so we may evaluate if they are actually part of a greater plan," Sandel offered.

"Has anyone talked to Lucifer or Elohim to get their take on the situation?" Justin asked.

"Elohim and Lucifer took a group of Angels to look for any sign of Jesus, Michael, and Gabriel," Sandel said. "They only managed to get into a few skirmishes with pirates."

"Are they safe?" Justin asked, a little concerned.

"Probably not, but they're enjoying the shit out of it," Sandel said, laughing. "I think it makes the old farts feel young again."

After the important part of the meeting was over, Zabkiel asked to speak with Rachel privately. "How are you doing, my dear?" he said.

"Very well, milord," she answered.

Zabkiel frowned. "Please be yourself. There's no one else around."

Rachel blushed a little and darted her eyes back and forth, to make sure no one was listening. "I am doing fine, Uncle Zab."

Zabkiel smiled. "Thank you. You don't know how much I love hearing that. How's the family?"

"Everyone is relatively well, considering the current crisis. How is Heaven coping?"

"It's a little tense, to be honest, but I think we're ready for almost anything."

"Please be safe. Let's talk again soon."

"You be safe yourself, my dear. Now, before you go, please let me hear it one more time."

She knew what he wanted and looked over her shoulder to check for eavesdroppers once more. She rolled her eyes, smiled, and said, I love you, Uncle Zab."

The reaction elicited from the Lord God himself was a sweet, comforting smile of his own.

"Please keep me posted on anything you find, and I will relay it to the others," Justin told them.

As they stood near the door saying their goodbyes, Stolas couldn't help having a little fun with Rachel. "Is everything okay with *Uncle Zab*?" he teased.

Rachel elbowed Stolas in the side, causing him to lose his breath. "Serves you right for eavesdropping." Then, as Stolas conversed with Laura, Rachel quickly turned and gave Justin a kiss on the cheek. "I love you, Dad. Tell Mom I will see her soon."

Justin couldn't help but smile fondly as he watched one of his oldest friends and his daughter walk out the door.

Chapter 9

After everyone was gone, Justin studied the research he had on the Dumah and Sauroptors. Although he was leader of a major galactic power, he had never met species so radically different from his own. He remembered Lucifer mentioning the Dumah, and he had meant to learn about his time during that battle.

Even though the Dumah home world was known as Insectus, the actual name was unknown. A clear, absolute translation had never been discovered. From space, Insectus was an incredibly beautiful planet. The blues of the oceans and the green hues of the foliage were breathtaking. Insectus boasted higher average temperatures than those on Earth and other humanoid worlds, and vegetation was abundant.

As Justin witnessed through the Illuminator, there were sure signs of intelligent civilization. Although buildings were visible on the surface, they were rather unattractive and industrial, for functional purposes only, and they were few and far between. The pattern of development was the same over the entire planet. Justin quickly realized that most of their society remained underground. When he witnessed the sensor readings of what lay beneath the surface, he couldn't escape similarities to the ant colonies on Earth. The main function of those buildings was to serve as conduits for the lower realms.

Rise of the Fallen

Justin directed the Illuminator to navigate to the files on the inhabitants, the Dumah. Clearly, the similarities to ants did not stop with their habitat. The Dumah closely mimicked the physical traits of ants, only on a much larger scale. They had six appendages, but they were bipedal. He watched in awe as the Dumah used their four upper arms with the efficient cooperation. Their mandibles reminded Justin of the Jaws of Life rescue equipment once used on Earth to free people who were trapped in the metal wreckage of vehicles; he had no doubt that they were just as powerful as the machines of the past and that they could do as much damage. As he thought about that, he remembered another incredible but terrifying fact he had been taught in his youth: *Ants on Earth can lift at least twenty times their weight. I wonder if the Dumah can...*

Once he had familiarized himself with the Dumah, he moved on to study their battle habits. Through the Illuminator, Justin saw the creatures through Elohim's and Lucifer's eyes, when they fought them thousands of years earlier, in the great war. Their technique for battle was very similar to that of army ants. What seemed like a million Dumah poured out of every ship, as black as ink.

As the Empire fleet neared, the Dumah swarmed around all who dared to cross their path. Justin watched in terror as the insect-like things seemingly swallowed up a battlecruiser with ease. The ship just seemed to disappear into the blackness of space as thousands upon thousands of the insect race covered its exterior surface.

It was hard to say what the Dumah had learned since that battle, but even if nothing had changed, they were a threat. The union of two desperate groups was dangerous, even if they were fighting for very different reasons. Jesus would do anything to regain the galaxy, and the Dumah would do anything to expand. Neither had anything to lose, and both had everything to gain.

His mental visits to the Dumah War scene gave Justin a whole new appreciation for his friends, Elohim and Lucifer. It was refreshing to see them defeat the so-called *immortal* enemies. Still, the smile on his face faded as a new thought invaded his psyche, the thought of Dumah moving across the surface of the Earth, swarming everything in their path and leaving only destruction in their wake. Chills ran through his soul, and he squirmed in his seat, suddenly feeling as if there were insects crawling all over him.

Chapter 10

Justin removed the Illuminator; he really needed a moment to recoup before he moved on to the Sauroptors. *What I really need is a drink,* he thought as he reached into his desk drawer to retrieve his bottle of Hennessy. After what he had just experienced, he wanted to tip up the bottle to his mouth and chug, but he decided he could be a gentleman about it and use a glass instead.

He stared at the glass in his hand for a second and finally took a drink. He welcomed the warmth as he swallowed. It was his preferred drink and the most popular on Hell. After he downed the last of it, he dutifully reached for the Illuminator to resume his research.

As it was with the Dumah, the Sauroptor home world was much warmer than Earth, but the vegetation was also much denser. Justin marveled at the sight of Sauros from space. It looked quite like the blue-green orb that was home to humanity. He was once again appreciative of his wife, as she had reversed much of the ecological destruction of humanity's arrogantly ignorant stewardship of the Earth and restored much of the balance with nature. He was proud of Salome for that, among many other things.

The Sauroptors were once part of a species known as the Saurians. They began their evolution on the planet Sauria, which orbited a star near the galactic core. As they became sentient, two distinct groups emerged. Although they were both of the same genetic line, those who would become the Sauroptors evolved much larger and more physically aggressive than their counterparts. The Saurians, smaller in stature, were higher developed when it came to functions of the mind.

For thousands of years, the two groups lived together on Sauria. Sometime after they began to reach for the stars, the Sauroptors resented being led by the much smaller Saurians, whom they saw as weak. Tension between the two groups escalated to a point when disagreements came frighteningly close to war, and the Sauroptors left Sauria and settled on Planet Sauros in a star system not so very far away, at least not in galactic terms.

Not long after the Sauroptors left, they began to attack surrounding star systems, former trading partners of their home planet. Soon, the Sauroptors grew quite powerful and ruled over fourteen star systems. After they established themselves as a powerful force in the galaxy, the Sauroptors offered the Saurians a place in their growing kingdom, but the Saurians refused to live under their rule.

The Sauroptors found that insulting and declared war on the planet of their origin. At that point, the history of the two groups became a bit murky. All that was known was that the warriors failed to take Sauria and limped back to their world with a fraction of the ships they had sent. Beyond that, there were no other records to rely on.

Many speculated that the Saurians had developed a new, tremendously powerful weapon. Stories passed around by the soldiers on the returning ships claimed the battlecruisers of the Sauroptor fleet began to mysteriously explode, even before they were within striking distance of Sauria. Only when the warrior fleet halted their advance did the unexplained explosions cease.

Whatever happened during the campaign, there was no further evidence of any Sauroptor attack on Sauria or the surrounding star systems. Neighbors did, however, become trading partners, though they lived with an uneasy peace between them. Although the Sauroptors never attempted another conflict with the Saurians, the warriors continued their bid to expand their empire.

Many years after the Saurian War, Elohim and Lucifer contacted both worlds, in an effort to invite them into joining the Empire. Although Sauria declined to join the Empire, they saw great value in signing trade agreements. Sauros, on the other hand, saw the Empire as a threat to their growing sphere of influence and refused any alliance.

The Sauroptors' main problem with the Empire was that they could not expand without encroaching on Empire space. The warriors made several attempts to conquer worlds within Empire borders, only to be defeated every time by the superior might of their opponents. That bit of archived history made it very clear to Justin why the Sauroptors so hated the New Empire.

When he watched them in battle, he saw ruthless, strong killers who were ready, willing, and able to tear their enemies apart with claws that jutted out of the backs of their hands. The lethal lizards could lie back on their tails and rip their opponent's flesh to shreds with clawed feet. Just as he dreaded the Dumah, he cowered at the thought of one day having to confront the Sauroptors in battle. As he understood it, there was no word for *retreat* in their language; they only knew how to advance, to keep pressing forward, no matter the cost.

Benjamin Oneal

Chapter 11

Once he was done learning about the Dumah and the Sauroptors, Justin moved on to the Titans. Cronus and the Titans were of particular interest to Justin. Their names figured into Greek mythology, something he enjoyed studying as a young man. Many years in the past, Uranus was their leader. Then, when they felt the time was right, he and his followers attempted a coup against Elohim's father, Jehovah.

After a short but bloody battle for control, the Titans were defeated. Uranus and his followers were rounded up and charged with treason. At the trial, because of the prodigious number of conspirators, it was decided they should be banished from the Empire, rather than overloading the prisons with them. Justin found it quite humorous that the Titans chose to remove themselves from Heaven, to a nearby star system. There, they could continue in their beliefs, just beyond Heaven's jurisdiction.

The Titans never forgot the sting of being cast out of Heaven, and many believed another coup was afoot. Cronus, now ruler of the increasingly powerful Titan system, had come to power after Uranus died under suspicious circumstances. Many believe Cronus killed his father, simply because Uranus had all but given up on his efforts to overthrow Heaven.

From the Illuminator, Justin got a true visual of Cronus.

He was surprised that the leader of the Titan, looked a lot like Karl Urban, an actor he enjoyed back before he knew there were other beings in the galaxy besides those who lived on Earth. His white hair and white beard did nothing to hide the resemblance. Justin also learned that Cronus ruled over thirty star systems that were just beyond the outer edge of Empire space. Although they maintained a strained trading agreement with Heaven and the Empire, they were still vocal in their belief that they were the rightful heirs to galactic rule.

After Justin was well into his research, he decided to give Zabkiel a call. "How confident are you that the details are correct in the report you gave me about the Titans?" Justin asked the face that loomed large on the video screen in his office. Thanks to the Factor, Zabkiel's features were youthful for a man over 5000 years old.

"To the best of my knowledge, everything is correct. Why? Is something bothering you?" Zabkiel asked.

"No, not really. It's just... Well, something I read in there could very well change the history of Earth." Justin said, as his thoughts moved inward.

"Hmm. I've got the report in front of me now. What's got your panties in such an uproar?"

Zabkiel's question brought Justin back from his thoughts. He laughed. "Don't you mean a twist? It was a surprisingly good malaphor though."

"A mala-what?"

"Never mind. I'll explain later. I'm just wondering about the children of Cronus."

"Okay..." Zabkiel said, trailing off for a moment. While Justin watched, he grabbed a book from a pile on his desk and thumbed through it to find the excerpt he was looking for. "What do you need to know?"

"Does it mention the offspring of Cronus ever living on Earth?" Justin asked.

"According to the full record, sometime after they established Titan as their home world, Cronus feared his children, led by Zeus, would someday rise up against him. So, he banished them from Titan. Since they could no longer return to Heaven, they set off across the galaxy and were lost among the stars. Their names were—"

"Zeus, Hera, Poseidon, Athena, Ares, Demeter, Apollo, Artemis, Hermes, Aphrodite, Hestia, and Hades, right?" Justin interrupted.

"That's right. How do you know? Are they part of your history?"

"Not exactly, but they do turn up in Greek mythology, in stories our ancients told to explain the unexplainable."

"As far as we can tell, Zeus, his siblings, and their followers tried to overthrow their father. Unfortunately for them, they overestimated their support on Titan and severely underestimated the strength of the military there. They were defeated and were forced to flee or be killed.

"Before the attempted coup, they lived on an unknown planet. During that time, they grew quite fond of the inhabitants. That information was obtained when some of those who were part of the attempted coup were captured and tortured. Somehow, they resisted giving their captors the name or location of the planet where they were hiding.

"All that is known about their years on the unknown world was that it was a time of rebuilding and peace. After the failed attempt to overthrow their father, they worried Cronus might find their new home and attack the planet and the inhabitants who'd welcomed them. Not wishing to bring harm upon their benefactors, they left. They haven't been seen or heard from since."

Justin sat in silence for a while. For the second time in his life, a long-held truth was shattered. First, he was shaken when he realized he could not take everything the Bible had to say at face value. Now, the Greek gods and goddesses were real, not just the stuff of urban legends or his childhood fancy. Suddenly, all those hours he spent poring over *The Odyssey* and *The Iliad,* salivating over those heroic and woeful tales, and dreaming about the Romans and the Greeks seemed like a fool's game. He didn't really feel he'd wasted his time, but his fantasies were now mocked by the truth.

As he pondered that, his mind wondered, *How the ancients must have marveled at the seemingly godlike powers Zeus and those around him displayed. If they only knew...*

"Are you okay, Justin?" Zabkiel asked.

"Huh? Oh, yeah. It's funny. Just when I think I've got it all figured out, I find out I'm dead wrong," he replied with a weak smile. "What our world once dismissed as mythology, as fiction or some sort of religious faith, was actually history."

"I know just what you need," Zabkiel said.

"What's that?" Justin asked, leaning toward the screen.

"Leave the gun and take the cannoli," Zabkiel said with a smirk

"What?" Justin asked, confused by the remark for a moment. Then, he smiled and asked, "So Sandel loaned you his copy of *The Godfather,* did he?" Justin asked.

"Soitenly! Whoop, whoop, whoop...nyuk, nyuk, nyuk," Zabkiel said, doing his best Curly Howard impression.

"No, no, no! Not *The Three Stooges* too," Justin said, laughing aloud.

"Seriously, though, just study the information I sent. The more you know about our potential adversaries, the better our chances to stop them."

"Thanks, Zabkiel. Let me know if anything comes up, and I'll do the same. Oh, and another thing..."

"What's that?"

"For your sake and the galaxy's, stop borrowing videos from Sandel!"

Chapter 12

The citizens of Purah 5 could not have anticipated the Resurrectionist attack. Ten ships each from the Disciple and Titan fleets, led by Archangel Michael, dropped out of deviant space with their forward guns at full force, shredding the star-studded vacuum of space with white-hot lines of destructive force. In quick order, Disciple ships targeted the eight communication satellites that orbited the planet.

At the same time, the Titan ships attacked the defense grid, in the hope of destroying any chance of retaliation. Those shots came soon after they entered normal space. The three ships posted around the planet were no match for the overwhelming power they faced, but, to their credit, the Purah 5 guard ships took out three attackers before being destroyed. Finally, the Resurrectionist ships destroyed the trading vessels that were parked above the planet, then concentrated the rest of their firepower on the capital city.

Purah 5 was alone on the outer edge of the New Empire, and all communications were rapidly cut off, eliminating the effectiveness of their desperate cries for help. The Holy Ghosts who were still loyal to Jesus had scouted Purah 5 and five other planets and deemed them ripe for the taking. The success of their Purah 5 mission was a strong indication that they would enjoy continuing and far-reaching victory.

While Michael led the assault on Purah 5, Gabriel focused his troops on Mihr. Three other Disciple captains took Planets Narcariel, Galgaliel, and Aeshma. Jesus just about pissed himself when he jumped for joy as the reports reached Dellos: "All five missions were successful. Victory is ours!"

It would be a week before anyone outside those planets would suspect anything was wrong and days after that before any ships could reach perimeter worlds. By that time, the invaders would be long gone, after they pillaged and looted anything worth the taking: food, technology, women, and every last morsel of the Factor that each planet possessed.

Two months later, five planets on the boundaries of Alliance space were attacked in similar fashion, with the same results. Dagiel, Harahel, Sabrathan, Sorush, and Jefischa all fell, just like the five before them. Some trading ships were spared, however, to be repurposed as spy ships.

***

"How many worlds?" Justin asked.

"Ten thus far," Sandel grimly reported, slumping a bit. "Five in New Empire space and five in Alliance space. They were peaceful worlds and had minimal defenses. In the grand scheme of things, most would have counted them insignificant, but they are no less important to the galaxy."

"Those occupy outer edge of Alliance and Empire space," Zabkiel observed. "The attacks were random, in both timing and location, with no determinable pattern. Neither the Alliance nor the Empire could have possibly anticipated where and when to expect them. After each attack, ships were sent to help push the aggressors back, but they arrived to find no enemy ships, only the devastation left in their wake. It seemed their goal was to attack, take what they could, indiscriminately destroy anything and everything, then retreat."

"Do we at least know *who* attacked?" Justin asked.

"That is not clear. It could've been pirates, but—" Sandel started.

"Jesus?" Justin finished.

"I'm afraid so. There is talk that the invaders referred to themselves as Resurrectionists," Sandel agreed.

"Well, that is consistent with the Bible story of Jesus rising from the dead, his so-called resurrection," Justin offered.

"It seems so. This has Michael written all over it. The attacks were too well coordinated to be pirates," Zabkiel offered. "They were also cowardly, targeting peaceful worlds with lackluster defense. Even pirates have enough sense to avoid indiscriminately destroying possible future targets."

"So why? Why those worlds?" Justin asked, baffled. He sensed that Zabkiel seemed more frazzled than normal but decided not to question him about that.

"My best guess? It was just...a test."

"A test?" Justin parroted, arching a brow in confusion.

"Yes. I believe they chose those relatively helpless worlds because they were safe targets, far from the home worlds of their galactic governments but still very fertile for plunder," Zabkiel continued.

"Some, like Mihr and Sabrathan, will require immediate help if they are to survive," Sandel added.

"Damn! If there is anything we can do, let me know," Justin offered.

"Thanks," Sandel and Zabkiel chorused at the same time.

"My main fear is that this is just the beginning. In fact, I'm sure it is. I would second the motion that it was some kind of test, an experiment and a way to build their confidence. I'm sure we have not seen the last of this heinous behavior," Sandel added.

"Sadly, without any idea of where they will strike next, we cannot concentrate our warships in an effective place. The outer boundary of Empire and Alliance space is too broad. Randomly sending ships here and there would severely weaken the defenses that protect our home worlds. For now, we must just do what we can," Zabkiel said, sounding a bit dejected. He paused, then added sadly, "I have family on Narcariel. I have not heard if they survived the attack."

"I am really sorry to hear that, Zabkiel. If there is anything I can do, even if you just need to talk to someone..." Justin said, then trailed off.

"Thanks. For now, just defend your territory. As you know, the Factor is crucially important to most species. Because of that, New Earth and Eden are the most coveted planets in the galaxy. There is no doubt in my mind that they figure into any scenario involving Jesus."

"We have concentrated our fleets around New Earth and Eden for precisely that reason. Of course, we will do our best to protect the other five systems in the cooperative, but it would be foolish for them to attack those protected planets. Regardless, when it comes to New Earth and Eden, I fear Jesus will not be able to help himself."

Benjamin Oneal

Chapter 13

The Resurrectionists continued their vicious attacks along the border of Alliance and Empire space. There did not seem to be any rhyme or reason to it, but with every planet they overtook, the Resurrectionists became richer and more powerful. To keep the Dumah on the hook, Jesus allowed them to visit a little world called Galizur. The indigenous population was no match for the swarm that moved across their planet.

Along with the warriors who advanced on land, winged creatures swept through the skies, cutting down anything that made the mistake of getting in their path. They were relentless and devastating. No matter how hard the citizens fought or how many Dumah they killed, the insects just kept coming. Their strength was not the result of superior weaponry or intellect; rather, they benefitted from massive numbers. Even though the Dumah suffered thirty-to-one losses in the beginning, they were victorious in the end. The citizens they didn't kill, along with the fallen Dumah, were quickly gathered and stored to be used as food.

As soon as the Dumah warriors secured the world, the workers began terraforming. They were not interested in building above ground, but they quickly booted up their special digging machines. As the monstrous contraptions scooped up dirt, they also lined the walls with a hardening agent that kept them from collapsing. To accommodate the

Dumah, nests were longer than they were deep. Each colony spread out over several miles, so the digging machines remained hard at work for a while. Interestingly enough, each Dumah home ship held two queens, one who was the designated commander and another in stasis, until she could take over rule of the emerging colony on the planet.

"We must be careful of the Dumah. They are single-minded and dangerous," Michael told Ophiel, his second-in-command.

"Did you see what they did to the people on Galizur?" Ophiel asked, still disgusted by it.

"Terrible! They have no regard for lives other than their own," Michael said.

"They don't even care for their own if they fall."

"Once this is over, we must remember to destroy this planet and all others the creeping things inhabit," Michael said. He then turned to his communications officer. "Open a channel to Dellos. I must inform Jesus of our success."

So far, the Resurrectionists had attacked twenty isolated star systems and all but destroyed thirty-five worlds. Try as they did, the New Empire and the Alliance could not discern any kind of pattern in the enemy attacks. There were hundreds of thousands of isolated star systems in New Empire space alone; preemptively determining targets to bulk up defenses there was nearly impossible.

***

Elohim and Lucifer decided a short junket to Narcariel was in order, to check on the wellbeing of Zabkiel's relatives. Even though they were still considered independent, not technically affiliated with the New Empire or the Freewill Alliance, Elohim and Lucifer had been pulled back into active duty. They were still free to go where they deemed necessary, but they were at the disposal of the Alliance and the New Empire. While they quite enjoyed being back in action again, they hated the reason for it. The thrill of putting their lives on the line for an honorable cause was something they had missed.

As they emerged from deviant space, they were immediately smacked with a plethora of debris. If not for their shields, they would have suffered real damage, but it was ultimately nothing more than an annoyance. The five ships that comprised their personal fleet fanned out around the planet, carefully checking for any sign of enemies.

After Elohim instructed his communications officer to hail the planet, the officer replied, "Sir, there is no answer. I have hailed them on every known frequency."

"Prepare the shuttle," Elohim ordered.

"The capital city has been totally destroyed, sir." He paused, worked the controls, then continued, "I detect a high concentration of lifeforms at many locations around Narcariel. One of the largest is a mere 100 clicks away."

"That will be my first stop. Signal the fleet to disperse around the planet and to contact as many Narcarielians as possible, without jeopardizing security."

Elohim was glad to contact Zabkiel on Heaven with good news. "Your loved ones are healthy and safe," he said. "Somehow, they survived the brutal attack." He and Lucifer lingered there for two days and only left when they were certain the planet was well protected and not as vulnerable to a repeat attack.

Before they resumed their normal duties, Elohim and Lucifer stopped on Earth, at Justin's request.

When they entered his office, Justin told his assistant he did not want to be disturbed, then shielded his office.

"What's going on, young friend?" Lucifer asked once they were under the ultimate privacy.

"I have a mission for you. It may or may not be helpful in our fight against the Resurrectionists. I've talked to Sandel and Zabkiel, and you have their go-ahead to take on this mission, if you choose to accept it," Justin said.

"What does the mission entail?" Elohim asked.

Justin laid it out for them and reiterated several times that it was confidential and top secret. "If any hint of this comes to light, it could destroy any value the mission may offer, even if it proves successful," he emphatically remarked.

Once he was finished filling them in on the details, he sat back and waited for their answer. He watched as the two great men stepped away from him to discuss the validity and the ramifications of what they were being asked for do. As they spoke about it, Justin noticed a lot of headshaking and shrugs, as if they were in a heated debate. There were frowns on their faces when they walked back to his desk.

"I would do it myself," Justin said, "but I am needed here, to watch over the star systems of the Long Life Cooperative, the LLC, just in case those bastards decide to go after the Factor." He hesitated for a moment, fearing rejection, then asked, "So? What do you say?"

"It's a good plan," Elohim acknowledged.

"A *great* plan," Lucifer said, upping the ante.

Justin sat back in his chair, relieved. "The way you two were arguing over there, I thought sure you'd turn me down. Worse, I figured you took me as crazy for even asking."

"Ah, we were just messing with you," Lucifer replied with a grin, followed by a laugh in which they all shared.

Chapter 14

Over the next five months, twenty-seven more worlds fell to the Resurrectionists. The attacks were fierce and devastating to the worlds who were left alone and in ruins. The morale of the leaders of the rest of the galaxy was at an all-time low. It was estimated that nearly one million lives had been lost, and that number was most assuredly low; they could not obtain an accurate count on worlds where Dumah now inhabited the surface. Even worse, they still had no way of getting the jump on the enemy.

The Resurrectionists, on the other hand, had grown stronger and gained more confidence with each new conquest. Every newly conquered world added to their fleet of warships. Even damaged ships were towed to Dellos, where they were repaired and made battle ready. The Dumah were amazingly efficient, and their single-minded nature gave them the ability to repair vessels in record time.

By command from the Lord Jesus himself, Dumah were forbidden from populating Dellos, save a very few representatives. It was feared that they would forget their place and destroy the home base of the Resurrectionists, so they remained in space around the planet. Their home ships were huge compared to other battleships, as they were required to be enormous to house as many as a half-million beings. Their battlecruisers were known to carry crews of over 50,000. They were more difficult to maneuver than other sleeker, smaller warships in the combined fleet, but that did not stop them from being a real threat.

The Resurrectionists came to realize during raids on so many worlds that the Dumah were relentless warriors. Every one of them was willing to sacrifice herself, and they did not mourn casualties, as long as all were fighting for the cause of the advancement of their species. Their dangerous nature was not lost on the Disciples or the Titans. What all but the Dumah knew, however, was their bitter fate: While they were part of the great force to take over the galaxy, they would have no place in it when the victory was complete. As far as Jesus and his followers were concerned, the Dumah would suffer a 100 percent casualty rate at the war's end.

Along with adding captured ships to the fleet, Disciples and Titans saw fit to retrofit their allies' ships with many necessary upgrades. That would give the Dumah a fighting chance to battle the New Empire and the Alliance.

***

"We must attack Heaven now!" Jesus commanded.

"No, milord. We mustn't," Cronus disagreed. "Patience is a virtue, as you know."

Ignoring Cronus's wisdom, Jesus snapped, "Did you hear me? I want my galaxy back right now!" With that, he released an audible growl.

"I have to agree with Cronus, milord. We are not ready," Michael bravely said.

"Since when does Cronus have the authority to give commands? Have you forgotten that *I* am the leader here?" Jesus yelled at his Archangel.

"You bast—" Cronus started, but before he could finish the insult, Michael grabbed his arm and pulled him away.

"Not now," Michael whispered.

"But—" Cronus protested.

Michael silenced him again with a finger against his lip, then pulled him farther away.

Once they were out of Jesus' earshot, Cronus continued,

"How long must we put up with the crazy bastard's insane ideas?"

"As long as the Disciples continue to follow him," Michael calmly suggested. "We cannot afford to move against him now. Once I have a majority of them on my side, we can make our move."

"And when will that be?" Cronus asked, finally beginning to calm down.

"Soon, I hope. More and more are recognizing the insanity. It will not be long, my friend."

As Jesus gradually slipped back into his old, childish, foolish, self-serving ways, Cronus and Michael, the true strategists, moved in the background, pushing the Resurrectionists forward. Their only hope of taking the galaxy hinged on the resources and vessels they plundered, an important fringe benefit of their raids on the fringe worlds.

Unfortunately for the Resurrectionists, however, they would soon be forced to move their attacks inward. The outer star systems were good for raw materials but lacked useful ships. Vessels were essential to increase their fleet so they could take on the Empire or the Alliance. Building new battlecruisers was a slow process. Even with the Dumah and slave labor garnered from the conquered worlds, it took more than two years to construct a battle-ready ship. On the contrary, captured ships could be repaired and ready in a fraction of the time.

One bright spot in the Resurrectionist campaign was the Dumah, who were proving to be very valuable allies. Not only were they willing to sacrifice many of their own to lay claim to new worlds, but after the initial attacks, they were willing to leave a large faction behind to further decimate the remaining population. It didn't matter to Cronus and Michael that the insects would likely be exterminated as soon as the New Empire arrived. To them, the Dumah were expendable, just a disposable means to an end and nothing more.

While Michael did his best to placate the frustrated Cronus, Jesus busied himself with primping in the mirror. It was becoming harder for them to keep Jesus on an even keel, and he was quickly showing more and more signs of the worst traits of his previous self. Meanwhile, Michael had gained a new appreciation for Seraphim One. He had no idea how anyone was able to guide Jesus and keep him from imploding for all those years.

Michael struggled to compose himself as he made his way back over to the Lord. "Savior," he said, barely able to stomach calling him that, "if we move before we have enough ships to conquer even one planet, we risk losing it all."

"But Heaven is mine, and I want it now," Jesus whimpered, sounding like a child once again.

"I know, and I want it as well, maybe more than you know. Nevertheless, it would be foolish to make our move too quickly. Just give us a little more time to gather the resources we need, and I promise we will return the throne to you." Michael paused for a moment. "Once again, you will reign as supreme ruler of the galaxy. I promise this on my life."

Jesus was angry, but he somehow found a way to settle down.

For his part, Michael continued to stroke the delicate ego of the deranged God-child he once served. *We are so close to having the ability to take just one world, but which one should it be?* the Archangel asked himself. *Heaven? Earth? Eden?* Michael knew Hell was not a feasible target, and Heaven was not much better. There was nothing to be gained from attacking it. For that reason, he was leaning toward Eden or Earth. Those worlds held real power, something they could hold up against the entire galaxy.

Chapter 15

A couple months later, Jesus was beside himself, happier than he had been in a long time. Giddily dancing around the place, he was overcome with excitement for the surprise he'd planned for Michael, something he'd begun to sort out over three months earlier. Of course, he had asked for help from his undercover Holy Ghosts on Hell, but they were more than happy to do his bidding.

"What is it, milord?" Michael asked when Jesus called for him. He looked around and realized what the Lord had done for him. The Holy Ghosts had kidnapped his daughter and spirited her away, and now she stood before him, a sight for sore eyes. Her red hair, that she had inherited from her mother, was long and tied back in a ponytail. In all his memories of her, her hair was short.

"I know who *you* are, asshole," Rebecca brazenly said to Jesus. She then glared at the Archangel with homicidal intensity. "But who are you?"

"I-I am Michael Hamon, y-your father," Michael stuttered.

"Bullshit! My parents are on Hell," she argued.

"He speaks the truth, my dear," Jesus interrupted. "You were captured by the Alliance, and they corrupted your mind."

"You're wrong. Why would they do such a thing?" she said, entirely unbelieving.

"No, it's true. Rebecca, you are mine." Michael opened his arms, desperate to embrace his long-lost child.

"My name is Mara Tyrre," she corrected, moving away from him.

Michael's face was the picture of guarded disappointment.

"Michael, with the help of the Holy Ghosts still on Heaven, I received an Illuminator file of Rebecca's mind scan, taken not long before she was captured. We can use that to restore your daughter to you," Jesus said, glowing with pride. Then, he turned his attention to the girl again. "Don't worry, dear. You will have your memories back, and then, you will be happy to be at your father's side."

"It appears the rumors about you are true," she spat. "You *are* absolutely insane!" she screamed at Jesus.

"Temper, temper," Jesus said, shaking his head. He was a bit taken aback by her spitfire, but he couldn't stop smiling. "Michael, she is truly beautiful," he said. Then, as guards held her, Jesus took her chin in his hand and turned her face from side to side, as if inspecting a new toy. "I just might keep her for myself."

Michael's joy from the unexpected reunion quickly faded, and he stared at Jesus with rage storming in his eyes. If looks had the power to kill, Jesus would surely have been dead on the floor in an instant.

Somehow, Rebecca managed to twist one of her arms free from the grip of the guards, and she slapped Jesus' hand away.

For that, the Lord gifted her a backhanded slap, so hard that it caused her to cry out in pain. A trail of blood came from her lip and found its way to her chin before dripping on the floor.

Michael made a move toward Jesus, but before he made a fatal mistake, Cronus grabbed his arm and pulled him aside.

"As you told me, we need him for now," Cronus said, unable to hide a little smile as he recalled his own previous outbursts.

"She is fortunate she is your daughter," Jesus said, squinting at Michael. "Otherwise, she would be dead already."

"Thank you, milord. You are merciful and generous," Michael said, bowing his head as he struggled to compose himself.

"Take her to the Room of Memories," Jesus ordered.

While the guards grabbed Rebecca again, Michael requested, "May I go with her?"

"Of course. I will call if I need you," Jesus said, feeling charitable, the very picture of a Lord being magnanimous to a peasant.

As they walked to the Room of Memories, Rebecca began to cry. Gone was the bravado she had exhibited before. She sniffled and quietly said, "I know I am not your daughter, sir. My name is Mara Tyrre." Between sobs, she tried to tell him of the life they had taken her from. "Please take me home. My husband and children are probably very worried by now."

"Husband? Children?" Michael asked, somewhat shocked.

"I am married to Nanael, and we have three children. Lailah, Raguel, and Dara are the loves of my life," she said. She hoped her captors would return her to Hell. As she thought of her family, she began to cry uncontrollably and jerked her body to and fro in an effort to get away. When a guard twisted her left arm violently, she screamed out in pain.

No longer able to see his daughter shamed and abused, Michael slammed the man against the wall. "Don't you ever touch her again," he growled.

"I'm sorry, milord," the guard said as he shrank away.

Suddenly feeling as if the man who now held her was different than the others, Rebecca fell against him and allowed him to hold her close as they walked down long corridor.

After a while, when her sobbing quieted a bit, Michael spoke again: "I am truly sorry," he said sincerely. He loved her beyond words, and the tears streaming down her face lured tears of his own. He could not bear to see her heartbroken, but he also knew he could not allow her to return to her former life. "Soon, my darling, the life you lived on Hell will be nothing but a distant memory. You will know I'm your father, and I will have you in my life once again. In time, if you still desire to be with them, I will do all I can to bring your husband and children to you. I promise you this."

Deep within, she knew he was telling her the truth. She was not Mara but Rebecca, even if it made no logical sense. *How is it possible?* she asked herself. *I had such a full, wonderful life on Hell, with a family of my own. How can I be the daughter of a man so...evil?*

Michael was struggling with an odd stew of emotions himself. He was elated to see her and desperately wanted his daughter by his side, but part of him would have preferred her to be left on Hell. After all, she was safe there, and she was obviously happy. For a moment, he reminisced with fleeting memories of Rebecca as a child, and then he marveled at the thought that he now had grandchildren of his own.

He mostly only recalled a grown Rebecca. He was gone for most of her younger years, busy on missions for Jesus, but all memories of her made him smile. A long-lost feeling of paternal adoration washed over him. If anyone would have dared to look at the mighty Archangel Michael as he walked his daughter to the Room of Memories, they would have noticed an uncharacteristic smile.

Benjamin Oneal

Chapter 16

Although their fleet had grown to 1,000 strong, the Resurrectionists were still not quite ready for a full-on strike against their enemies. That said, it was time to hit a major target to assess their strength. The unfortunates would be those in the Laoth System, so close to Earth it would make everyone in the galaxy quite uncomfortable.

The Laoth System was highly advanced, a civilization consisting of five planets, with strong ties to the Alliance. However, the Alliance presence there was strained, due to the growing need to be elsewhere. The Resurrectionists were counting on that, and they had, for the most part, orchestrated things to be precisely that way. Just as the morning light from their star began moving across Laoel, the Laoth capital city, 400 Resurrectionist ships dropped out of deviant space.

Next, 200 forward guns ripped white-hot energy beams through the cosmos, the Disciple and Titan forces tearing away at the shields of the Alliance battlecruisers and the Laothen security force that hovered just above Laoth. At the same time, 100 Dumah vessels attacked 2 of the outer planets in the system, and another 100 enemies, the Sauroptors, mounted an attack on the 2 remaining worlds.

The lopsided assault on the capital planet was quick and deadly. With the element of surprise and the numbers on their side, the Disciple and Titan fleets made short work of destroying any and all defenders. In just two hours, the planet was theirs. Even though it was a vicious tragedy for them, the poor four outer planets suffered a much worse fate: The Sauroptors basically burned every major city to the ground, then let their ground forces slaughter the defending armies that tried to rise against them.

The Dumah did not destroy the major cities, but they did take out any weapons that might prevent them from landing on the planet. They set down near the major cities and swarmed in with wave after wave of single-minded, insect-like terror. No matter how many Dumah died, they just kept coming, climbing over the bodies of their own and killing everyone in sight.

***

"The Laoth System is under attack!" Stolas blurted as he rushed into Justin's office. "We are the closest to that system. I think we need to help."

"All right. Let's send our nonessential vessels in. I'll call Sandel and Zabkiel and try to coordinate with them. They will know how to best to manage the situation," Justin said.

Immediately, Stolas commanded part of the New Earth Security fleet to move into deviant space.

Twelve hours later, that fleet found Laoth in complete ruins. The space around the planet was littered with the remnants battle from both sides, along with thousands of Dumah bodies, casualties who had simply sacrificed themselves by fighting until they ran out of air. Although debris was scattered above Laoth, no complete ships were located; just as before, the Resurrectionists had towed away any vessels they felt they could repair and/or modify to add to their own fleet.

The capital city, Laoel, along with every major city on the planet, suffered the same grim fate. They were now just burnt-out holes in the landscape. Those fortunate enough to escape death were forced to live without power or any of the modern conveniences they had grown accustomed to. Even with the help of the Alliance, it would be many years before they could resume any semblance of normal. Even then, they would have to carry horrible memories with them for the remainder of their lives.

Forty battleships lingered in the space around Laoth, while sixty spread out to the other four systems. The two planets that were attacked by the Sauroptors were devastated. Just like the space around Laoth, the whole place was littered with debris and bodies, and there were no ships to protect those planets. Both planets were under the oppression of significant Sauroptor ground forces.

The fifteen ships that surrounded the other planets deployed fighters to locate and neutralize as many Sauroptor ground forces as they could, giving the inhabitants a fighting chance to defend themselves. They were also able to land enough troops to completely eradicate the invading reptiles. The Sauroptors were not difficult to locate, as they considered themselves brave warriors who refused to hide and relentlessly attacked, no matter the odds.

When the thirty New Earth Security ships reached the two planets that had been attacked by Dumah, they found that a huge insect ship was stationed in the space above each. Following protocol, they minded the gap between themselves and the enemy as they opened fire. That was the only way NES could avoid the only real weapon of the Dumah, the swarm.

Dumah fighter ships poured into space, along with countless insect creatures. Since NES ships wisely kept their distance, many of the swarm clung to their fighters, hoping to be pulled within closer range of NES ships, so they could breach the hulls and disable them.

The valiant New Earth Security fleet took out as many fighters as they could but still had to launch their own to repel the rest. Because of the precautions they took as they approached the Dumah warship, their casualties were minimal. After the Dumah ship was destroyed, NES ships moved into higher orbit to avoid the many thousands of Dumah that continued to gush toward them.

The situation on the ground was not as easy to correct. Once ground defenses were all but eliminated, the insects swarmed the planets, eager to eradicate anything or anyone who got in their path. No matter how many Dumah fell to the inhabitants of the planets, replacements followed. In just a short time, large sections of each planet were overtaken by insect warriors.

The was not sure how to retake the planets. NES fighters flew missions to the front lines to kill as many Dumah as possible. They slowed and even stopped their advance, on some fronts. That bought them a bit of time to decide how to proceed, whether they should continue to eradicate the insects or focus on rescuing the survivors.

Eleven hours later, 200 Alliance ships dropped out of deviant space. Once the Alliance arrived, NES ships filled them in on everything they needed to know. Then, it was time to let them take over.

Chapter 17

"A test?" Justin asked redundantly.

"I believe it was," Zabkiel posited. "A major one, to be sure."

"But was it the *final* test? I fear what comes next," Sandel confessed.

"Do you really think they will attack Heaven, Hell, Earth?" Justin asked.

"I'm afraid so," Zabkiel said.

"Are you ready for that?" Sandel asked Justin.

"Stolas, my head of New Earth Security, says we are as ready as we can be. We have ships posted around the seven planets of the Cooperative," Justin assured him. "How about you?"

"We are ready," Zabkiel said.

"As are we," Sandel agreed.

"They must be riding high after their success on Laoth," Justin surmised.

"Yes, their confidence has surely grown with each successful raid," Sandel agreed.

"I just thought of something that might work to our advantage. If they plan to use the Dumah in a final attack, there is really only one world where that would be feasible," Justin offered.

"Hell!" Sandel said.

"Why there?" Zabkiel asked.

"Because they cannot take the chance of Dumah destroying the precarious balance of nature on Eden or Earth, where the Trees of Life grow. They will not risk losing that. Also, since their main goal is to regain the Empire, they will not let the Dumah loose on Heaven, the symbol of galactic rule."

"Hmm. That makes perfect sense," Sandel agreed.

"That said, it does not guarantee that Hell is the target of the next major strike," Zabkiel said.

"Regardless, it's imperative that we figure out where and when they are going to attack, or we could lose the fight."

The three sat in silence for a while, pondering many scenarios in their minds before they shared their thoughts with the others.

Chapter 18

For two months, the scientists in the Room of Memories worked feverishly to bring Rebecca back to Michael. The Archangel watched through the observation window as they asked his daughter questions to evaluate her progress. Only when she passed those tests would she be free to leave and join her father. With each correct answer, Michael's hopes grew.

"What is your name?" a scientist asked.

"Rebecca Mikhal Hamon."

"Who is your God?"

"The Lord God Jesus."

"Who is your father?"

"Archangel Michael Hamon, the supreme leader of the Lord God's army." Rebeca straightened when she answered, as if standing at attention.

Pleased with the results of the questionnaire, the scientist deemed her mentally fit for duty. When she saw her father, she smiled and offered him an awkward hug. Even though she'd been returned to her previous state, with her memory restored, there was no real affection between them; their association was more of a military hierarchy connection.

"How do you feel?" Michael asked.

"Ready to get back to work, sir," Rebecca answered.

Michael had spent quite a bit of time thinking about the grandchildren he knew he would probably never meet, and he could not forget the profound love Rebecca had expressed for them when she first arrived. Their rigid reunion and the "sir" were like a knife in his heart. He did his best to play it off, but his feelings were mixed.

No matter how Michael felt, it was not the time to pay much attention to his emotions. They had a war to win. Besides, it felt good to have Rebecca back at his side during the true battle for the galaxy. *Maybe, just maybe, we'll be able to rescue my grandchildren from Hell, so we can finally be a family,* he thought, but he kept those hopes to himself.

Although he wanted to spend more time with his wayward daughter, he knew Jesus had already been told that her resurrection was complete. She would have to be presented to the Lord God. He wasn't sure what he would do if Jesus tried to take her as a consort, though, the thought of Jesus touching his daughter in that manner tore at his soul.

***

Over the course of their campaign to regain control of the galaxy, they had decimated many worlds on the fringes of Empire and Alliance space. In some instances, they slaughtered entire populations. At the very least, they stripped them all bare of any and all precious resources.

When Michael and Rebecca entered the conference room, Jesus and Cronus were already discussing the next move for the Resurrectionists.

"Let's take them all," Jesus spoke matter-of-factly, as if he would hear no other thoughts or opinions on the matter.

"We only have enough ships to take on one target, milord. We must choose between Heaven and Earth," Cronus explained.

"I believe we should seriously consider the importance of Earth, Lord," Michael offered.

"Heaven! I want Heaven! To hell with Earth."

"But we—"

Before Cronus could offer even a shred of reason and

logic, Jesus barked, "Never think you are too important to escape punishment for disagreeing with me! You either, Michael," Jesus admonished.

"I was just saying I must agree with Michael, milord." The disgust on the face of Cronus as he uttered the title spoke volumes. "As the main producer of the Factor, it would be wise to consider Earth a better target. It is also far less fortified. Then, after we establish ourselves as controllers of long life, we can easily buy the Empire…and likely any other worlds we desire."

"Damn you! I want my Heaven back," Jesus screamed. "And another thing… Once I have it, you will bring my father to me. I have dreamt of killing him for far too long. The thought of watching the life drain from his eyes as the blood flows from the wound I deliver to his heart fills me with the utmost joy." Jesus smiled as his eyes glared into space, dancing about and glittering as if he completely enjoyed the thought. When his mind came back to him, he continued, "This is *my* command. You *will* do as I say. And no other shall touch my father, for he is mine to kill."

"That's it!" Cronus said, having heard what he deemed the last straw. "I have had enough of this crazy, juvenile ranting. I refuse to cater to a spoiled brat of a man for even one moment longer," he said, beside himself with anger.

"How dare you talk to me in that manner? Michael, kill him!" Jesus screeched.

Michael stood next to Rebecca, silent and still as a statue, obviously opting to stay out of the conflict between the two.

"Just shut up, you pathetic fool," Cronus barked.

"You dare to challenge my authority?" Jesus again looked toward Michael. "You must kill him at once. I knew it was wrong to form an allegiance with the likes of him."

"I am sorry, Jesus, but you are no longer in charge. To be completely truthful, you never have been," Michael admitted with a callous shrug, as Rebecca stood by his side, struggling to catch up.

"Blasphemy!" Jesus shrieked. "Michael, do as I say! I command you!" Jesus growled.

"I'm sorry, but I cannot," Michael said, shaking his head.

When Jesus finally realized that Michael was no longer under his control, intense rage consumed him. "Guards, kill them both."

Mimicking Michael's insubordination, the guards did not move.

"I am your Lord, damn you. Kill them! Kill them all!"

Cronus smiled as Michael just stood there with a blank look on his face, watching Jesus tremble with concentrated anger. He smiled even more broadly when their former Lord walked up to him and waved an accusatory finger in his face. When the guards started to move toward Jesus, Cronus did his best to stifle a laugh, then held up his hand to stop them.

"I am your God, like Elohim, Jehovah, and Yahweh before him. As your Lord and master, I order you to bow before me!"

For an answer, Cronus backhanded Jesus, knocking him to the floor.

Jesus, dumbfounded, looked helplessly up at Cronus. Tears began to course down his face, mixing with the blood from his split lip.

"Elohim is not your father, you stupid bastard. *I* am."

"What!?" Jesus asked, aghast and certain he had not heard Cronus correctly.

"I am certainly not proud of it, but you are my son...as well as my greatest failure." Cronus frowned. "As a baby, my daughter, Dilyla, was placed on Heaven with a prominent family who were loyal to me. From the time she was very young, she was groomed for her mission. Her sole purpose was to become Elohim's queen. When she came of age, all we had to do was wait.

"After Elohim and Lucifer returned from a particularly successful mission for the Empire, they were in a festive mood. My agents on Heaven made sure Magdalene was part of that celebration. When the time came, she made her move. Although she was strikingly beautiful, we still used some...

chemical assistance to give her an edge over other females who may have sooner garnered your father's attention. The pheromone enhancer did exactly as we hoped. After that night, he was completely in my hands, like clay for the molding.

"Not long after they married, your mother bore my child. It was Dilyla's sole purpose to groom you to become God. Then, you could pardon me and my followers and invite us back to Heaven. When the time was right, I would take my rightful place as God of Heaven and all the galaxy. So, *son*, do you see how you have served as both my greatest hope and my greatest disappointment?"

"Liar!" Jesus yelled, seething. "Elohim is my father, and I am your God. I will not allow you to speak to me this way. I should've had you killed when we first met, you traitorous scum." Even as he said it, somewhere deep within him, Jesus knew that Cronus was telling him the truth. Nevertheless, he ordered again, "Michael, kill him."

Again, Michael stood in place, darting his eyes to Jesus, then to Cronus, then back to Jesus again.

When he did nothing, Jesus screamed, "I said kill him, Michael."

"I'm sorry, but I cannot," Michael repeated, with another shrug to go with it.

Rebecca, who had just regained her memory fully, was very confused and wide-eyed with fear.

"Why?" Jesus asked, glaring at the Archangel. "I do not understand. I have treated you as a brother, even brought your spawn here to be with you. Why do you deny me this one small request?"

"Like a brother?" Michael questioned, taken aback. "I have been a lapdog at best! No matter how hard I worked to help you reach your goals, you never showed me the slightest bit of gratitude, never even thanked me. You used me, then just sent me on my way. To be honest, Jesus, it has taken everything in my soul not to kill you myself over these many years."

"How dare you?" Jesus spat.

"How dare I? How dare *you*!? You are a spoiled brat, a fool with a false sense of entitlement, with no respect for the feelings or the accomplishments of anyone other than yourself. You continually take credit for the ideas of the very ones who help you. Because of your petty tantrums, countless lives have been lost, many by your own hand. This has to end."

"I am your God!" Jesus said weakly, with only the faintest hint of authority.

"Perhaps you *were*," Michael said. "When you had real power and a plan for the glory of the galaxy, I gladly followed you. Now though? Now, you are impotent, nothing more than a figurehead to rally our forces."

"Figurehead?"

"Yes. You will continue to be our leader in title only, but you will have no actual power. You brought this on yourself. I hoped you would grow stronger during your years of imprisonment, but you only stagnated. You could have channeled your pain into making a great leader out of yourself, a true and worthy God, but you failed," Michael said, his face a portrait of disappointment. "You had 100 years to show the prisoners on Naberus what it means to be God, but instead, you wasted that time on a downward spiral of shameful, drunken self-pity."

Jesus looked from one person to another, bewildered, obviously still unable to grasp the meaning of Michael's powerful words. He finally returned his blank stare to Michael again, but he could not seem to come up with a response.

"You have fallen into your old ways, and you no longer have the guidance of Seraphim One. I now know that he led you to wiser decisions, probably without you even realizing it. In the few short years since he led the Empire, it has grown strong, much too strong to conquer. If your mind were not so foggy and self-serving, you would know that. I agree with Cronus on this. I can no longer follow the mindless desires of a spoiled child. If we are to win this war, we need a leader who can look beyond mere want, a leader who will set his personal wishes aside and do what is best for all, a leader who is capable of listening to reason."

"Why have you forsaken me, Michael?" Jesus said, in a pitiful whimper of a voice.

Michael reached out to help Jesus to his feet. "I have not forsaken you. Your refusal to grow into an adult is why you lost the Empire, and now, it threatens to derail our current fight. There is too much at stake, Jesus."

"If you still want to be a part of this, just shut up and let the adults win this war. Then, I can finally take my rightful place as leader of the galaxy," Cronus sternly stated.

"But I am…" Jesus started, only to cower and hush when Cronus raised his hand. After a while, he found his voice again and sheepishly asked, "Are you really my father?"

***

After the humiliated Jesus was taken to his chamber, Michael had a question for Cronus: "That was a lie, was it not? Surely, you're not his father."

"Unfortunately, I am."

"What!?" Michael said, doing a double-take. "That lunatic is *your* son?"

"Yes. As I said, my agents on Heaven impregnated Dilyla with my seed." Cronus laughed. "I have always considered it a slap in the face to Elohim and his family. Unknowingly, he raised my child as his own."

As Michael considered that, a cruel thought came to his mind: *Inbreeding? No wonder Jesus is such a madman.*

Chapter 19

After it was revealed to Jesus that his mother was the daughter of Cronus, he struggled to find his place in his new reality. If he understood it correctly, Dilyla was groomed on Heaven by agents from Titan, with the sole purpose of deceiving Elohim into falling for her charms. She was meant to wed Elohim and ultimately bring a child into the world. No one could have guessed the depravity to which Cronus would stoop to become God. Even Jesus was sickened by the fact that Cronus had impregnated his own daughter. *This cannot be true. I cannot be the son of the worst traitor Heaven has ever known. I am the son of Elohim. I am God!* he silently fumed.

Jesus was now a broken man. Gone was his swagger, his energy, and his arrogance. He was still allowed to sit in on strategy meetings but rarely offered any opinion; he only spoken when he was directly addressed. He felt alone because he was. There were Disciples who still saw him as God, but there was no one close to him with whom he could share his thoughts and dreams.

He sat in his elegant, palatial bedroom and wondered, how did things go so wrong? *Why has Michael forsaken me? Did Cronus somehow corrupt the mind of my most valued servant?*

"Figurehead?" Jesus asked himself in a forced whisper.

"I am God!" He screamed. His words echoed through the vast expanse of his chambers. While it was not a prison cell, it was clear he could not leave. Soon, his anger shifted to self-pity. The sorrow he felt for himself was overpowering, and more tears came.

Sometime later, Michael visited the man who had once dominated his life. He felt pity for the once-powerful deity who had the galaxy at his pleasure. His thoughts were filled with regret about the years he had wasted trying to please his child God.

As Michael moved closer to Jesus, the man he had given his life to, raised his tear-stained face from his hands and grimaced in anger. "Why, Michael? Why?" Jesus asked, barely able to form the words.

"You should be able to answer that yourself, milord... and that is why," the Archangel said, showing his disappointment.

"I-I don't understand."

"I know. There is a saying on Earth, spoken by a man named John Dalberg-Acton. 'Absolute power corrupts absolutely.' That will be your legacy, how you will be remembered. When you became God, the power you held over the galaxy was absolute.

"Not only did that power corrupt you in material ways, making you thirst for riches and power over others and the worlds they lived on, but your childish mind was also corrupted beyond repair. You never outgrew the tendency to be spoiled, never wanting to share your toys and always feeling you deserved more. Not once did you consider the feelings or the wellbeing of your servants, those who worked so hard and sacrificed much to keep you in power. You never proved yourself worthy of the position you were fortunate to be born into. You were never more than the smallest fraction of the leader your predecessor was."

"But, Michael, I *am* your God, not just a figurehead," Jesus whined.

Michael sighed. He knew it was a losing battle to try to

make Jesus' feeble mind comprehend the reality of his new role in the Resurrectionist war against the New Empire. "It is entirely up to you," he finally said. "Your destiny, how we will move forward with you, is your decision. You can be a willing participant in our taking of the Empire and claim a position of respect, or you will be as your father was in the end, a drugged shell of himself. Either way, you will serve as an important symbol for the Resurrectionists."

In an uncharacteristically selfless vision of clarity, Jesus recalled a speech he once made to all the worlds of the Empire. Behind him was his father, a drugged and broken man. The thought of either future frightened him. *Are those really my only choices?* he wondered, with great horror. *Am I to be a figurehead, with no real power, or a dead soul, sitting behind Michael or Cronus, giving them validation for ruling the new Empire?* After a moment of thought, Jesus came to a decision: *I most certainly will not! Both are unacceptable!*

Michael studied the face of the Savior he once served. He truly felt sorry for him, but there was no way they could let him continue to lead the Resurrectionist. He stood there silently, letting Jesus digest what he had just heard, in hopes that he might get an epiphany.

Then he had his own epiphany. He put his finger to his mouth, to indicate that people might be listening. He leaned in close and spoke in a whisper. "They could be listening."

"Who?" Jesus said in a normal voice.

"Shhhh." Michael again put his finger to his lips. "I need to tell you something, but we need to be careful. Spies could be listening."

That caught Jesus' attention. He knew about spies. This changed everything. "What is going on Michael?" Jesus whispered.

"I am loyal to you milord, as I have always been. Everything that I have time, and that I will do, is in your service. Right now, I must treat you this way, for Cronus has spies everywhere, and the only way I could get him to join with us, was to make him believe that he would take the throne."

"No!" Jesus said aloud. "No." He repeated in a whisper.

"You have my word my Lord, as soon as we have conquered the galaxy, you will set on the throne, not Cronus. Cronus will be dead by my hand, long before he gets close to the throne. But my Lord, you must play along. You must act as if you are okay with being a figurehead."

"But I am God." Jesus implored.

"Yes, yes you are God, and always will be, but we must pretend as if you are not. Your life depends on. Can you do this for me?" Michael asked, putting his hand on Jesus' shoulder, and looking deep into his eyes.

Jesus was starting to understand. It would not be easy, but he believed he could do it. "I will do as you say, but every time I see him, I want to kill him."

"Believe me my Lord, I feel the same way. As you are my witness, I promise to kill him myself, and you will once again be in your rightful place, as God."

Michael could see that there was something else on his Lord's mind, and that it was causing him great concern. "Is there something else on your mind, Lord?"

Jesus looked at Michael, and started to say something, but stopped short of saying the words. He was wringing his hands together, and clearly nervous. "My Lord God, please tell me what bothers you so." Michael pushed.

Jesus again seemed to go inward, and it was clear to the Archangel, that there was a deep inner struggle. Finally, he looked straight at Michael. "Is Cronus my father?"

Michael just shook his head and shrugged.

Chapter 20

Uzza Flauros, a freelance cargo ship pilot, was contracted to deliver a shipment to a planet well outside the normal trade routes. In her 12 years as a pilot, she'd only been to the planet Dellos twice before. It was the only inhabitable planet in this its system.

There was not much known about the inhabitants of Dellos. It was a fairly new society, being around 200 years old. Flauros knew that the Dellosians were approached by the new Empire, soon after they established their government. Due to the abundance of natural resources that the planet had to offer, and preferring a solitary existence, they declined entry into the new Empire, or to enter into a trade agreement. Soon they were all but forgotten.

Even though it wasn't part of her usual trade routes, she made it a point to find out as much as she could about every planet where she delivered supplies. The one thing that she did know, was the population was between 15,002 to 16,000.

As she traveled to Dellos, she began to wonder why the Dellosians had changed size of their order so drastically. As she cut through deviant space, she decided to give in to her curiosity. She accessed the manifest, to see what she was actually delivering to the solitary planet.

This is strange. Florio's thought, as she noticed that most of the things were thermostabilized or freeze-dried foodstuffs;

enough to feed and army. *Their farmers. They have always grown their own food.* Along with the crates of food, there were luxury items that they could ill afford. *The Dellosians this extravagant?* She asked herself. Then she saw a list of crates, with no indication of what they contain. *What the hell?*

She did not like the fact that she was delivering cargo that was not declared. If she was caught delivering banned weapons, or the like, she could lose her pilot's license. It would be another four hours before she reached Dellos, and decided to find out just what she was carrying. She made sure that all was well with navigation, and headed for the hold.

Once in the hold, she quickly found the crates of the undisclosed cargo. She checked the crates for any indication of what was inside, but there was nothing on the outside to tell her what was inside. "This is bullshit!" She said aloud, but it was a wasted sentiment, since she was the only one on the ship.

"Camael." Flauros, said to her onboard computer.

"What can I do for you, Uzza?" The computer spoke to her, in a soft feminine voice.

She checked the manifest again. "Please scan crates 27 through 48."

After a few moments Camael related her findings. "The crates 27 through 48, are shielded. I cannot read their contents. Is there anything else I might do?"

"No Camael, standby." Flauros said, and absentmindedly scratched her head. For a moment, she seemed to be having some sort of an inner struggle. Then she gave a little smile, when she made a decision. She walked to the end of the cargo hold, to a supply closet. She found her toolbox and pulled out a crowbar.

She walked back to the closest crate, 48, and thought about what kind of trouble she might be in, if she opened the crate. *But hell, if these are weapons, I could lose my license.* She thought, before she jammed the blade of the crowbar into the gap in the lid of the crate, and prided it open.

She slid the lid away, and looked down at a refrigerator unit. *What the hell?* She asked herself. She had already gone this far, so she had to see what was in the unit. *It could still be weapons.* She thought. She carefully worked the latch and open the unit. What she saw, rocked her back on her heels.

Chapter 21

"The Factor?" Asked herself, again wondering, *what the hell?*

This was even more strange than weapons. As far as anything that she had ever known about the Dellosians, they had always been adamantly opposed to the Factor. *Always.* She thought. *Why would they suddenly change their minds?*

At that moment Camael announced, "We are approaching beacon, Uzza."

"On my way." Flauros answered.

As she dropped into normal space, she noticed that the space around Dellos was crowded with a myriad of vessels, some she had never encountered before. There were a couple that looked familiar, but she could not place where she had seen before.

Once she connected with space dock, she was surprised that the workers started unloading the cargo within moments. She really hoped that they wouldn't notice that she had tampered with one of the containers. Flauros thought about asking someone about the unusual cargo, but she didn't recognize any of the men offloading the cargo, or staff that checked off each as they were loaded on to shuttles bound for the planet. She had a strong feeling that she was being watched.

She wanted to ride down to the planet, to see the few friends that she had made delivering cargo, but got a serious notion that that was not going to happen. The one person in authority that would talk to her, said something about a virus, and a quarantine. Something didn't sound right, but she wasn't in a position to argue.

Everything seemed wrong. Flauros had the intense feeling, that she needed to leave now. As soon as she got the okay to detach, she quickly moved away from the station, so she could safely enter deviant space. One of the ships that appeared familiar to her before, seemed to follow her as she moved away from the station.

"Camael, scan the ship that is following us. It looks familiar, but I cannot place it." Flauros said.

"It seems to be a Class D Battlecruiser, once used by the old Empire, but with significant modifications." Suddenly, Camael took on a more frantic tone. "They are powering their weapons!"

"Camael transfer yourself to the fighter and make ready for a fast exit." Flauros barked. She quickly set the ship to run on auto pilot, making it look like they were unaware of any danger, and merely preparing to enter deviant space. Then she ran for the fighter, hoping she would make it in time.

As she climbed into the fighter, Camael informed her that they locked their weapons on her cargo ship. Just as the battle cruiser's energy beams tore away at what little shields she had, and tore through the skin of her ship, and caused a massive explosion. She looked like a piece of shrapnel, as her fighter burst into space. The shockwave from the blast, caused her fighter to rock violently. She was barely able to keep her grip on the controls.

She activated the jump into deviant space, but nothing happened. The concussion that resulted from her exploding cargo ship, jarred something loose. "Camael , something's wrong with the jump engines. See what you can do, while I try to outrun them."

After a moment, Camael came back. "Uzza, there's nothing I can do. The circuits are fried."

"We need to warn the New Empire."

Without the ability to move to deviant space, she was on borrowed time. "Camael, Code-Rachel-One." Knowing she didn't have much time, she made the message as brief as possible, still hoping that anyone who intercepted the message would understand. The message was disguised as a distress signal. As she dodged the energy beams from the battleship, she worked out a message. Her fighter buffeted from near misses, as she composed her message that might never be received by anyone.

Her time was running low as enemy fighters burst from the belly of the battleship. Dodging and weaving to avoid the barrage of energy beams, she made the decision to go down fighting. Uzza pulled the fighter into a wide loop and came at the Battleship firing everything she had. She took down three of the enemy fighters and was able to launch a missile before the sheer number of enemy fighters became impossible to avoid.

"Goodbye, Camael" Uzza said, knowing the end was near.

"Goodbye, Uzza. It has been an honor to serve you."

Through the view port, it was clear that her missile found its intended target. Although it could not help her current situation, it was some small measure of satisfaction, that the Battlecruiser's main engines were severely damaged, and the resulting chain reaction, ruptured the haul. She smiled as the blinding explosion of the Old Empire ship, coincided with the total disintegration of her own, as multiple energy beams hit her all at once. There was an explosive white flash, and she was gone.

Chapter 22

Justin opened a secure line to the *Vepar*, Elohim and Lucifer's ship, the namesake of Lucifer's first wife, who died near the beginning of the galactic war.

After a few pleasantries, Justin got down to the business at hand. "How goes the top-secret mission, my friend?" Justin asked.

"We are currently chasing down a most promising lead," Lucifer told him.

"How long before you'll know?"

"We will arrive at our destination in twenty-five hours. We should be able to report back to you soon after that. How are things going on your end?"

"After the successful Resurrectionist attack on Loath, a reliable source indicated that an all-out attack is imminent. Our main problem is that our source is not yet in possession of the location of the Resurrectionist base or the details of the target," Justin informed him.

Elohim, who was listening to the conversation, joined Lucifer on the screen, and he and Lucifer chorused, "Damn!"

"Either way, your mission is vital in our fight, my friends," Justin said.

Elohim and Lucifer both nodded.

"We will contact you as soon as we arrive at our destination. Stay safe, my friend," Lucifer signed off.

***

"I am afraid that is the way it lays out, my friend," Sandel said.

"You know Sandel is right," Zabkiel offered.

"Yeah, it's the only thing that makes sense," Justin agreed.

"We all need to make the necessary decisions right now to protect the New Empire, the Freewill Alliance, the Long Life Cooperative, and all the citizens. Very soon, the Resurrectionists will move into their endgame," Sandel said.

"I hate to bring this up, but Eden or Earth would be the most strategic target for an all-out attack. Where Heaven or Hell would be prime targets, the ships and resources that they would have to expend would leave them venerable to a counter attack." Zabkiel offered.

"If they were able to take either of the planets, where the factor is grown, would give them strategic advantage, against an all-out attack. And holding the Factor as a bargaining chip would be a powerful weapon. Sandel added.

After Justin signed off, he called for Stolas and his daughter Rachel to meet him in his office, so he could update them on the latest information. His meeting with the three leaders of the galaxy shed the light on the only scenario that made sense. If their assumptions were correct, the defenses of the Cooperative needed to be at their peak, to give them every advantage.

"It is exactly as I thought," Stolas said, nodding. "Heaven will be extremely difficult to conquer. Also, because of the resources required to obtain the planet, they will not be able to defend the prize."

"Hell would me much of the same, but the residents there will not be controlled," Rachel added.

"It has to be Earth or Eden. The Resurrectionists can ill afford to make more than one attempt. They must grab the brass ring now."

"Brass ring?" Stolas asked.

Justin smiled, amused. "Long ago, carousels were equipped with dispensers that contained many iron rings and one brass ring. Riders tried to grab those rings as they passed by, hoping to snag the coveted brass one. When the ride ended, the rider who captured the ring of brass received a prize," Justin explained.

"Well, they won't get *this* brass ring, damn it!" Rachel said, with determined anger that brought a smile to Justin's face.

After shaking the hand of Stolas and giving Rachel a hug, Justin decided he was due for a bit of downtime. He was happy to see that Salome was home when he got there. He took her into his arms and gave her a loving, very lengthy hug.

"Are you alright?" Salome asked.

"Yeah, but I think the shit is about ready to hit the fan. Zabkiel, Sandel, and I are all in agreement on this. There is a good chance the Resurrectionists are going to attack Earth sometime in the next six months."

"That soon?"

"Yes, I am afraid so."

"Are we ready?"

"Stolas and Rachel assure me that we are. Oh, that reminds me. I saw Rachel today. She promised she'll come see you when things settle down a bit."

"I really feel safer with her watching over us all."

"Me too. She has always been the best of both of us."

"Yes, she has," she agreed. "I'm sorry, my love, but I am exhausted. I need to go to bed."

"Bed?" Justin said, with a naughty twinkle in his eye. "I like the sound of that." He started to dance her toward the bedroom, but she put a hand up to stop him.

"No, I need to get some sleep for my trip to Eden tomorrow. We are on the verge of a major ecological breakthrough."

"Salome, I don't think that's a good idea. It's too dangerous to travel right now."

"I have no choice. I am to meet Chief Elder Lornash. We

have finally turned the corner on making Eden the paradise it was before Jesus overtook it."

Justin knew Lornash was the leader of Eden and somewhere in the vicinity of 20,000 years old, perhaps the oldest living being in the galaxy. For that reason, he understood the importance of the meeting, but he was genuinely concerned for his beloved's safety. "Can't you accomplish the same results with a video conference?" he asked.

"I really wish I could, but you know Lornash does not like modern technology. This stage is really important, so I must be there."

"Salome, I just don't feel comfortable with it. How can I protect you when you're so far away?" Justin asked, with a worried look on his face.

She smiled. "I'll take Father with me. Would that make you feel better?" she asked, giving him another hug to console and convince him.

"A little better," Justin said. Jarod, her father, was Justin's instructor on Hell in the early days of his Angel training. He knew if anyone could protect her, Jarod could. "I would like to speak with him first though. There are a few things you both need to know before you go."

"All right. First, would you like to continue our dance to the bedroom?" Salome asked as she put her arms around Justin's neck and pulled him in for a kiss.

"I thought you'd never ask," he said, finding his silly schoolboy grin once again.

"They made love like it was when they first married, but with the knowledge of things that only people who have been together for a while could understand. Suddenly she pushed against him, and he responded. The complete rapture that they felt, seemed to go on and on.

"I love you, Salome. Justin whispered.

"I love you, Justin. Always." Salome said and kissed him deeply.

After they made love, Salome lay asleep in Justin's arms. Slumber did not come for him, however. He was worried about the impending attack, but he was even more worried about the woman in his arms. *I don't know what I would do if I ever lost you,* he thought, gently combing a stray hair off her face.

***

Early the next morning, Justin received a call from Zabkiel, to let him know they had finally obtained the results of a request Justin had presented to him a while back. Zabkiel also let him know that his suspicions were right. All they were waiting for now was for Elohim and Lucifer to return to Heaven.

"Hey, Zabkiel, what's up?" Justin began.

"We finally have conclusive evidence on that project you assigned to us," Zabkiel said smiling.

"That's great! What did you find?" Justin asked as he literally moved to the edge of his seat.

"I was skeptical at first, Justin, but damn! You were right," Zabkiel said, wearing with a bogus frown.

"I knew it! It is nice to have confirmation though," Justin replied, feeling vindicated. "Have you told him yet?"

"I expect them to arrive later today. I will tell him then."

"Patch me in when he gets there."

"Why? Do you really need to gloat that badly?" Zabkiel asked with a smirk.

"No, not at all. I just…want to see his face," Justin said, backpedaling.

"Relax, my friend. I am only kidding." Zabkiel laughed. "I'll call you when he arrives." With that and one final giggle, he signed off.

Chapter 23

Elohim and Lucifer were back on Heaven, in part to gather necessary supplies but also because Zabkiel had requested to see them. He said he had something to tell Elohim, and he didn't feel it was best to reveal it via video conference.

"So, what's so important that you had to see us face to face, my Lord?" Elohim asked Zabkiel. "And why can he video in?" Elohim asked pointing toward Justin, patched in on the vid screen.

"Okay, first of all, stop the 'my Lord' crap. Second, we finally have some answers," Zabkiel said.

"To what questions?" Lucifer asked.

"Let me give you a little history. It was all sparked by something Justin said about Elohim during a conversation we had not long ago."

"Uh, I am not sure which conversation we're talking about, but go on," Justin chimed in, only patched in because it involved him in the first place, and wearing a sly grin.

"Wait. Why am *I* here? If this is about Elohim, it can't be that important," Lucifer offered. Zabkiel smiled, as Justin outright laughed.

"I think you'll find this quite interesting indeed," Zabkiel said, still suppressing a smile. "It seems that since the day of Jesus' birth, all sources of his DNA have been purposefully and systematically destroyed."

"What? For what purpose?" Elohim asked, baffled.

"I wondered that myself, especially when Tubiel, a servant, came to me and said her master Dilyla had ordered her to thoroughly clean or destroy anything Jesus touched, discarded, ate, excreted, and so on. It included diapers, napkins, silverware, cups, dishes, and anything else he came into contact with in any way," Zabkiel announced.

"Now that you mention it, I remember Tubiel's odd behavior. She seemed obsessive about cleaning up after him, but what does a neurotic nanny have to do with anything?" Elohim asked, a little peeved.

"There was a very important reason for her obsession. They deliberately hid something from you. To discover what it was, I sent a team of scientists to Naberus, the prison planet, and ordered them to escort Dilyla to Heaven, where our scientists could collect her DNA. We also needed to scan her thoughts with the Illuminator. To put it lightly, and no pun intended, the results were quite...illuminating." Zabkiel smiled at his own joke, then paused.

"Come on, damn it! You brought us here to tell us this big secret of yours, so do not leave us hanging," Lucifer pushed.

Zabkiel was happy he had gotten Lucifer's attention; he definitely needed that, because the newest revelations were very important.

"Yes, go on. What did your scientists find?" Elohim asked.

"Well, it took a while to research the old files, but, after careful analysis, it was determined, with the utmost certainty, that Dilyla is the daughter of...Cronus." Zabkiel paused again, this time wearing a more serious look as he let the information sink in.

"Huh? Cronus?" Elohim growled. "You mean, my son is the grandson of Cronus?"

"Not exactly, Elohim," Zabkiel said. He hesitated once more, trying to break the news softly. "The DNA also proves you are not the father of Jesus."

Elohim was uncharacteristically silent and utterly dumbfounded.

Lucifer, on the other hand, had plenty to say. "Then who the hell is the diseased little shit's father? Do you even know?" he blurted.

"Of course!" Justin said.

Zabkiel really wasn't sure how to proceed, because the truth was going to be painful. "It is bad, my friend," he gently warned.

"Zabkiel, just tell me," Elohim implored.

"The DNA is conclusive. Jesus is not the *grandson* of Cronus. Rather, he is Cronus' son."

"What!? You mean he impregnated his own daughter?" Lucifer asked. "That's disgusting."

Elohim was quiet for a long moment, so long that it worried Zabkiel, who finally asked, "Are you okay?"

"I feel like a fool," Elohim lamented, then hung his head.

"Please don't beat yourself up. No one could have anticipated such a devious, long-range plan. It was almost flawless…almost."

"But—" Elohim started.

"But nothing," Zabkiel interrupted. "They also fooled me, and I was in the position to watch over Heaven in your absence. I never questioned his servant's obsession with getting rid of his brushes, even when she burned them after every grooming. It did not dawn on me what was going on. I blindly dismissed it as one of Dilyla's royal quirks."

"There is something you both overlooked," Justin offered.

"What?" they chorused.

"Cronus stepped in poopy and made a fatal mistake," Justin started.

"Don't drag this out. How did Cronus, as you say, step in poopy?" Lucifer inquired.

"Cronus, desiring to produce a pure progeny, failed to take into account the effect that inbreeding would have on his offspring. This could be the cause of the obvious abnormalities of Jesus' mind. He sees everyone as a threat, but perhaps that is because his brain is actually biologically damaged. Cronus has never been able to approach Jesus, his own son, without being the target of his diseased rage. That kept Cronus from realizing his ultimate plan to rule the galaxy himself," Justin said with confidence, knowing that the logic behind his words left little room for any challenge.

"If this is true—and I believe it is—Cronus must only be pretending to help Jesus now, while moving to some sort of Plan B behind his back," Zabkiel suggested. "He has found another way to exploit and use his son to make the galaxy his own."

Lucifer looked over at his old friend, who was several feet away and lost in his own thoughts. He touched Elohim on the shoulder and asked, "Are you okay? I know this is a lot to take in."

"Not since the days before Dilyla have I truly felt good about my life. Her beauty beguiled me somehow. When Jesus was born, I knew something was not right with him and his mother, but she had a way of making me forget my misgivings.

"As Jesus grew, I felt the two were distancing themselves from me. I compensated by making up excuses to travel off world. Our adventures helped me cope with the painful loss. I had always yearned for a family I could love and cherish, and I was fooled into thinking I had one. To be honest, though, I never truly felt like a father or husband." He paused, sighed, then finished, "You asked if I am all right. My answer is yes, my friend. For the first time in a long time, I am truly well. Now that the wound has been exposed, perhaps it can heal."

Benjamin Oneal

Chapter 24

Sandel lay down after a long day of coordinating defense plans, only to be immediately alerted by the simultaneous, ear-splitting blaring of what seemed like every alarm and communication device in his home. He almost fell out of bed scrambling to get to the video screen.

"We are under attack! They came out of deviant space just moments ago," shouted Asbeel, Sandel's head of defense.

"How many?" Sandel asked.

"So far, 115."

"It is a good thing our planetary defense grid is shielded. That's the first thing they targeted when they emerged."

"Battleships?"

"We have deployed our forces and are engaging the enemy now."

"Is the *Cassiel* ready?" Sandel asked.

"Why, Sandel? You can't possibly go out there and—" Asbeel tried, hoping to dissuade his leader.

"This is my world, and I will fight for it," Sandel interrupted, looking resolute.

Asbeel knew there was no way to change Sandel's mind, so he conceded, "It will be ready by the time you arrive, sir."

"Good. Send word to all Alliance ships. They need to be on standby. Also, inform the New Empire and the Cooperative of the attack," Sandel ordered.

Once Sandel joined the battle, he realized, much to his dismay, that a great number of Dumah were among the attackers. *That means only one thing,* he surmised. *Damn. They are going to do everything they can to land ships on Hell itself.*

"Hail all ships!" Sandel ordered. "Those creepy crawlers are beginning to swarm. Move to higher orbit to avoid the nasty things and target the other warships. We cannot let any Dumah ship land! I repeat... It is imperative that we prevent all Dumah from touching down."

As Sandel relayed that urgent message, he noticed something odd: As many members of the Alliance fleet concentrated their weapons on the Dumah, the Disciples removed themselves from the fray and focused their firepower on protecting their insect comrades, as if trying to help the Dumah in their attempt to reach the surface. When he witnessed that, Sandel knew he had to act quickly, before the Alliance fleet suffered enough damage to create holes for the Dumah to penetrate.

Sandel directed ten ships to strike out at the Disciple battleships. The tactic worked, but it drew Disciple fire to Sandel in the *Cassiel*. As the ships under his command took on the Disciples, more enemy vessels dropped out of deviant space.

The inhabitants of the planet below found their peaceful night interrupted when they were treated to an impromptu light show like none other. Energy beams of varying colors spat streaks through the starry background of space, resulting in spectacular and terrifying explosions, bright blue-white coming from the Cooperative and the Alliance and dark red coming from the Disciples. Not long after that, the Dumah joined in with light green, and the Sauroptors added their high-intensity purple. What the observers on Hell did not know was that the streaks of white that resembled falling stars were not only debris from the battle above entering the atmosphere but also Alliance fighters diving into the exosphere to burn away Dumah who were tearing away at their outer skin.

The war waged on for hours. Both sides took damage,

but more and more Alliance ships entered the fight. Soon, there were no more enemy ships to drop out of deviant space. While the battle seemed to be moving in favor of the Alliance and the LLC, they knew there was always a chance for a third or fourth wave.

Even in the heat of battle, something continued to bother Sandel, something that just did not seem right. There were not enough enemies there to see their presumed plan through to fruition. With that on his mind, he called Asbeel and asked, "What can you tell me about the makeup of the attack force?"

"What do you mean?" Asbeel inquired. He hesitated for a moment, a little confused, but quickly recovered and gathered his thoughts. "Oh!" he said as he looked away for a second to do a few quick calculations in his head. "During the first wave, there were twenty-five Sauroptors destroyers, ten Disciple battleships, ten Titan battleships, and seventy Dumah warships. The second wave brought seventy-five enemy vessels in all, with five more Disciple battleships, five Titan battleships, fifteen Sauroptor destroyers, and fifty Dumah. Their total attack force was 190."

"What!? They couldn't possibly take Hell with less than 300 warships!" Sandel paused as the horror sank in. "Shit!" he wailed. "It was only a diversion. Patch me through to Heaven and the Cooperative right away."

"Yes, sir."

"The attack on Hell is a diversion!" Sandel screamed from the deck of the *Cassiel*. "I repeat… The attack on Hell is diversion." He almost yelled it a third time at the images of Justin and Zabkiel as they appeared on the video screens.

"We just got word that warships are dropping out of deviant space around Eden," Justin said. His demeanor became more grief-stricken as he announced, "Salome is on Eden."

"Zabkiel and I both have ships near there." Sandel looked at someone beside him, then said, "They are on their way, my friend."

"Thank you. I'll call back as soon as I know more," Justin

promised, looking beyond worried as he signed off.

***

In all, the Alliance lost twenty-three ships to the enemy, though the actual death toll was yet to be determined. Only thirty-one enemy ships escaped into deviant space: twenty-two Disciple battleships and nine Sauroptor destroyers. Before the last of the Disciples escaped, they disabled two Dumah who attempted to follow them.

The space around Hell was littered with the remnants of destroyed ships from both sides of the battle, just random, jagged, burned-out and smoldering clumps of metal and plastic, floating in the cosmos, grim markers of the passage into oblivion. Hundreds of thousands of Dumah had joined the fight; some were still alive and stubbornly continued attacking any ship that came close. To their credit, they fought until the very last insects succumbed to the vacuum of space or were lucky enough to die quickly as their warships exploded. The only silver lining to the dark cloud of destruction was that no Dumah made it to the surface of Hell.

Sandel and everyone else knew it would take months or even years to clean up the debris, but that was a worry for another day. The defense of Hell and the galactic war was at the forefront of everyone's thoughts and would be until the Resurrectionists were no more.

Chapter 25

A lot had been done to bolster the defenses of Eden and New Earth since the formation of the Long Life Cooperative. No one knew how many ships the Resurrectionists had at their disposal, but it was clear that they were confident enough to engage in a battle they thought they could win. History would designate this another dark day in history, as 147 of those enemy ships dropped out of deviant space, their forward guns blazing.

The only bright thing in the otherwise dire situation was that Eden was somewhat prepared for the imminent attack. Not only that, but at the precise moment when the enemies attacked, the LLC was in the midst of a readiness drill. While no attack was welcomed, the timing couldn't have been better; it was easy to switch from practice to actual combat mode. The ratio of enemies turned out to be quite different in this attack, with only thirty-seven Dumah warships, eighty Sauroptor destroyers, and fifteen each of Disciple and Titan battleships.

While Eden was not completely ill prepared to face invasion, it still came as something of a surprise. When the Resurrectionists began their attack on Hell, all eyes were on the Alliance defense of their home world. No one actually thought Eden would be the real target. It was bait-and-switch at its best, and it gave the Resurrectionists a distinct advantage. Due to the suddenness of the attack, twenty-four LLC battlecruisers were quickly disabled or destroyed. Nevertheless, it was no time for kicking oneself.

Along with the planetary defense grid, 200 more LLC battlecruisers entered the conflict, with Dumah again leading the way. Hundreds of insect-like fighters oozed out of their warships. The LLC engaged the Dumah, using tactics created by Elohim and Lucifer. Still, as each Dumah warship was dismantled, thousands more bugs gushed out of others to replace it.

The Dumah were followed by Sauroptor destroyers and fighters. Although the space around Eden was vast, it suddenly seemed remarkably crowded. As bright, white energy beams from LLC battlecruisers tore at the shields of the attacking warships, their fighters skillfully weaved in and out, repelling the enemies.

Just as the Long Life Cooperative began to overwhelm their adversaries, a second wave dropped out of deviant space. Another 120 enemy ships surrounded the defending fleet and opened fire. Far too soon, thirty more LLC ships fell prey to the contest. Still, when it looked as if all was lost, 200 Alliance ships joined the fight.

***

Justin watched the battle with rapt fascination. He was very interested in the defense of Eden, but Salome's safety was paramount. Although no Dumah landed on Eden, many Sauroptors did, and they were better on foot than they were in space. Word from Eden indicated that ground forces had contained all the reptiles for the time being, but the battle was far from over.

He was not surprised that the Resurrectionists used Dumah in their attack on Hell, because there was no downside to letting the relentless, innumerable creatures ravage the home world of the Freewill Alliance. What Justin couldn't figure out was why they employed them during the Eden attack. *Why would they risk the Dumah destroying the Trees of Life?* he struggled to fathom.

His worry over his wife almost clouded what was truly happening. When no third wave attacked, he had his answer:

Damn them! They allowed those monsters on Eden because they do not care! Eden is not the prime target! My God, we've been deceived once again!

Quickly, Justin opened a signal to the head of New Earth Security. As soon as the first snowy pixels of Stolas appeared on the video screen, Justin barked out an order: "Prepare for attack! Prepare for attack!"

"I assure you, sir, we are as prepared as we can be," Stolas said, sounding far too calm and looking more than a little confused.

"You don't understand, Stolas. They are coming for Earth, and they are coming now!" Justin hollered.

At that moment, the atmosphere around Earth filled with dark green rings as the Resurrectionist fleet dropped out of deviant space. Ground sensors counted 700 separate incursions into normal space around the planet.

Although Justin was still quite worried about Salome, his focus shifted to the defense of Earth. *So many precious people and resources to protect,* he thought, *and so little time...*

Chapter 26

Archangel Michael, the leader of the Disciple attack on Earth, was certain the three-way diversion would work in their favor. As he dropped out of deviant space, it seemed his predictions were right. His sensors told him Earth defenses numbered around 700 battleships. He knew a good number of the members of their fleet were en route to Eden, and he couldn't help but smile at the thought.

The plan he and Cronus had devised worked like a charm. Initially, they were the only ones who knew the first two attacks were a ruse, nothing but diversions. The Dumah and Sauroptors were unwitting pawns in their plans, carelessly sacrificed for the greater good—or the greater bad, depending on how one looked at it. It had already been decided that the Sauroptors would find a place in the Empire, provided any survived, but the Dumah would be systematically eradicated.

"Commence fire as soon as possible!" Michael ordered his fleet. That command resulted in the destruction or disabling of fifty-six Long Life Cooperative ships before they even had a chance to fight back. It was a crushing blow to an already outnumbered Earth force.

The Titans, on the other hand, were under the command of Cronus. He employed the same attack plan as Michael, and his ships managed to take out thirty-seven of the Earth fleet. The Sauroptors, not nearly as skilled in space warfare as their comrades, only took out nineteen vessels with their destroyers. The combined number of casualties was devastating, nonetheless.

If not for the Earth planetary defense grid, it might have been a quick defeat. That helpful resource did much to level the odds and even gave Planet Earth a decent chance of repelling the assault. Just as a turnaround seemed imminent, though, a second wave of enemy ships joined the fight.

In all, 300 Disciple battleships, 200 Titans, and 40 Sauroptor destroyers came to the party. Although Earth defenses managed to remove 174 enemy ships, that still left the odds at 1,016 to 588. As the battle roared, the odds tilted in the favor of the enemies of Earth and Eden.

Justin sat in the control center, carefully analyzing the data and reports he received from his communications and surveillance teams and from those on the battlefront. He quickly realized two things. First, there were no Dumah ships involved in the attack on Earth. That told him the planet was the final target. They had obviously disabled the Dumah ships that attempted to retreat from the assault on Hell, and that told him they were not taking any chances that the Dumah might land on Earth and destroy the Trees of Life.

Second, once he heard that Michael was in command of the Disciple fleet, he struggled to justify it in his soul. Most of all, he just could not resist the chance to face the Archangel in battle. Justin felt it was his duty to fight alongside his NES ships. So, against the protests of all his advisors, he boarded the *Ronwe* and joined the battle.

Even with the additional ships, Earth did not seem to be faring well. New Earth Security put up a valiant fight, but the numbers were 892 against 476, leaving every NES vessel to fight two enemy ones.

Justin looked around him and saw a rainbow of energy beams cutting through the dark cosmos. They reminded him of another time, a time long before the people of Earth were sure they were not alone in the universe. Back then, a laser directed at the moon could spread to a diameter of over three miles. In time, they found a way to manipulate those energy beams to make them destructive and dangerous. Other weapons that illuminated the cosmos reminded Justin of machine-gun blasts, just vicious bullets of light peppering targets with consecutive explosions, tearing away at the shields. Once the shields were breached, the armaments easily tore through the exterior skins and hulls of the unfortunate victims.

He did not want to admit it, but, barring any help, they were on a path to losing Earth. The Long Life Cooperative fleet continued to fight, and he was proud to be among such great warriors, but he was saddened by the fact that he could not seem to fulfill his duty to keep his beautiful planet safe. The thought of Jesus once again taking control of Earth tore at his heart.

With those thoughts weighing heavily on his mind, Justin opened a direct line to Stolas. "Stolas, I have a very important assignment for you," he said.

"Okay, but I am kinda busy here, Justin," Stolas replied.

"Listen, if things become...hopeless, we—" Justin started.

"It's going to turn around soon, sir," Stolas interrupted.

"Damn it, Stolas, just listen! If we get to the point where we're certain we have no chance, I want you to take Rachel to Eden. See if you can find Salome," Justin said, resolute.

"But, sir, I—"

"No buts! Just please promise, okay?"

"Of course, but only if there is no other way."

"Thank you, my friend. Now, let's win this war," Justin said, then commanded his crew of the *Ronwe* to blast every ship that came within striking distance, until they took one violent hit after another.

"We take another shot like that, sir, and they will breach our shields," said Harut, Justin's second-in-command.

In a blur of terrifying firepower, three Disciple ships converged on the *Ronwe*. There was no way Justin's ship could withstand the devastating combined assault of their arsenal. *Damn. If only there were but one or two of them,* he thought, but there were far more attackers than that and little chance of surviving such an onslaught without assistance.

Conceding to his sad fate, Justin prepared to send a grim communique to the surviving NES fleet. It was then, at that very moment, that something quite amazing occurred, something entirely unexpected; in fact, it could have been considered something of a miracle.

Chapter 27

"Need a little help?" Lucifer asked over the communicator.

"What the...?" Justin's eyes widened as he watched multiple concentrated, blue-white beams run parallel with the dark red ones, doing their best to eliminate the Disciple ships.

As it turned out, 760 Olympian fleet ships, led by Zeus, followed Elohim and Lucifer into normal space. For the first time since the battle began, Justin felt hope. *If there is no third or fourth wave,* he realized, *we might actually have a chance at victory!*

After taking a moment to let his mind catch up to what he saw with his eyes, his thoughts traveled to Michael. "Does anyone have a location on the Disciple command ship?" Justin asked.

"Not yet," Stolas and Maalik chorused, a reply echoed to everyone in the fleet.

As Resurrectionists were pushed back, a call came from Sorath, captain of the *Enola*. Justin had met him on his first journey to Hell, what seemed like a lifetime away. "I have eyes on the command ship," Sorath said. "I'm sending the coordinates now."

"On it," Justin replied. He then looked at his navigator and commanded, "Max speed...now!"

The *Ronwe* cut a path through the many points of battle, homing in on the command ship. Justin was, quite literally, on the edge of his seat, counting the seconds before they were in range. Time seemed to slow as he waited to give the command to fire.

Michael, a prudent and observant commander in his own right, caught sight of the retaliation as soon as the *Ronwe* moved within firing range. In a defensive move, the Disciple command ship and the 307 remaining ships in their fleet entered deviant space.

Still, Justin yelled, "Fire!" At the very least, he hoped to disable the Archangel's ship, but Michael managed to disappear from normal space as the crippling blast ripped through empty space.

After a long moment, Justin lessened his grip on the arms of the captain's chair. More than anything, he wanted to take Michael down, but his enemy had foiled him once again. Frustration gripped his soul, so much so that he almost audibly screamed. Ever since Michael first tortured him in the Angel compound on Earth and attacked Salome and him in their home, the Archangel had been his quarry. The predator had yet to catch his prey.

Suddenly, Elohim's voice broke into his discouraged thoughts: "It seems the Titans are leaving as well."

Justin's sensors picked up 168 Titan battlecruisers making an exit. It had been one of the longest days of his life, and it was refreshing to force the retreat, but he knew the battle was not over. Only 37 Sauroptor destroyers remained, unwilling to run. Although they were enemies, Justin couldn't help but be impressed by their valor and commitment. They fought hard and were willing to make great sacrifices. The war would not really be over till the very last stubborn Sauroptor destroyer boiled away in the vacuum of space.

Justin sat back in his command chair. "Elohim, Lucifer, thank you," he said sincerely. "You really saved the day."

"Hey, it was *your* idea to seek help from the Olympians. The credit for this small victory goes to you, puny earthling." Lucifer laughed.

"Not such a small victory but definitely a costly one. We lost a lot of good people today, as did Eden and Hell. We must end this once and for all. Cronus, Michael, and Jesus must pay," Justin said with a controlled growl in his voice.

"And they will," Elohim vowed with confidence. "But right now, I'm not quite done with the ones who are trying to get away. I got one in my sites right now." With that, the Vepar followed the retreating ship into deviant space. They followed the Resurrectionist ship through deviant space. Their scans of the damage to the enemy ship, indicated that there was no way that they could know they were being followed, as long as they stayed at a safe distance.

After three hours, the enemy ship dropped out of deviant space. Lucifer and Elohim, aboard the Vepar, followed. Once they were in normal space, the sensors picked up the enemy ship traveling at maximum speed, away from the drop point. As they moved to follow, Maalik, the Communications officer, broke the tension.

"Captain, we are getting a distress signal."

"Do we have a location?"

"Trying to lock on now sir." As he worked the controls to determine the location the signal abruptly stopped. "We lost it sir."

"Play back what you got."

"Under attack, unknown vessel, can't outrun." The message from the unknown source repeated until it suddenly stopped.

"Sir, there seems to be a coded message hidden within the distress signal."

"Can you retrieve it?"

"Yes, but I cannot unlock it."

"Let me see." Lucifer said, looking over his shoulder. Something about the code seemed familiar. "I think it is a Ghost code." He tapped a few keys, and the message became clear.

"Uzza Flauros, Holy Ghost, Priority message for the New Empire, the Free Will Alliance, the Long Life Cooperative.

Regular cargo run to the planet Dellos. curious cargo, including the Factor and strange luxury items. After unloading, attacked by Old Empire battlecruiser. Cargo ship destroyed, escaped in fighter. Fighter damaged, cannot make jump." The message continued to repeat until it suddenly stopped. "Uzza Flauros, Holy Ghost, Priority message for the New Empire, the Free Will Alliance, the Long Life Cooperative. Regular cargo run to the planet Dellos, curious cargo, including..."

After the recent attacks on Hell, the Free Will Alliance, and the New Empire, the need to find the Resurrectionist home base was paramount. Although, they were victorious, the danger of continued aggression was a real fear. The home worlds of the Dumah, the Sauroptors, and the Titans were well known, and plans for their futures were in in the process, the finding and dealing with the combined force of the Resurrectionist was a priority.

Lucifer sent scout ships to Dellos, to see if there was any validity to the message. At the same time, the message was communicated to the three major powers. Justin sat with Rachel and Stolas, in his office, when the message arrived. Rachel sat back hard in her chair, causing Justin to ask, "What's wrong?"

After a moment, to calm her nerves, she finally looked up teary eyed. "Uzza was my oldest and dearest friend. We went to school together. When I came back to New Earth Security, she was recruited into the Holy Ghosts. We still found time to get together a few times a year."

Justin watched as her daughter fought back the tears. He knew that she would find time to mourn later. He still took her in his arms and hugged her.

"Uzza was a Holy Ghost?" Stolas asked truly surprised, and as an attempt to help Rachel compose herself, which he knew she was struggling to do.

"Yes. Sorry, but I was not allowed to tell you, or even my father Rachel said, as she gave her father final squeeze, and broke away.

"That is so cool." Stoller said.

Rise of the Fallen
***

"Are you sure the base is on Dellos?" Justin asked.

"Oh, yeah! The scouts we sent to the Dellos system, have assured us that that they have counted at least 200 Resurrectionist battlecruisers, along with almost 100 Titan vessels, with at least as many Sauroptor and Dumah ships, parked in space around Dellos." Lucifer assured him.

"Thank you, Uzza Flauros." Justin offered, and put his arm around Rachel.

It was time for immediate action. They had to organize the offensive on the Resurrectionist home base, and they had to do it now. An attack force comprising ships the new Empire, the Free Will alliance, and the Long Life Cooperative set out toward Dellos.

Benjamin Oneal

Chapter 28

After their failed attempt to capture Earth, Michael returned to Dellos. He was happy with he made it out alive but was furious that he had failed to take control of Earth. He was also surprised to find that the thing he wanted most was to be with his daughter, Rebecca.

As soon as he landed, Michael rushed to the control room to see if Cronus was on his way. *Perhaps he fears they'll attack Titan, after the Olympians aided in repelling the attack on Earth,* he reasoned. When he was unable to contact Cronus, he decided to find Rebecca.

He couldn't get her on the video screen, so he decided to visit her room. He knocked and pressed the doorbell, but no one answered. When a Dellosian custodian walked by, he took a chance and asked, "Have you seen my daughter."

The Dellosian shrugged. "I have not, sir. Perhaps she is visiting Lord Jesus in his room. I saw her go in there earlier this evening."

Michael thanked the servant and walked away, but he could not hide the dismay on his face. After Jesus' threat to keep Rebecca for himself, Michael was quite concerned about his former Lord's intentions. Given the history of the self-proclaimed God, he feared for Rebecca's safety. *After all, he is a crazy bastard,* Michael thought. He had known Jesus for thousands of years, and in that time, he had witnessed some of the most depraved behavior he'd ever seen. Genuinely worried, he picked up the pace; he was almost running by the time he knocked on Jesus' door.

"Come in, Michael," Jesus snidely said from the other side.

Michael burst through the door and found Rebecca in the middle of the room, held hostage by two guards on either side. Jesus was standing behind her, with a plasma ion weapon pointed at the side of her head. Her clothing was torn, and she looked dazed, as if she'd been drugged. The tears running down her cheeks told Michael all he needed to know: *That bastard! He raped her! He put his filthy hands on my little girl!*

"Throw your weapon to me!" Jesus ordered, then smirked as Michael released his weapon and threw it across the room. "I am not happy, Michael. You don't really think that I'm foolish enough to fall for that play along act. I saw how you acted when Cronus was around. Michael, you have forsaken me. You went against my wishes and failed in your attempt to take that wretched little Earth. Furthermore, since you wasted all our resources in your pitiful effort to go against me, you also failed to give me back Heaven."

"Please, milord, I—" Michael started, only to be interrupted.

"Milord? Milord?" Jesus growled. "You don't even see me as your Lord!" Jesus stomped a sandaled foot on the floor, as if to emphasize his point, and Rebecca shuddered in fear. "Instead of trusting in me, you sought counsel with Cronus, a traitor who only has eyes for the throne that is rightfully mine. To whom do you owe and offer your allegiance? To the Lord God of Heaven or to a man whose wretched family was cast out of Heaven by my grandfather, Jehovah? Are you a traitor, too, Michael?"

"No, milord. I have been your faithful servant for thousands of years. I only used Cronus to make your wish come true. I offered him something he could not walk away from, because he is so greedy for power."

"Liar! The two of you were in league together the whole

time, working against me."

"Please, Jesus, just listen. I... You were still healing, not quite yourself. I planned to take Earth first, then serve the head of Cronus to you on a silver platter," Michael said. He bowed his head and spread his arms out in front of him, hoping to feign respectful honesty to the fool in front of him.

"I am not so easily swayed by words anymore," Jesus admonished. "You will not change my low opinion of you by trying to stroke my ego."

"Fine," Michael said, losing his patience, "but if you have a problem with *me*, why are you holding a weapon to *her* head?"

"Because she is a traitor, just like her father—a beautiful one, surely, but a traitor nonetheless." Jesus leaned over to lick her cheek. "And so damn talented too."

"Traitor? How did Rebecca betray you?" Michael asked.

"I caught her in the communications room, sending a message to Lucifer."

Michael stared at his daughter in shock. "Is that true, Rebecca?" he asked, stunned.

"I-I'm s-sorry, Father. It's just that I so miss my ch-children and my husband," she said, struggling to speak without slurring.

Michael was suddenly angry with himself. In a moment of weakness, he had instructed the scientists who worked in the Room of Memories to let her keep her fond recollections of her family on Hell.

"Your bloodline is one of treachery," Jesus posited. He was angry that Michael had failed to put him back on the throne, and he was eager to see the Archangel pay for choosing Cronus over him. "The Lord giveth," Jesus said, moving the weapon closer to Rebecca's temple in a most threatening way, "and the Lord taketh away."

"Milord, please!" Michael begged, fully aware that an ion plasma blast would kill her instantly.

"You have betrayed and forsaken the Almighty, the one who gave you so much and was willing to let you serve at my side for all eternity. You never genuinely believed. Not only am I *a* god, you fool. I am *the* God. See? I once again have the power to choose between life or death. Beg for her life, Michael. Beg for forgiveness," Jesus said, sneering.

"Lord, please forgive my transgressions. I've been...weak. I do not have your strength. If you let her live, I will pledge my loyalty to you until my dying day."

"You know nothing of loyalty!" Jesus screamed. "How can I ever trust you again?"

"I will prove it to you, milord."

"How?"

"Let me kill my traitorous daughter myself," Michael said, with great resolve, reaching for the weapon in Jesus' hand.

Chapter 29

"F-Father?" Rebecca whined.

Jesus was taken aback by the offer he had not anticipated. "You would kill your own daughter?" he asked, clearly suspicious.

"If that is what is required for me to regain your trust, yes, milord," Michael answered without a hint of deception in his voice.

Jesus thought for a long moment, then turned to one of the guards next to Michael. "Give him your knife," he ordered.

Michael took the knife from the guard and looked at it for a moment with a pained expression on his face, as if trying to wish the cruel blade away. He turned his gaze on Jesus once more, nodded, then clutched the knife so tightly that the tang made an impression in the flesh of his hand. Moisture filled his eyes as he stared at Rebecca, still flanked by the Lord's guards, with rivers of tears on her face.

In an instant, Michael broke free and lunged at Jesus, only to be shot in the back by one of the guards. He hit the floor with a thud, and blood flowed freely from the wound on his back.

Jesus walked over, kicked the knife away, and stood over the fallen Angel. "Dear Michael, I had such high hopes for you. Now, you will die here, alone and unloved. As for Rebecca, I think I'll keep her. She will make an excellent mother to my children, or, perhaps I will just use her as I see fit, then slit her throat when I have no more use for her."

Michael tried to rise up to challenge Jesus, but the guards easily held him down. "Please!" he said with a groan. "Please spare my daughter."

When Jesus was sure Michael was watching, he approached the terrified, woozy, young woman and tore open her blouse, exposing her upper body. As she struggled in vain to move away, Jesus grabbed one of her breasts, licked her cheek slowly, then looked at Michael once more, with a most lascivious, taunting glint in his eye. "I will make her scream from both pleasure and pain," he said. "Let that be the last thought on your mind. Guards, make sure he doesn't leave this room!"

"Nooo!" cried Michael as the guards began to brutally pummel him with their weapons and hands.

"Bring her along," Jesus calmly instructed the ones who were holding Rebecca, stripped and humiliated.

Michael could only watch as his daughter was dragged out of the room behind her rapist and captor. It was the last thing he saw before one of the guards kicked him in the head and his world went dark.

***

Once he was out of Michael's sight, Jesus' true panic revealed itself. He ran as fast as he could and breathe heavily, heading for his ship, for he knew they were coming for him. *I need to leave Dellos now!* he thought. The guards behind him struggled to keep up. To make matters worse for them, Rebecca was beginning to come to her senses and was flailing about like an angry wildcat, causing them to fall even farther behind their Lord. Although she and her father had never been close, something deep within her told her that she wanted to be with him, and her heart ached with grief when she was forced to leave him behind.

Finally, Jesus stood in the doorway of his ship, but he was conflicted. With the passing of every second, the New

Empire drew closer. He knew if he didn't leave right away, his capture—if not his death—was imminent. The true dilemma was what to do with Rebecca. He desperately wanted Michael's daughter, wanted to make her his to finalize his revenge on the insolent and deceitful Archangel, but he was wasting precious time hauling her along as she tried to fight off his guards. After a few moments, Jesus frowned and yelled to his men, "I have to depart immediately. Hide her, and I will send for her when I can." His disappointment was palpable.

As the door of his transport closed, he looked back at the prize he was denied. It angered him even more as his transport lifted off and was soon lost in the darkness of space.

Within a few moments, twenty Disciple ships followed their disgruntled God into deviant space.

Chapter 30

Some 1,000 battleships, from the three major powers, suddenly appeared in the space around Dellos. Most of the ships, that the scouts had witnessed, were still there. Because their attack was unexpected, the enemy ships were quickly dispatched after a short, yet heated battle, the space above the planet Dellos was free of any threat from the Resurrectionist. Forward planning, made sure that no enemy ships made it to deviant space. Next, the threat of retaliation on the surface was quelled and the planet secured, the home world of the enemy was conquered. Once their control is absolute, Elohim and Lucifer landed.

"Let no one leave this planet without my authorization," Elohim commanded, in no uncertain terms. His next order of business was to initiate a search for Jesus. "This is our top priority, since it appears Cronus has not yet returned here," he said.

As instructed, those under Elohim's command undertook a search for Jesus, but there was no sign of him anywhere. They cleared the command center in under an hour and had to assume Jesus was either hiding or gone.

Although Jesus was nowhere to be found, Michael was located, bloody and battered and sitting against a wall near the door. It was clear from the crimson stain on the floor that he had dragged his broken body to where he now sat.

Elohim and Lucifer stood over the dying Michael. As they carried him to a cushioned chair, he grunted in pain.

"You two..." Michael began, every syllable torturing his body with agonizing aches and throbbing. "How fitting that *you*, of all those in the galaxy, are here to witness my death. I will not bother trying to justify what I have done, but I..." He paused again to take an excruciating breath, then said, "There is something I must tell you."

"Go on," Lucifer urged, knowing Michael's time was short.

"I-I truly believed I had chosen the right side. In the beginning, it was an honor to follow Jesus, but in time, he began to change. His dive into lunacy was gradual at first, but by the time he truly went off the deep end, I felt it was too late for me. I had already committed crimes against my people, awful acts no one could ever forgive me for. Those atrocities, along with the hate I harbored in my heart for you both, kept me from accepting the truth.

"See, when we were young, in Angel training together, all those years ago, I was jealous. That was before I knew you were Jehovah's son, Elohim. I came from a prominent family, so I had an air of superiority about me, a false sense of entitlement. I thought I was better than you, than either of you. Truly, I thought everyone was inferior to me. I felt as if I deserved everyone's respect, simply based on who I was and where I came from. For that reason, envy boiled within me. I saw how others respected you and applauded your accomplishments. I also coveted the close friendship between the two of you. I had never enjoyed such brotherhood with anyone.

"When I found out you were Jehovah's son, I was furious. I let myself believe that you only fared well because you were the son of God. The truth is, you are a great leader, just like your father. Deep down, I knew that all along, but my jealousy and bitterness caused me to refuse to admit it to myself. If only I would have realized my error and chosen with my head and not my heart, my life might've been different."

"The past is behind us, Michael," Elohim said.

"Perhaps, but it does guide our future, doesn't it? Even

if our future is short," Michael wisely said. "Wait though. I-I need you to know something else."

"What is it?"

"Jesus is... He is not your son. Cronus is his father," Michael said, shuddering with every word.

"I know."

"Oh. Well, that's good then. You should not have to live with the burden of thinking that diseased seed came from you," Michael said before he coughed up a glob of blood. "I will not, cannot ask for your forgiveness, for I deserve none. All I do ask is that you find my daughter, Rebecca, and take her back to Hell. Please return her mind to the time when she was at peace there, before Jesus had her brought to me. She yearns to be with her children and husband, in the place she knows as her home. I know you owe me nothing, but please grant a dying, disgraced Archangel this one wish. Please give my Rebecca a life that is happy and free of memories of me and the shame of that knowledge."

"If that is her desire, Michael, we will do it," Lucifer assured him.

"Do you know where she is?" Elohim asked.

"Jesus took her," Michael answered, then stirred a bit, as if he were trying to get up. He coughed up more blood, then weakly fell back into the chair. "Please find her. Please save my daughter."

"I promise," Elohim earnestly said.

Lucifer suddenly excused himself and left the room. Ten minutes later, he returned and asked Elohim to follow him.

"Where are we going?" Elohim asked.

"Let's just say I've found a Disciple who is...willing to talk to us."

"Willing or persuaded?" Elohim said, when he saw the Disciple who looked as if he'd been through a knock-down, dragged-out fight.

"Let's call it...forcibly coerced," Lucifer said with a grin. He gave the abused Disciple a shove and barked, "Tell us...

now!"

"Jesus... He took a transport to his ship, just before you descended on Dellos," the Disciple said.

"Damn it all!" Elohim cursed. "Was the girl with him?"

When the Disciple hesitated to answer, Lucifer took a step toward him, wearing a menacing grimace on his face that left no doubt about his lack of patience.

The Disciple flinched. "Yes!" he screeched. "Milord left the pretty redhead behind, but I-I know where she is."

"Tell us!"

The punished Disciple looked at Lucifer. "I will. Just keep *him* away from me."

Elohim smiled, despite the disappointment of losing Jesus. He knew Lucifer could be quite persuasive when he needed to be. Within seconds, they were made aware that Rebecca was locked in a hidden, underground bunker.

It did not take Elohim and Lucifer long to find the girl, and they quickly escorted her back to the Jesus' room.

Instantly, she ran to kneel by her dying father's side. "Father," she softly said.

"Rebecca, my love," he quietly said, almost a whisper.

"Please, Father, don't leave me," she begged as she laid her head on his chest.

He reached up and stroked her hair. "I love you."

"I love you too."

Michael looked up at Elohim and Lucifer. "Thank you," he managed. He then paused, coughed, and labored through another breath before he muttered, "Imagine it. Me, a grand-fa—" Before he could finish, he expelled his last breath, and his hand fell away from his daughter's soft, red locks.

Chapter 31

Although Heaven was not the main target, it did not excuse them from the fight. Cronus was still a dangerous threat, since had he had not returned to Dellos. Most believed he was heading for Titan. With that in mind, Zabkiel sent 1,000 New Empire battleships to join the Olympian fleet as they converged on what they believed to be Cronus' destination.

The combined fleet dropped out of deviant space above Titan, only to be immediately fired upon. Clearly, the enemies were expecting an attack. Unfortunately for them, many Titan battleships had been lost during the three previous attacks. Although the remnant numbered in the hundreds, they were no match for the nearly 1,700 ships that surrounded the planet.

After the New Empire and the Olympians successfully stifled the ground defenses, they received a signal that Planet Titan had surrendered. The main concern was Cronus; just because the planet had given in, that did not mean he had. As the New Empire and Olympian fleets continued to surveil the space around Titan, Zeus and 5,000 troops landed near Othrys, the capital city. Within two days, Planet Titan was under Olympian control. An extensive search ensued, and it was soon determined that Cronus had not returned there.

The ten star systems under Titan rule were subsequently

approached, much in the same way: Threats were systematically eradicated, and control was established. After three weeks, they found Cronus in the third Titan star system, on Tartarus. That planet was once used as a prison, but while there was still a rather extensive population of inmates, it was also now home to a vibrant, functional society.

Cronus was soon privy to the truth of reaping what one sows. He tried to hide, but those he trusted to help him were bitter, because he had abused them in the past. The family was once highly respected on Titan, but a false accusation prompted Cronus to banish them to Tartarus, denied a fair trial or any evidence of their guilt. They had not forgotten his cruelty, and they were happy to pay it back in kind when he dared to ask for their help once more. Once they were made aware that he was a fugitive and could no longer lord over them, they gleefully sent word to the forces searching for their former dictator.

When he was found and arrested, Cronus seemed surprised; he claimed to have no knowledge of his former wrongdoing against those who had turned him in. In fact, he was the poster child for undignified surrender. Kicking, screaming, crying, and throwing a tantrum like the Jesus he so despised, he was carried into the ship that would take him back to Titan.

***

Cronus stood trial on Heaven, for crimes against the galaxy and was promptly found guilty. He was then extradited to Titan and was also found guilty there, of crimes against his own star systems, and the people who once called the Lord. It was agreed that he would be held in solitary confinement on Planet Tartarus. He would be denied the Factor, but he had to consider that something of a mercy; although it would take from 600 to 800 years for the effect of longevity to wear off, dying of old age was far better than suffering through 6,000 to 8,000 years in captivity.

Of course, Cronus was safe nowhere, despite his access to the Factor or his former high position. He had made enemies in all corners of the galaxy, and even solitary confinement was no protection. Just a month after being thrown into his cage, he was murdered. As it turned out, two guards who could not resist a container of the Factor disabled the surveillance cameras and entered the cell of their former master. They beat him severely, then poured flammable liquid on him. Just before they ignited him, they delivered the message they had agreed to deliver: "Jesus says, 'hello.'"

The guards laughed as Cronus spent his last few moments of life wondering how his deranged son had managed to get the better of him, but all thoughts of his offspring's treachery disappeared, when he was set aflame. The two richest guards on Tartarus, if not within the entire galaxy, just watched as Cronus screamed and writhed in excruciating pain. Then, they casually walked away.

The joke was not only on poor Cronus, however. When the guards opened the container that held their promised prize, presumably enough Factor to last four lifetimes, they found only sugar. There was no Factor and never was, for they had been deceived by the real Master of Deceit, Jesus himself. At that point, there was nothing they could do but run. Unfortunately, much like the man they'd just incinerated, they found that there was no place for them to hide. The two were captured while attempting to board a trade ship that was preparing to leave Tartarus. No one gave them much of a chance, and they soon found themselves incarcerated in the same prison where they once worked, and that is never a good thing.

Chapter 32

Once the Titan system was secure, most of the New Empire fleet moved toward Insectus, and the Freewill Alliance fleet moved toward Sauros. There was a little unfinished business to take care of, for the part the Dumah and the Sauroptors had played in the war could not be ignored. Although they were just pawns in the Resurrectionist quest for control of the galaxy, they were still knowingly responsible for the deaths of many.

As was the case on Dellos and Titan, all ships that rose up against the New Empire or Freewill Alliance were destroyed or disabled. The viciousness of the Sauroptor attack became even more terrifyingly real when they were fighting on the surface of their home world. Fortunately, resistance was minimal, since each world lost many vessels in combat.

After the space above each planet was secured and ground defenses were neutralized, a message was dispatched: "Citizens of Sauros, you have declared war on the Freewill Alliance and the New Empire. You will pay for the destruction you have caused and for the lives lost in battle. Aggression or retaliation will not be tolerated, not from you or from any worlds under Sauroptor control. Signal your surrender now, or we will be forced to take further action."

The Sauroptors had an inherent resistance to surrender; in fact, it was a concept wholly foreign to their species. They had retreated before but had never actually admitted defeat. Thus, they responded to the warning by refusing to heed it and by firing a weapon that seriously damaged a Freewill Alliance ship. This elicited an immediate response, and energy weapons left a crater at the origin of the attack. The Freewill Alliance was forced to destroy five more locations before they were notified that aggressive action from the Sauroptors would cease.

The New Empire fleet that arrived at Insectus experienced a similar response. The only difference was that most Dumah facilities were subterranean, so the buggy creatures mistakenly thought they were protected. The Dumah were given the same ultimatum, though it was not clear whether they understood, since translation to their language was tricky. The basic message was given, however, but the insects soon realized there was no room for bargaining in the surrender-or-accept-your-fate message. When they tried to fire against the New Empire, they quickly learned that their opponents' weapons could reach all but their deepest tunnels.

The Dumah reluctantly surrendered, even as the workers were going about repairing the damage from the counterattack. It was amazing how rapidly they cleaned up, albeit without making any distinction between the debris and the bodies of their dead.

After Planets Insectus and Sauros complied, they were granted only enough ships to carry out trade with their own star systems. All vessels deemed unnecessary were emptied and destroyed. New Empire and Freewill Alliance battleships were also stationed in the space around their star systems to ensure that they remained in compliance.

The Sauroptors and Dumah gained no benefit from the Factor, so there was no need to threaten withholding it. The agreement was that after 100 years, when everyone who participated in the war was dead and gone, they would be approached and offered a place in the galactic community. Ambassadors from both sides would meet regularly to discuss grievances, answer questions, and, hopefully, keep each planet on track for the transition of power.

Benjamin Oneal

Chapter 33

  While Rebecca missed her life on Hell with her husband and children, she did not want to lose the memories of her father. It was decided that Michael's identity would be kept secret from those who did not need to know. Her husband and children would continue to think of him as just the parent who had been a part of her conditioning when she first arrived on Hell. She really had very few memories of him from before that time anyway; he was often absent during her childhood, and even when he was with her, he almost treated her as if she didn't exist.

  The memories she now cherished were of their few hours and days together after she was spirited away from Hell. Although the time she spent with him was short, she caught rare glimpses of his tender side. When he asked her about her life, her husband, and his grandchildren, he was genuinely interested. She would never forget how his eyes lit up when they talked about his granddaughters, Dara and Lailah, and his grandson, her beloved Raguel.

  On her way back to Hell, she spent many hours with doctors, who offered to help her remove any memories she did not wish to retain. She would not relinquish her thoughts of time spent with Michael, when they talked for hours, about nothing and everything all at once. She also desired to remember Jesus as a diseased, evil man-child, the one who had tried to rupture her soul, the maniac who corrupted her father, then killed him.

Sandel and Lilith had been in close contact with Rebecca's family since her abduction. The memories of a schoolmate, Lilith, given to her when she first arrived on Hell, made it possible for them to keep tabs on her and check her progress. Lilith and Sandel developed a wonderful friendship while watching over Rebecca; thus, it was not unusual that they had Rebecca's family brought to the spaceport and stood with them as they awaited the arrival of her transport.

When Mara Tyrre, formerly Rebecca, walked off the transport, Lailah, Dara, and Raguel ran to her. Her husband, Nanael, seemed frozen for a moment before he slowly joined his family. He waited patiently for his children to free their mother from their embrace, then hugged her himself. As the lovers held each other, their bodies trembled, and they all cried the happy tears of a family made whole.

When Mara calmed enough to speak again, she asked the one thing she'd been wondering about since she realized she would return to Hell: "How is Café Tyrre?" Upon her arrival on Hell over a century earlier, she had found employment in happily waiting tables at a small restaurant. In time, she and Nanael acquired a place of their own, an eatery that specialized in Earth cuisine. As on Earth, the people of Hell had long since left behind their desire for animals as a food source, but the smell, texture, and flavor were spot on.

"I closed the doors after you were taken. I-I just didn't want to be there without you," Nanael sadly answered. "Besides, the children needed me. We all missed you, Mara. We... I didn't think we would ever see you again," he admitted with a sniffle.

"That's all right," she said. "That just gives us a chance to hold a grand reopening!" Mara Tyrre said, and she practically skipped out of the spaceport with her beautiful family in tow.

Benjamin Oneal

Chapter 34

Along with the sanctions placed on the Sauroptors and the Dumah after, changes were afoot in the Titan system after the Olympian takeover. The government would be modeled after the New Empire and the Freewill Alliance. Top leadership would consist of a council of representatives from the ten planets, headed by a grand leader. Although it was his birthright, Zeus did not prefer to automatically claim the position; he preferred to give that decision to the people. Much to his shock and awe, now that his father was no longer a threat and could not control the lives and thoughts of his citizens, support for Zeus was overwhelming, and he was unanimously elected as grand leader of the council.

Zeus was both flattered and humbled to be selected by the people, but he knew it would take a good amount of time for the new government to mend the wounds caused by the previous leadership and to dismantle the oppressive caste system of his father. In that system, the minority of the entitled class had the most to lose. In the Cronus government, one didn't necessarily have to be useful to enjoy the finer things in life, and workers were looked down upon and devalued. In the new Zeus government, the playing field would be leveled out.

No longer would perceived usefulness trump actual usefulness. Free and fair elections would be held, a democratic process to give the citizens a voice in which officials would run the planet. Those who were previously trapped in the worker caste had the potential to use their skills and abilities to propel them into leadership positions. Suddenly, the falsely entitled ones found themselves having to prove they were worthy to remain.

In addition, a security force would be formed to enforce the laws. All members would be carefully vetted and subject to testing by Illuminator, which would weed out undesirables and Cronus loyalists. Then, they would be trained in ethics, with focus on fairness and honesty, so they would know that all were equal in the eyes of the law, rich, poor, or otherwise. There would be no differences among persons when it came to obeying the law; no one was above it, and even an Olympian could be prosecuted when and if laws were broken.

When Cronus held the throne, many individuals and even whole families found themselves on trial for crimes they did not commit. Honest people who once felt the sting of injustice and false accusations now enjoyed solace as they watched criminals from both castes be rightfully prosecuted and punished for their crimes.

The Factor, the secret of extremely long life, was considered a right of all, not a luxury for the rich, the bribed, or the entitled. No innocent person of any race, stature, or creed would be condemned to age and die while the wealthy thrived eternally. Only criminals sentenced to life in prison were deprived of the Factor. It would be cruel, to make them suffer any longer than necessary. In those cases, the convicted were sent to prison planets to live out their normal lifespans, along with others who were without the benefit of the Factor. Instead of thousands of years, their fate would be numbered in the hundreds.

Until worthy officials were found to campaign and be elected, it was decided that the siblings of Zeus would take on leadership roles for the ten star systems of the Titan empire. Once the new government was in place, Olympian leaders could retain their offices if they were elected and chose to do so.

To help alleviate the negative legacy left behind by

Cronus and Uranus, it was decided that the name of Titan should be changed, since it left a bad taste in the mouth of almost everyone. By unanimous vote, the capital planet became Olympia and the capital city of that planet was dubbed Olympus. In the years that followed, Zeus took his rightful place as leader of his home world, and all the galaxy was better for it.

Chapter 35

While galactic matters healed, personal joys also abounded for many. Justin was ecstatic to learn of his dear Rachel's engagement to Stolas Tezalel, a Hell-born man and head of New Earth Security.

Justin might have described his future son-in-law as a Wes Study lookalike, with strong, rugged features and his long, dark hair always held in a ponytail. He couldn't ask for a better man to marry his daughter. He first met Stolas when he was trying to infiltrate the Angelic organization that was secretly controlling Earth. He was part of a group of followers of Justin's website, Serpent's Gift. In fact, Stolas was a spy, sent by the Freewill Alliance to protect Justin when Rebecca, in her previous life as an Angelic spy, tried to kill him. If not for Stolas, she would have succeeded.

Others in the galaxy were also very excited about the upcoming nuptials, as evidenced by the fact that wedding guests began to arrive a week ahead of the event, with Sandel and Lilith being the first. They claimed they just wanted to "enjoy an extended vacation," but they readily volunteered to assist Salome in any way to make the wedding perfect. Mara Tyrre, formerly the spy known as Rebecca, brought her husband along, and they traveled with Sandel and Lilith.

Salome, Rachel, Mara, and Lilith discussed wedding plans, while Sandel, Nanael, and Justin had a few drinks and whined about the stresses of their respective jobs. When Justin and Sandel complained, "It is far more difficult to run an entire world," Nanael was quick to tell them stories about the horrors of being a restaurateur. Perhaps it was the alcohol, or perhaps it was simply the truth, but they soon agreed that rowdy diners and kitchen fires were far more daunting than the everyday minutiae of overseeing planetary proceedings.

When Zabkiel and his wife Tashamire arrived from Heaven, Rachel was overjoyed. After all, he was her favorite uncle. She ran to him when she and Justin met them at the spaceport, and her heart leapt with joy at the sight of him. "Uncle Zab, you made it!" the bride-to-be squealed as she jumped into his arms.

"We wouldn't have missed it for all the worlds," Zabkiel said, tightly hugging her.

Justin looked at the two of them, laughed, and shook his head. *Way back, when I was teaching that Religious Studies class, I wouldn't have imagined God attending my daughter's wedding!*

The father of the bride had another surprise for Rachel, so he managed to pull her attention away for her Uncle Zab just long enough to point back toward the spaceport in time for the arrival of a very special guest. There, walking through the doors, was Lornash, flanked by Elohim and Lucifer. The esteemed chief elder of Eden was thought to be over 20,000 years old, but he didn't look a day over 200. When they were just children, listening to their father tell the story of the plight of Eden, Rachel and Jarod, her brother, had suggested to Justin that it would be a good idea to save the Edenites from the old Empire, and Lornash had previously traveled to Earth to personally thank them. Since then, they had remained close and kept in touch. She was very happy to see Elohim and Lucifer as well, but the hands she held as they walked out of the spaceport belonged to Zabkiel and Lornash.

Heading up the New Earth Council had its perks, one of which was enough rooms for everyone. They all sat outside by the pool, enjoying food, drink, and conversation. It was a wonderful party on a wonderful day. Of course, Salome's environmental initiatives made things even more pleasant, for those efforts had elevated mankind into a nearly perfect symbiosis with Planet Earth. With a broad, proud grin on his face, Justin toasted the day and his wife's success.

As they continued eating, drinking, and being merry, Rebecca looked at Justin and reached out and touched his hand. "Remember the apartment in Chicago, when you tried to...get in my pants?" she asked, fully aware that Salome, Sandel, Lilith, Stolas, and Rachel were within earshot.

Justin sat back in his chair and felt the heat of his face reddening. "Well, I, uh... I remember it in a different way." He looked at Salome, reeling with embarrassment and hoping to quickly change the subject.

"Relax. Salome put me up to it," Rebecca said before she burst out laughing.

Everyone joined her with heavy chuckles of their own. Justin's were especially loud, once he caught up to the fact that he was the punchline.

Justin shook his finger at Salome teasingly, but after the laughing died down, he decided it was time for his own dig. "Maybe," he said, looking sincerely at Stolas, "but that was also the night I kicked your ass in that apartment. If Salome hadn't stopped me, you may not have made it out of that place alive."

Stolas grabbed Justin in a headlock. "Is that right? Is it? Is it?"

"Okay, okay!" Justin tapped out, as if forfeiting a wrestling match.

Wearing a grin of his own, Stolas let him go.

"You don't know how lucky you are, you big oaf," Justin said. "See, my wife was about ready to kick your ass to protect her man."

In response to that little bit of carefully edited history, Salome just shook her head.

"Now *that* threat scares the shit outta me," Stolas confessed, causing another chorus of side-splitting laughter all around.

Chapter 36

A very unexpected guest soon called ahead to make sure it was all right to attend. "Of course!" Justin said. "You didn't even have to ask, and it will be an honor."

Justin, Elohim, and Lucifer went to the spaceport to welcome Zeus, and Justin was in awe when he stepped out of his ship. The first thing he noticed, was something he learned in his recent research. The average height of the Olympian males was 5 inches more than humans. He was easily six foot eight. He reminded Justin of the actor Dolph Lundgren when he played in the movie *Masters of the Universe*, when his long blonde hair blue in the wind. Justin was quite familiar with the Olympian history.

As a youth, he had a passion for Greek mythology. For him, meeting Zeus in person was better than bumping into Superman or Santa Claus. Justin was star-struck for a while, but it did not take long for him to realize the legendary hero was really quite ordinary.

A couple days before the wedding, Zeus approached Justin with a simple request: "May I visit Mount Olympus while I am here?"

"It's real?" Justin said before thinking. "It must be real, I mean, the Olympians did live on earth for a while. I'm sorry but my mind is still coping with the fact that you are not a myth."

"It is real, indeed. Since we were just guests here for a while, and this is your world, it's only right that I asked permission. What you say?"

"Well, only if I can accompany you," Justin said, as if he would or could ever prevent the God of thunder and lightning, from going anywhere he wanted. His whole being screamed out, *please say yes*, as it was all he could do to compose himself.

"Certainly! I was hoping you would ask," Zeus said.

"Really?" Justin said, as excited as he was flattered. As if it were not enough to meet someone right out of the pages of his childhood storybooks, now he would visit a place that he'd dreamt of countless times. It would be a boyhood fantasy come true.

"There is something I want to show you," Zeus said, sporting a curious smile.

"What is it?" Justin asked.

"Just come with me. I don't believe you will be disappointed."

On Mount Olympus, near Litochoro, Greece, Justin darted his eyes in every direction, full of wonderment. He had always wanted to visit but had never had the chance. The area around the mountain was now protected, known as the World Biosphere Reserve, and it boasted remarkable biodiversity with a plethora of beautiful fauna and flora, some seen nowhere else in the world.

"Do you know how to use a personal AGU?" Zeus asked.

"An antigravity unit?" Justin snickered. "I might be a little rusty, as I haven't in a while, but sure I do," he said.

Zeus handed the unit to Justin, then began to fasten one on his own body. Once Justin donned his and was ready, Zeus smiled. "Let's go," he said, then rose into the air.

Justin followed Zeus up over 9,000 feet, almost to the top of a nearly vertical rock face near Mytikas peak. He wondered why Zeus was so fascinated with that particular location. It was full of splendor, but it was hardly anything to get excited about. Nonetheless, he shook his head at Zeus to indicate he was ready to follow him wherever he went.

Just then, Zeus pointed a device at the rock face. Suddenly, a huge door appeared. It was white, shiny, and solid, as if made of ivory.

Justin shut his eyes for a moment and wondered if the door would still be there when he opened them again. He was grateful to find that it was, so he knew he was not just dreaming up another epic adventure. "H-Has that been here all along?" Justin asked, when he finally rediscovered his voice.

"Yes, always. When we left, we could not risk anyone getting their hands on what we had to leave behind. Thus, we had to hide it behind an illusion, this rock façade."

When Zeus pointed the device again, the huge ivory doors began to slide apart, with a profound cacophony of deep rumbling thunder, as they slid to either side.

"Wow, that is impressive. I am surprised you guys got any sleep." Justin posited.

"Oh, that was just for the people below. Actually, it's completely silent."

"That's quite effective. For sure." Justin was impressed.

As they entered Olympus, they deactivated their AGUs. Justin stood in amazement, gasping at the immensity of the room, merely the entryway to a grand palace. He struggled to find his breath as he was overcome by veneration. Everything in the vestibule was so enormous, so immaculate that he couldn't imagine how truly gargantuan the palace had to be.

Following Zeus down a long corridor, he could only marvel at the majesty of it all. He was most surprised to see only a thin layer of dust. When he asked about that, Zeus explained, "This palace was sealed in a special way, constructed with dust-repellant material."

Although everything about it was wonderful, most of what Justin saw seemed antiquated by modern standards. That said, he knew the ancient Greeks must have found it magical. He could only imagine how it looked through the eyes of the people who once lived here, who had witnessed it thousands of years before his time. *A dust-proof palace inside a mountaintop? Indeed, fit for the gods!* he mused.

They traversed the expanse of a communal area where the gods had spent hours performing their godly duties, and then they entered the personal domicile of Zeus himself. In that room, Zeus retrieved a few items of sentimental value. "I really was saddened that I left these behind in my rush to leave Earth," he said. "Thank you for coming with me."

"No...thank you. I have dreamt of this since I was young. Back then, I read everything I could get my hands on concerning you and the Greek gods. So, again, thank *you*, Zeus."

Before they left Olympus, Zeus wanted to put on a bit of a show for Justin and the people below, to show them why he and his siblings were such phenomena to the ancient peoples of Earth. He worked a few controls and somehow summoned a loud crack of thunder, so strong it shook the mountain. Next, electronic bolts cut through the air around the mountaintop. As Justin laughed with delight, the people below looked on in questioning wonder and a bit of fear. Their shock turned to cheers when they realized they were in no danger.

Zeus and Justin activated their AGUs again and floated out the magic door. Before they descended, Zeus gave Justin the device he was holding. With great glee, Justin activated it, and the huge door closed and vanished, to be replaced by barren stone.

"Amazing!" Justin screamed, still fascinated.

"Consider that yours, to do with as you please," Zeus said.

"What?"

"Earth belongs to you, my friend, and Mount Olympus is part of it. Besides, there is little reason for us to return."

"I... This is great," Justin stuttered, mystified. "Thank you." His mind spun as he considered the greatness of what he had been gifted and all its possibilities. *We already have the World Biosphere Reserve, thanks to Salome and her team. Now, we can make the palace into a museum! It'd be the perfect place to display ancient Greek antiquities.* "Watch out, Smithsonian! Here we come," he mumbled to himself as he made a mental note to bring it up at the next New Earth Council meeting.

Chapter 37

At the rehearsal dinner the day before the wedding, old friends reconnected, and new friendships were forged. It was shaping up to be a wholly wonderful event. Justin's parents were in attendance, along with Alex, his younger brother by 100 years or so. When his mother and father began taking the Factor, their lives changed in ways entirely unexpected. Most surprising at all was, at the ripe, old age of 126, Justin's mom learned she was expecting. Nine months later, along came Alex.

Justin did not keep in touch with Alex often, for they were both very busy. Then, one day, he discovered that his brother was employed at a Tree of Life farm. Alex wanted to pave his own way, without relying on his older brother's reputation as chief counsel. He started out as a picker and climbed the ladder of success through hard work and dedication, till he was promoted to manager of one of the largest farms in Florida. At the rehearsal dinner, Justin also found out that Alex and Salome had been working together, trying to coordinate the Tree of Life farms with responsible environmental ideologies and sustainability concepts.

As they reconnected, Justin realized just how remarkable a young man his little brother was. "I'm really proud of you, Alex," he said. "You started at the bottom and ended up on top!"

"Meh, it's nothing. I'm just following in my big brother's footsteps," Alex said, giving Justin a pat on the back.

Justin smiled sheepishly at the compliment. "Truly, I never could've done it on my own. Many people are the wind beneath my wings, and some of them had to really push me." He smirked as he remembered being practically dragged, kicking and screaming, every step of the way.

"Yeah," Alex said, unconvinced. "I've read your story, and I have it on expert authority that you deserve to be exactly where you are."

"Expert authority? Whose?" Justin asked.

"Mom's and Dad's. Duh!" Alex retorted, sending them both into a laughing fit.

As the siblings continued talking, Rachel walked up. "Hey, Dad. Hey, Uncle Alex," she said, then gave them both a hug.

"Well? Have you decided what you're going to do?" Alex asked.

"Truth be told, I don't think it's going to work out well, being my soon-to-be husband is in command at NES. We'll get plenty of that at home," she said with a grin.

"Huh? You're going to be *second*-in-command once you're married? I've never known a wife to do that," Alex teased.

Rachel laughed. "I just think it's best for me to be reassigned."

"We've decided to break Long Life Cooperate security into two units. Stolas continue to be in charge of securing the space around our seven planets, and Rachel will head up planetary security," Justin informed him.

"I'm still not sure I'm up for the job though," Rachel lamented.

"What!? You're my favorite niece. You'll do fine," Alex assured her. "Besides, I've taught you everything I know." He reached toward her face, then held up his hand, with his thumb protruding between his index and middle fingers. "Got your nose!"

Rachel slapped his hand away and giggled. "I'm 100 years older than you. D<u>on't</u> you forget that, Uncle Alex." She then punched him in the shoulder playfully.

"Did you see that, Justin? She hit me. I think you need to give her a spanking," Alex whined, rubbing his arm.

"You're on your own, pal. I'm pretty sure she can kick both our asses without even breaking a sweat," Justin acknowledged, raising his hands in faux surrender and backing away.

A while later, Justin stood by himself and looked around. Again, he found it hard to believe, the odd course his life had taken. *I thought I was so smart when I taught at the university, but I was so ignorant of the universe around me,* he had to admit. *Now, I run my world and six others. I have friends from other galaxies, and my family is my ultimate joy. I'm the luckiest man in the universe. Hell, I'm the luckiest in all the universes!*

Chapter 38

Like the perfect frame for the perfect picture, a beautiful day wrapped itself around the wedding. Justin felt tears flowing down his cheeks as he gave sweet Rachel away. The tears continued through their vows and lasted until the officiant announced them as man and wife. Along with being the luckiest man in all universes, he now felt like the happiest. Although he knew he would continue to protect his daughter until his final breath, she now had another man who would do the same.

The reception was a delight for all, and Elohim and Lucifer were the lives of the party. Justin laughed as he watched Lornash, possibly the oldest being in the galaxy, dancing the Macarena with Salome.

As everyone sat down for a delicious dinner of culinary delights from all over the galaxy, Justin added a few notes to the speech he'd prepared. When it was time, he stood and clinked his glass a few times to get everyone's attention. "I appreciate you all coming to see me, and it is especially thoughtful of you to pretend to be here for the newlyweds," he said, drawing a bit of laughter from around the room. "Seriously, though, I couldn't ask for a better son-in-law..."

The waitstaff began to serve the food while he spoke, and everyone looked at their plates of gourmet eats with mouthwatering anticipation.

Rise of the Fallen

Suddenly, Justin looked toward the bride and groom, and a sinking feeling overtook him. He wasn't sure why for a moment, but then the thought struck him, as bold and heart-stopping as the lightning of Zeus. "Stop!" he blurted.

Everyone looked at him in surprise, and some nearly choked on the bites they quickly gulped down. All eyes soon traveled to Rachel, and they were horrified to see a waiter putting his arm around her neck and pulling her from her chair.

The server placed his free hand against the side of her head and yelled, "Do not move! No one move, or I will end her!"

The voice was familiar to everyone, especially to Justin. He rose from his seat but found himself speechless and momentarily paralyzed with fear.

"Stay back!" Jesus yelled. "If anyone comes close, I will fry her brain."

The energy weapon was very well camouflaged, but it soon became apparent that there was a dark blue glow coming from the palm of his hand. As long as it remained at that setting, Rachel would only feel some discomfort, but with the slightest adjustment, a bright blue glow would be the precursor to the menacing thing burning a hole straight through her head.

"Jesus, stop. You will never make it out of here if you do this. Let her go, and you can take me for a hostage," Justin begged.

"Be still, peasant!" Jesus looked around the room and snarled. He felt strong again, in a roomful of his enemies but still in control, with all of them hanging on his every word. It was as if he were on the throne once again, and the surge of power was almost orgasmic. Still, when he looked into the faces of the ones who took it from him in the first place, his mood was quick to sour. "Look at them, my father and Lucifer, such good friends. Your great, benevolent, so-called God Elohim abandoned his only son to spend all of his time with Lucifer! I had to learn how to be great on my own," he said with a growl.

Even though Elohim knew Jesus was not really his child, he still felt some guilt and a measure of regret. *Maybe if I had spent more time with him, things would be different. Maybe it would not have come to this,* he tortured himself.

"Oh, and there you are, Sandel, son of Lucifer and my best friend when I was young. I still don't understand why you left my side. We could've been like our fathers, ruling the universe together. Was it Lilith? Did you forsake your God over something as insignificant as a woman? To this day, it puzzles me. You are a mere mortal, but I am God! You knew she was mine, yet you beguiled her, corrupted her mind so she chose you over me. Of course, none of that matters now. In my infinite benevolence, I forgave you for your transgressions. All that matters is that you forsook me. That, I cannot forgive.

"Lilith, you could've been queen of all the galaxy. I gave you the gift of my love, but you would not repay me with yours. Someday soon, I may let you beg me for another chance, but know that I have had and will have women far more alluring than you."

Jesus' berating moved from person to person, with insults after insults heaped upon all whom he blamed for forsaking him. His anger seemed to grow as he progressed, and Rachel weakened with every passing moment, enduring the pain of his grip and the sweltering heat of the weapon near her head, which was beginning to adversely affect her ability to stand.

"Zabkiel, you stood by my side and bore witness to the glory of my being. Do all of you here know it was his treachery, his bad counsel that destroyed Heaven? Someday, I will come for you."

"Rebecca, like your father Michael, you are a case of wasted potential. We could have been remarkable, with him at my right hand and you on my left, but you both turned out to be traitors. Now, instead of a long and wonderful life in the service of your Lord God, basking in my light and glory, you will walk in darkness, with the vile creatures that reside in Hell. How pathetic and foolish you are!"

Rise of the Fallen

Jesus then turned his harshest gaze on Justin. "You puny vermin! You are more worthless than those foul insects called the Dumah! *I* found what you now claim as your world. *I* nurtured it to greatness. I was willing to let you and your kind join the Empire, to let you become something greater than you were. In the end, you and Planet Earth are at the core of all the terrible happenings I've endured. Don't think yourself responsible for Earth being lost to Heaven. Zabkiel, Sandel, and the damned Freewill Alliance are to blame for that. No worries though. What I do here today will affect almost everyone in this room, in a very impactful way. Because you took Earth away from me, I will now take something from you."

As soon as Jesus started to back away, brave Rebecca moved toward him. She had noticed that he had a propensity to talk with his hands, unconsciously moving the energy blaster away from Rachel's head every once in a while. She knew it was not enough time to rush him before he was able to carry out his threat, but she hoped she could get Rachel's attention somehow.

The moment came while the self-involved Jesus was swallowed up with a need to justify his life choices. Rachel finally looked toward Rebecca, and, with both hands near her face, Rebecca pointed her index finger downward. She made a slight motion, as if she were dropping. When it was clear that Rachel understood her signal, Rebecca gave one nod of her head.

"I will leave now, and the bride will go with me. All of you will stay here," Jesus resolutely said. When many ignored him and tried to stop him, he adjusted the weapon to a more her powerful setting, and Rachel screamed in reaction to the pain. It was not enough to kill her, but Jesus smiled as the jolt became more intense and everyone stood still again. "Once we are safely away, I *may* release her." He paused to kiss her on the cheek. "Then again, I may not. For the spawn of an insect, she is quite beautiful," he said, then punctuated the cruel remark with a vile laugh. Then, looking straight at Justin, he taunted, "I was your God when time began, you idiot. I am still your God now, and I will be your God forever, whether you like it or not." With that, he moved his hand away from her head.

What he didn't realize was that his captive had not taken her eyes off Rebecca. Rebecca nodded, and Rachel bent her legs at her knees and dropped down. Her head slipped from the deranged ex-God's grip as she fell. In a blur of action, Rebecca leapt forward and knocked Jesus to the floor with an elbow to the face, and a knee to his ribcage. Reactively, he lashed out, and the energy weapon tore a gash across her cheek. Before he was able to cut her again, though, she skillfully grabbed the wrist of his weapon hand, jumped on his chest, and punished him with several punches to the face. The force of the blows caused her to grunt, and blood soon flowed from his nose and mouth.

"You will never hurt another woman, never again! Do you hear me? Never, ever again! Never, never, never!" she chanted as she continued to lay siege upon his face.

Jesus, no longer able to hold the weapon, let the energy weapon drop to the floor.

Stolas pulled Rachel to her feet and hugged her close.

Sandel moved to pull Rebecca away from the defeated Jesus, but Justin caught his arm. "Don't. She needs this... and he deserves it."

Jesus was down for the count, no longer able to feel pain. So, once Rebecca began to feel exhausted and her punches steadily weakened, she decided he'd had enough. She sat back on her heels, breathing hard. "No use beating a dead horse's ass," she said, with an ornery grin stretching across her face.

"I doubt he's dead, but you're right about the horse's ass part. Feel better now?" Justin asked, helping her to her feet.

"Yeah, actually, I do," she said, still smiling as she wiped blood from her knuckles.

In spite of the awful beating, Jesus was not as incapacitated as they thought. Slowly and sneakily, he reached into his pocket, watching to make sure no one noticed. The weapon he retrieved may have done him some good, had Rachel not still had her eye on him. In an instant, she broke free of Stolas' hug and kicked Jesus in the head, so hard that it knocked him backward. This time, his head hung to the side, and his mouth was agape, with drool pooling on the floor beneath it. There was also a growing wet stain in the crotch of his pants, as his bladder emptied.

"You knocked the piss out of him," Stolas said, so excited he was actually vibrating. He laughed and pointed at the growing wet stain at the wannabe Lord's crotch.

"Literally," Rachel said, dusting her hands together as if cleaning them off after a job well done.

"I don't know about the rest of you, but I've never been more entertained at a wedding reception!" Alex shouted, and his big brother had to agree.

Benjamin Oneal

Chapter 39

For the second time in his life, Jesus was extradited to Heaven to stand trial. The Long Life Cooperative and Freewill Alliance agreed to abide by whatever decision the courts of Heaven made, as long as both were permitted to present evidence of the many crimes he had committed in their respective jurisdictions.

Jesus' violations against the galactic communities were beyond egregious. Entire worlds had been destroyed by his hand or his command, and countless lives had been lost or ruined. Although he was not technically in charge, as Cronus and Michael were responsible for most of the battle decisions, Jesus was obviously complicit.

With a bang of the Stone of Justice, an object that had not seen the light of day since the time of Elohim, Zabkiel began the trial. The charges against Jesus were many, and he had little chance at any defense. As was done in his first trial, Jesus was made to occupy a chair in a clear, shielded box; this was not necessarily to protect others from him but to protect him from his many enemies from across the galaxy. Also as before, he declined counsel and chose to represent himself.

His opening statement was brief and to the point: "I am God. I have no peers, and you have no right to judge me." With that and a dismissive wave of his hand, he took his seat once more.

Elohim was conflicted, so much so that he wondered why he even bothered attending the trial. As he sat in the courtroom, he knew there was no justification for the evils committed by the man on trial, but he still felt some guilt for being so absent during Jesus' childhood, even if he was not his biological father.

Zabkiel again grabbed the court's attention and addressed all who could hear him. "People of the Empire, we are here today to try Jesus El-Elyon for his crimes. Since there is no way to ensure an unbiased jury, as no one on Heaven is untouched by his malfeasance, in accordance with the laws set forth by the council under the reign of God Elohim, Jesus will be judged by a council of his peers. You will hear testimony from the accused and the accusers, and the council will decide his fate. We will now hear opening arguments."

The prosecution began with witnesses presenting detailed, personal accounts of the crimes Jesus had wrought against the three major powers since his escape from Naberus.

"Jesus, do you have anything to say about the charges brought against you?" Zabkiel asked the ex-God.

Jesus was clearly unimpressed and oblivious to the proceedings as he sat in his transparent box. Even when he realized Zabkiel was talking to him, he refused to stand. He wanted everyone to know he did not recognize the legitimacy of the court or the trial. He put up a strong front, but those closest to him saw the fear in his eyes. He tried to appear bored and apathetic to the legal goings-on, and he offered Zabkiel no response other than another condescending wave of his hand.

Even as testimony was offered and Jesus' guilt became undeniable, the trial carried on for six days before he was officially found guilty on all charges. On the seventh day, they rested, but on the eighth day, the largest audience the galaxy had ever known waited anxiously for the sentence to be handed down.

In the end, Jesus was sentenced to life in prison, forbidden from the Factor. This time, he would serve his time on the same high-security prison planet in the Purgatorian sector where Michael was once imprisoned and where Gabriel had returned to serve his sentence. His would not be an easy life. While most felt he deserved a death sentence, they were sated in the knowledge that he would spend the rest of his years laboring in the dark, smoldering mines of Vapula, a torture far less merciful than execution.

Security on Vapula had undergone a complete, systemwide upgrade since the Archangels escaped, and detail around the planet had doubled. Ground defenses were now equipped with the latest technology. Every guard who worked on and around the prison planet was screened via Illuminator, to ensure that none were unfit nor loyal to Jesus. A mosquito couldn't fly about the planet without the security team being aware of it; there were eyes and ears on everyone at all times.

Jesus did still receive some special treatment though. While it was usually disallowed, he had a visitor during his first week of imprisonment. While Elohim waited for Jesus to be brought to see him, he was still not sure what he intended to say. Part of him wanted to beat Jesus to within an inch of his life for his crimes against the galaxy, but another part— the part that was once the young Jesus' absent father— yearned to apologize to the fallen Lord.

A guard walked Jesus into the room and secured him with thick chains to a table directly across from Elohim. Jesus looked more like a frightened little boy than a sadistic dictator. He was dirty and stunk of profuse perspiration, a side effect of working in the mines. The foul stench was nearly unbearable, as Elohim fought the impulse to back away. There was a paternal urge within Elohim, and he briefly thought of taking him in his arms to comfort him and tell him all would be all right, but he was ultimately glad the prison restrictions prevented that, because the thought of touching him almost made him sick.

"Father, I am so very glad you came to see me. Please help me," Jesus begged, with what little humility he could muster. "Look at me! I am a filthy wretch. They make me work in the mines till I nearly pass out from the heat and exhaustion. My muscles cry out when I collapse in bed each night, but there is no relief, no respite. I must only rise and endure it again every morning. Please help me, Father," Jesus pleaded.

"I'm sorry the consequences are so difficult for you to bear," Elohim said, with genuine pity in his tone. He sighed deeply and confessed, "Jesus, deep inside my soul, I feel somewhat responsible for how things have turned out for you. Nevertheless, you know I have no power to change your situation or free you from the justice that has been handed down to you. I can only say I am sorry for any part I may have played in your...downward spiral."

"No power?" Jesus scoffed. "But you were once God of the Empire. Surely word from you would convince them to transfer me to Naberus," Jesus argued.

"Even if I had such power, I would not use it," Elohim said, with a finality that scared Jesus.

"But you are my father, and—" Jesus started.

"You know better than that. Cronus is your father," Elohim said.

Jesus was uncharacteristically quiet for a moment, as if lost in his own thoughts. He bowed his head, and when he raised it again, he was no longer a frightened child. Rather, his eyes burned with anger, and his face twisted into a snarl. "I should've killed you on Nod, when I had a chance."

Elohim sighed once more. "Part of me wishes you had. Now, I must live with the knowledge that I may have been able to stop your reign of terror, if only I had been more present in your life," he said, his voice filled with anguish.

"Damn you!" Jesus yelled, forcing a stream of sticky spittle to fly out of his mouth. "How dare you!? In my infinite love, I found it in my heart to spare you that day. You must take me away from this place. You owe me that much."

"Have you so quickly forgotten my beautiful Anael?" Elohim asked as a tear escaped his eye.

"Anael?"

"The woman I loved. You took her life just to hurt me, and you forced me to watch. You say you wished you would have killed me in Nod. In many ways, Jesus, you did. You ended my life by ending hers," Elohim said, rising from his chair. "Of all the people who now reside in this awful place, you most deserve to be here."

Jesus jumped to his feet and violently pulled at his chains as he jumped up and down, screaming obscenities at Elohim.

Elohim did not react, other than to wipe away a small tear that formed in his left eye. He said nothing more before he turned and left the room. When he left Planet Vapula, he felt as if a great burden had been lifted. For the first time, he felt some measure of closure concerning Jesus.

***

A few months after his fateful meeting with Elohim, Jesus went missing after his hour of exercise. There was talk of Jesus possibly being lost in one of the many old branches of the mines, but an exhaustive search proved unsuccessful. There was only one place they had not searched; the surface. The reason they had not searched it before, is because Jesus was strictly for bidden to be there.

The guards donned their protective gear, and braved the hundred and 120° heat. It wasn't a good idea, to spend very much time out during the day. The first place they look were the recreation areas. It wasn't long before they found the former Savior's body. The guards were stunned, and were at a loss to explain the condition of Jesus' body.

His condition and cause of death was reminiscent of an ancient form of punishment once used on Heaven: crucifixion on a makeshift cross. Something akin to barbed wire was used to secure Jesus' arms, legs, and neck to the crude death trap. Not only that, but he was severely bruised and bloodied, with broken bones. It was obvious that Jesus was alive when he was bound to the cross, because of damage he suffered, as he struggled to free himself from the barbed wire. He was unable to scream out, due to the dirty rag that was stuffed into his mouth. It appeared he had been left to die on the cross, to bake in the oppressive heat of the Vapula daylight hours. As much as many wanted him to suffer, they were sure he didn't suffer long, for it would have taken only a short time for him to succumb to the boiling temperatures and the severity of his wounds.

***

Justin sat with Sandel, Lucifer, and Elohim in the garden behind his home on Earth, looking at a photo of Jesus' corpse. "How mind-bogglingly ironic," he said.

"How so?" Elohim asked.

"Jesus, on the cross. In the Bible, the book of propaganda to get us to join their side during the war, it was claimed that he died that way, only to be laid in a tomb and rise again on the third day."

"Ah, yes, the resurrection," Sandel said.

"Well, he's not coming back this time," Justin said with a frown and not a hint of humor behind his words.

Benjamin Oneal

Chapter 40

The three great powers of the known galaxy settled into a time of comfortable, much-needed peace. Even still, there was much to do: worlds to be restored, memorials to be built in honor of lost lives, and governments to be reestablished. For the most part, however, everyone was looking forward to a better, brighter future.

Justin assured all that Planet Earth would help with the restoration efforts in worlds ravaged by the preliminary Resurrectionist attacks. In some cases, entire infrastructures had been wiped out. It would take years to bring everything back to any semblance of normalcy, but fortunately, volunteers from all around the Cooperative offered to assist, knowing that many hands would make light work.

Once the major projects were addressed and delegated, there were a few special undertakings Justin needed to assign and some proposals he wanted to implement. He shared his ideas with the council and was thrilled with they gave him the green light. With their permission, he began making plans to bring his goals to fruition.

He was a bit miffed that he had not implemented one particular idea before, due to the inevitable deaths of the oldest among the Earth population. Almost immediately, he put together a group of individuals tasked with researching and cataloging any and all Illuminator memories that depicted the past eras of the planet. They did not find much in the way of vital information, but the historical value of the memories they captured was incalculable.

The older population, those fortunate to be alive when the Factor was first made available, provided memories from the 1940s and some as far back as the 1930s. Most did not revolve around eyewitness accounts of events, but even their personal impressions and reactions to those events were great learning tools.

Justin also tasked the team to retrieve memories from the Angels who were ordered by Jesus to deliver the Bible to the inhabitants of Earth thousands of years earlier, as well as memories from those ordered to remain on Earth to guide the earthlings. Even if most of those memories were benign, they occasionally captured some that were truly wonderful.

Some of the memories of particular interest to Justin were those of Jared, Salome's father, who had traveled to Earth long ago. In 1505, he visited Florence, Italy, where he met an older gentleman by the name of Leonardo da Vinci. At that time, the *Mona Lisa* was only a series of sketches, not yet the famed, timeless painting it would become. Leonardo was also working then on his second attempt at a flying machine.

Jared was invited into Leonardo's home and spent time with him in his workshop. The historic value of those memories was immeasurable. As great as those were, however, the memories that most interested Justin were those of the nights Jared and Leonardo spent barhopping. The recollections of Florence nightlife was a real revelation, but even more so, the conversations between the two were amazing and quite revealing.

On his next trip, in 1547, Jared traveled through France. One place he visited was Salon, and he met a man named Nostradamus there, a healer. Jared seemed to sense a bad omen in Nostradamus right from the start, and those hunches were proven true when he caught Nostradamus going through his personal belongings. Unfortunately, unbeknownst to Jared, Nostradamus ran off with his Illuminator.

Two days later, Jared caught up with the thief and retrieved the device, but it was too late; the damage had been done. Nostradamus asked Jared about the things he witnessed via the device. Even though Jared tried to downplay the memories as mere fantasies, Nostradamus did not believe him. The man's mindset was already moving toward the occult, and he was sure he had seen the future of Earth.

On his third and final trip, Jared found himself in London, England, in 1687, at the home of Sir Isaac Newton. Newton's book, *Philosophiæ Naturalis Principia Mathematica*, had just been published. Along with a few notable socialites, another scientist Edmond Halley, was also in attendance. In Justin's opinion, the conversation between Haley and Newton was one of the most wonderful pieces of history he witnessed, and it was a memory that would've been lost in the ether if not for the Illuminator.

Jared met Anh that very night, and it was love at first sight. After a whirlwind romance, they were married, and she eventually became Salome's mother. Under the pretense of moving to the American colonies, Jared escorted his beloved back to Hell, and they never looked back.

The council also agreed with Justin that Mount Olympus should be made into a museum. It became a popular tourist destination for beings from all over the galaxy. Justin made an agreement with the Olympians that a couple times a year, one or more of the gods who had spent time there before would visit to share some stories, and Justin made sure to claim a front-row seat for every one of those presentations. It was as if the pages of his Greek mythology storybooks from his childhood were coming to life right before his eyes, and he listened to every word with bated breath.

Truly, it is a good time to be on Planet Earth, Justin thought to himself as the world began to change for the better, and many had to agree with that.

Chapter 41

Although there were many outcries for Elohim to reclaim the throne and become God of the New Empire, he declined. He decided to address the issue via communique to the entire New Empire, while sitting in the throne room. "Zabkiel is doing a better job than I ever could," he said. "He pushed back an old enemy in Cronus, stopped the evil despot Jesus, and brought you through a war."

"But you are a wonderful leader!" the citizens of all the worlds cried.

"I am flattered you think so, but I am not so sure you are right. Although Jesus was not truly my son, I failed him. In doing so, I failed you. Yes, Zabkiel was with Jesus for many years, but it was not his place to know of Jesus' evil intent, nor was it his place to stop him. You may not be aware of it, but throughout the years when Zabkiel served Jesus, he also managed to save countless lives, even when the incredibly deranged Jesus ordered the deaths of so many people. During his time with Jesus, he was trusted with the day-to-day operations across the Empire. For this reason, he knows more about running things than I ever could. I see no reason to change that.

"But it is your birthright!" many chorused.

"I understand why you feel that way, because my bloodline has ruled Heaven and the Empire for thousands of years.

My father and the Gods before him were all great leaders. Zabkiel is the great leader you deserve, and he will serve you well."

A question came from somewhere in front of him: "Almighty Elohim, if you will not lead, what will you do?"

"I may have retired the throne, but I will still serve the New Empire in some capacity. I will continue to travel throughout the galaxy as a freelance soldier, and it will be my privilege to help in any way I can. Thank you all for your support and your trust in me, and it is my hope that you will give the same respect to Zabkiel."

With that, he stepped back and motioned for Zabkiel take center stage, so he could continue the State of the Empire speech. Elohim was quite impressed with him, and he knew Zabkiel was the best man for the job, for no one on Heaven knew half of what he did about the workings of the New Empire.

After the speech, they sat in Zabkiel's office for some friendly conversation.

"You laid it on a bit thick out there, don't you think?" Zabkiel asked.

"I had to. You're not a very likable guy, you know," Elohim said before playfully punching him in the shoulder.

"Careful, old man. Don't make me kick your decrepit ass," Zabkiel responded.

Elohim laughed. "Very well. I have to go anyway, tough guy." He stood, shook Zabkiel's hand, then pulled him in for a hug.

"Hey, you two, save that for a *private* room, would you?" Lucifer admonished as he walked in.

"All right, if you need me, you know where I'll be, Zabkiel," Elohim said. "Just know there is no one more deserving of that throne." Elohim smiled as he and Lucifer left the room.

***

When Elohim and Lucifer weren't chasing pirates or settling border disputes, they just explored. They reached beyond the boundaries of the New Empire and the Freewill Alliance to discover new worlds and make contact with technologically advanced ones. Most of all, they just had a great time.

In their travels, they discovered a world just beyond Alliance borders that greatly resembled Earth, except that the evolutionary state of the beings there had not yet carried them to the level of sentient, early primates found on other planets. What made the world special to them was its offering of great fishing. They named the planet Sanctum, for that was exactly how they saw it: an almost holy place where they could get away from the rest of the world. From that moment on, much of their downtime was spent casting lines into the pristine lakes there while they fondly reminisced about old times.

Chapter 42

On the 1,000-year anniversary of the signing of the peace agreement between the three great powers in the known galaxy, Justin invited everyone to Earth to celebrate. He decided to hold the party in the great halls of Mount Olympus. It was a beautiful setting and would certainly accommodate the many guests who were sure to attend.

As was the custom whenever they got together, Zabkiel, Sandel, and Justin sat around complaining and generally feeling sorry for themselves for having to tackle the growing responsibilities of being leaders of the three great powers. Meanwhile, Elohim and Lucifer celebrated with glee and their typical carefreeness. Every time one of them passed or danced by the grumbling, old men at the table, they chanted, "Na-na-na-na-na," as if to rub it in their faces, that they were free spirits, unencumbered by the day-to-day responsibilities of running the government. Of course, their teasing was never mean-spirited, for they knew exactly how their friends felt.

After a while, the good-natured taunting brought the three leaders out of their funk. They got up, found their wives, and skipped out to the dance floor to join "the two old bastards," as Justin so eloquently put it.

To make the event even more memorable and spectacular, all the Olympian gods and goddesses were in attendance, and Justin's special request was for them to re-create the special effects used to impress the ancient Greeks. While he claimed it was for the benefit of the children in the audience, his ulterior motive was to see it for himself. He intently watched every illusion in awe, as if through the eyes of the ancient Greeks, and he tried to imagine the wonder they felt as they tried to make sense of the powers that could only be magic reserved for the gods.

There jamboree was a long, boisterous one, with good reason. Except for the time of the Resurrectionists, the galaxy had enjoyed a long interval of peace. Although they didn't know it at the time, that wonderful tranquility was destined to last. Other than sporadic and minor border disputes and random attack by a few space pirates, there were no major conflicts to contend with, so the years that followed were a time of rebuilding and growth.

The Long Life Cooperative, once a group of only seven planets, now consisted of seventeen worlds. To everyone's amazement, Trees of Life flourished on three of those planets. While those orchards would never be as productive as those on Eden or Earth, it was comforting to know there was a greater supply of the Factor for the galaxy to harvest.

Alex was in charge of the Trees of Life production for the Cooperative. No matter how far removed he was from the day-to-day operations of growing the incredible arbors, he still found time to get his hands dirty. When he wasn't busy in his office, it was a good bet he could be found on one of the three new worlds, planting and nurturing his baby Trees of Life.

Thanks to Salome, the seven original planets of the Cooperative were ecological paradises, and the other ten were well on their way. Her environmental initiatives became the standard throughout the known galaxy. Many worlds that had brought their ecology to the brink of no return were making great strides in recovering from the missteps. Not only did she want to stop the unnecessary destruction, but she also wanted to reverse the damage and make the nature of each planet healthy again. Her unofficial title throughout the New Empire, the Long Life Cooperative, and the Freewill Alliance was Mother Nature, and she lived up to it in every way.

At one point during the party, Lornash pulled Justin aside and asked to speak with him privately. When they were out of sight and earshot of the guests, he said, "What I tell you now may not seem relevant at the moment, but it will greatly impact your future."

"What is it, Lornash?" Justin asked, with growing foreboding.

"As you are aware, the inhabitants of Earth are descendants of those taken from Eden," Lornash started.

"Yes...and?" Justin coaxed.

"The Trees of Life are prominent on Eden, permeating every aspect of our lives—the ground we walk on, the water we drink, and the air we breathe. Although I cannot comprehend or explain it correctly, the Factor, as you call it, eventually became part of our DNA. Because of this, we have received an increased benefit from it. While people on other planets can expect 10 to almost 15,000 years to be added to their lifespans, I have already experienced life for 26,000 years."

"Remarkable," Justin said.

"On Eden, there is a place where some ancient souls live. They were already old when I was still quite young."

"Really?" Justin found it hard to believe that there were some even older than Lornash, but he also knew Lornash would never exaggerate or lie to him. "Why are you telling me this?" he asked.

"Justin, you and the people of Earth are direct descendants of those taken from Eden. Thus, you will also reap the enhanced benefits of the Factor." Lornash paused to let his words settle in Justin's mind.

Justin's brain began reeling with the ramifications of what he just learned. "What!?"

"Barring accidents, you will have a greatly extended length of life. This is a blessing, yes, but you must know that it can also come with some regrets."

"What regrets?" Justin asked, confused once more.

"Your friends from other worlds will die before you. You will not have that chance to grow old with them."

"Oh. I hadn't thought of that," Justin said, with a tinge of sadness in his voice.

"I'm afraid the blessing comes with a bit of a curse," Lornash said. "What you do with this information is up to you." He then patted Justin on the shoulder. "Today, though, is a day to celebrate. Besides, if I can get Rachel away from Stolas, she owes me a dance," the old one said, smiling as he got up and walked toward the music.

Chapter 43

That day, a new agreement was signed. Some 500 years earlier, on the same date, the three major powers in the galaxy joined as one. The New Empire, the Freewill Alliance, and the Long Life Cooperative came together to become the Galactic Union.

The three powers would still be self-governing within their respective regions, but they would function as one when it came to galactic matters. It was also decided that Zabkiel, Sandel, and Justin would lead the Galactic Union Council. The lower councilmembers would consist of representatives from throughout the known galaxy.

One of the first major decisions of the Galactic Union Council was that they would explore and catalog the unknown regions of the cosmos. The Galactic Union only made up around 40 percent of the galaxy, so that left 60 percent for them to discover.

After the party, when most of the attendees had already departed to return to their home worlds, Justin sat with Salome, Jarod, Rachel, Stolas, and his grandchildren. *Not so long ago,* he thought, *I was sitting in a classroom, teaching hungry, young minds about religion and the growing relevance of it in a time when belief in God was under attack. Back then, Earth was alone in the universe, and a benevolent God watched over us all...or so we thought.*

He had only encountered one of his former students, as she was one of the volunteers who traveled to Eden to help reclaim the environment after Jesus lost the planet to the Freewill Alliance. He truly hoped more of those he had unknowingly poisoned with his teachings of the Bible would find the truth and forgive him of his ignorance.

As the great era of exploration began, Justin could only imagine what they might find. He and all earthlings were direct descendants of the inhabitants of Eden, where the secret to long life, the Trees of Life, were first discovered, a secret later found on Earth as well. As he pondered that, he thought of Bible stories of the Garden of Eden, home not only to a Tree of Life but also a Tree of the Knowledge of Good and Evil. *Could there be a planet somewhere in the vast unknown that houses something that could enhance our minds to a point of near omniscience?* he wondered. If he had learned nothing else, he had discovered that almost anything was possible.

Justin also wondered if there were other empires on the other side of the galaxy. *Could there be societies with power greater than our own?* With that, he had to consider whether or not it was a good idea to reveal his peoples' existence. *If there are others, are they humanoid, reptilian, insect? Maybe their evolutionary path has taken them beyond the need for a physical presence.*

Later that night, as he lay next to Salome, Justin felt some peace after his conversation with Lornash, but there was also a bittersweetness to it. He knew now that, excluding any unforeseen accidents, he and his family would outlive everyone they knew and loved. With that on his mind, he deeply kissed Salome and held on to her, as if he never wanted to let her go. He loved her more than life itself and was once again so humbled by the thought that she wanted to be with him that he actually began to cry.

"What's wrong?" Salome asked, pushing away to look into his eyes. "Tell me, Justin. What is it?"

Justin sat up in bed and, with her lying against him, told her about his conversation with Lornash. As the full weight of that knowledge came down upon her, Salome began to weep.

They held and consoled each other for what seemed like an hour. Justin wiped tears from her face and again kissed her deeply. No matter what the future held, they both knew they would face it together.

Chapter 44

    Over the years, they reached out and explored new regions of the galaxy, setting beacons in deviant space that would help them return to new areas. They approached many new worlds and their inhabitants with offers to join or establish trade agreements with the Galactic Union. Some declined, not quite willing to accept change, but many found value in what the Galactic Union had to offer.

    After countless years went by, the galaxy was closer to 70 percent known. Justin never ceased to be amazed at the diversity of intelligent lifeforms they discovered in the expansion. They encountered worlds whose inhabitants were technologically superior but not hostile. One planet was unique, in that their major form of communication was very close to entirely telepathic. It wasn't clear whether they could read the minds of other species, but it was something to be explored.

    The age of expansion was a wonderful time of peace and prosperity. Citizens of the Galactic Union established colonies in newer regions of the galaxy. During that time of profound growth, Justin sat as chief counsel of the Galactic Union, long after Zabkiel and Sandel passed on. Lucifer Satanis, Sandel's great-grandson, and Hahasiah Dominic, grandson of Zabkiel sat by his side. They were strong leaders, and Justin greatly respected and admired them. He also knew the ones who came before them would have been justifiably proud.

On Justin's next birthday, he knew Salome would be waiting for him to return home. When he walked in the door, she met him with a hug and kiss, and Rachel Anh ran up to join them. Sadly, lacking the benefit of human DNA, Stolas had passed on long ago. Many of his grandchildren and great-grandchildren were with Justin to celebrate his birthday though.

"What are you now, Dad, 27,501?" Jarod asked.

"Sounds about right," Justin replied.

Salome had baked a cake and put one candle in the middle. He tried to imagine what a cake with candles for each year might look like, and he chuckled under his breath at the thought.

A while later, after their guests had gone, he pulled his darling wife in for another kiss. "Is everything ready?" he asked.

"Almost, my love. I just need to grab a few more things, and we can be on our way."

Soon, Justin was exactly where he most wanted to be, his favorite place in all the worlds, on the shore of a pristine lake on Planet Sanctum. He took a deep breath, it was clean and fresh, without the least hint of civilization. He imagined that Earth must've smelled much the same, before the rise of humankind. It was the greatest way to celebrate yet another birthday, alone with his loved ones, fishing and laughing about old times and smiling with the warm memories of the dear ones they have lost.

Carrying their fishing gear, they walked to the lake hand-in-hand. They stopped as they reached the end of the dock. He sat his fishing gear down, and looked out upon the lake. He couldn't imagine the scene more beautiful. He gave Salome a kiss, then cast his line into the lake. As they sat in the end of the dock, with her feet enjoying the cool of the water, Justin looked at the woman that he had loved so deeply. "I love being here, but most of all I love being here with you."

The Alpha

Before They Were Gods

Benjamin Oneal

Chapter 1

It was the first time the boy had ventured past the boundaries of his home world. At 17, he found himself alone and a little scared, awaiting his future. Although it was an honor to be chosen for training in the Lord's Army, he deeply missed his friends and family. As he sat through orientation, he wanted nothing more than to run away, but he refused to dishonor his father or his home world. Fighting back tears, he thought of his parents, envisioned them standing on the space dock and waving goodbye as he entered the ship. He also had another thought, a memory of the girl named Vepar, the girl that might have been. He wondered if he would ever see any of them again. Late into the night, he quietly wept himself into fitful sleep. It wouldn't do for the others to hear him cry.

The next morning came quickly. Around 5 a.m., he was torn out of his slumber by the sound of metal slamming against a metal wall. Everyone fell out of bed and dressed quickly as their group leader paced the length of their dorm, barking commands and promising punishment to the last man to make it outside to stand at attention. Many of the boys had tears in their eyes, but Luc's were dry; he had cried his last the night before. Dutifully, he did as he was told, without so much as a sniffle.

By 5:15, everyone had gathered outside in reasonably straight lines, and all were making their best attempt to stand at attention, hoping they would not upset their terrifying leader. True to his word, Sergeant Bethor assigned Private Armen Turel to double-duty, as punishment for being the last to join the lineup.

Sergeant Bethor shouted orders, and the boys spent the next thirty tortuous minutes vigorously exercising in unison. After that, it was time for the morning meal. They filed into the mess hall to receive their breakfast. It was reminiscent of the school cafeteria line, except that there were no smiling lunch ladies to serve the grub. Instead, angry-looking personnel slapped piles of goop into various compartments on each tray.

Luc sat down at a table with his group, but he was as disinterested in the conversation as he was in the olive-drab blobs of sustenance on the tray in front of him. So, he sat in silence, contemplating their uncertain futures. Twenty minutes later, a worn-out Turel dragged his weary body to the food line. It was obvious that Sergeant Bethor had worked him hard, and Luc was sure Turel would never be late for the morning lineup again.

After breakfast, they were permitted to enjoy a brief rest, before the real training began at 8:30. Sergeant Bethor, a man who either refused to smile or simply wasn't capable of it, briefly told them what he expected of each and every one of them; how to correctly stand at attention, and their proper appearance. They marched for two miles then exercised some more. Bethor worked them hard. It was almost as if he were *trying* to make them cry, as if he took some pleasure in getting in their faces, yelling, and pushing them harder and harder.

At noon, they stopped for lunch. Luc had worked up an appetite, and although the food was a far cry from the wonderful meals his mom made, he managed to scarf down every bland, unidentifiable bite. The thought of his mother's home cooking almost brought a tear to his eye, but he pushed it away. There was not much time for fond recollections, because training started again at promptly 1300 hours.

Another two-mile march was followed by an even more

strenuous exercise regimen, then hand-to-hand combat. Since fighting was new to Luc, he found himself bested repeatedly, but he didn't stop trying until ordered to do so. When the evening meal was served, he had no trouble gobbling down every bite.

After the evening meal, Sergeant Bethor spent a bit of time getting to know his recruits. One by one, they told their stories of home, explained why they were there, and expressed what they expected in the future. Most seemed likable, but Luc silently categorized a few as arrogant assholes.

One in particular stood out, Michael Hamon. Rumor had it that he came from a prominent Heavenly family. Nevertheless, his connections did not leave him immune to fear; in fact, Luc had noticed him openly crying on their first morning. The sergeant must have sensed those feelings, because he stressed at every given opportunity, "We are now a team, men. We must all work together to make it through training." Their group leader seemed almost uncharacteristically friendly during those seemingly casual conversations, though he always exhibited an I-will-kick-your-ass-if-you-get-out-of line air.

The sergeant left the recruits to themselves before bedtime but added, "It would be wise for you to study the manual whenever you have a chance." He then ordered poor Turel to three hours of cleanup. As cruel as that was, neither Luc nor any of the others dared to protest.

Luc took the sergeant's advice and read the first three chapters of the manual. Then, a few minutes after lights-out, he slipped out of his cot, and slipped on a shirt. Once he was sure the coast was clear, he sneaked into the bathroom to help Turel finish the chores. They worked together in silence, but Turel looked up at Luc once in a while, with something akin to disbelief on his face. It was never spoken, but his gratitude to the young man scrubbing the floor tiles beside him was visible in his expression.

Unfortunately for the pair, Sergeant Bethor stopped by to check on Turel. "What in Heaven's name are you doing, Private?" he bellowed.

Rise of the Fallen

"I-I had to use the restroom, sir," Luc responded, not as convincingly as he would've liked.

"Get your scrawny ass back in the rack!" Sergeant Bethor growled.

Luc rushed out of the room like a scolded child, hoping the little misstep wouldn't land him in the same boat as Turel. Not long after, Turel came in, whispered his thanks to Luc, then collapsed onto his cot.

Worn out and a little bruised, Luc slept hard, and the next morning came all too quickly. Hurting all over, Luc quickly pulled himself out of bed and readied himself for a new day. *No way I'm gonna be the last one in line,* he vowed to himself. He even found time to make sure Turel made lineup. As it happened, no one was late for the morning lineup for the remaining duration of basic training.

During hand-to-hand combat later that day, the sergeant's tough side really came to life when one of the arrogant assholes stupidly challenged Bethor's authority. *This is going to be interesting,* Luc thought. Private Ardouisur was in phenomenal shape and had at least thirty pounds on the sergeant. He also spent a lot of time boasting about being a regional high school wrestling squad champion.

As expected, the sergeant promptly kicked the asshole's butt. Ardouisur advanced when the sergeant prompted, threw a few punches that caught air, then took a knee to the gut and an elbow to the back of his neck. Just like that, Ardouisur was down for the count. Luc and Michael were ordered to take him, bruised and unconscious, to the infirmary.

Later that day, the battered and humiliated private walked into the barracks, keeping his head low so as to avoid eye contact. Neither he nor the sergeant ever mentioned it again. It was as if it had never happened, and it might have been forgotten, except for the fact that no one ever came close to challenging the sergeant or disobeying any of his orders again. From that day forward, every soldier regarded their leader with respect and a dash of fear.

Benjamin Oneal

Chapter 2

The first week went much as the first day had, except that Sergeant Bethor pushed them a little harder each day. On the last day of the first week, they had their first shot at the obstacle course.

Luc did his best but failed to complete the course. His arms and legs trembled with strain as he tried to scale the rope wall, and he felt the barbed wire snagging his clothes and threatening to scrape his skin as he crawled under it. Eventually, he collapsed in exhaustion at the tall hurdles. He tumbled to the ground and lay in the dirt before being dragged out of the way. He felt like a failure, but only two of the fifteen recruits made it through. Neither of the successful ones were arrogant assholes, and that gave Luc a little satisfaction.

On one of the rare days set aside for rest, Luc went on a clandestine mission: a practice run on the obstacle course. When he arrived, he noticed one of the other guys from his outfit already running the course, one whom Sergeant Bethor had been particularly hard on all week. Eli was about the same age as Luc, and he was just as determined as Luc was to conquer the course.

"Mind if I run through it with you?" Luc asked.

"Nope. Go ahead. This thing keeps kicking my ass," Eli said.

"Then let's do it," Luc said, holding out his hand for a shake.

"Yes, let's," Eli said, offering a handshake and a grin in return.

They spent the next four hours pushing their bodies to the point of absolute fatigue, until they were far too exhausted to move another muscle. Their arms and legs burned, and their hands were scraped and torn, making way for inevitable blisters. Still, they felt accomplished, considering they'd completed far more of the brutal course than they'd been able to earlier in the week.

As they struggled through it, the two discovered that they shared some common interests. For the next few weeks, they continued to push each other in their studies as well as their physical training. By the fourth week, Luc and Eli had mastered the obstacle course, and they had become experts in many areas covered in their manuals. They tackled each new challenge head on, always striving to best one another while continuing to work together.

They particularly enjoyed hand-to-hand combat. Neither allowed the other to go soft; for them, it was all or nothing. Many nights, they ached in their cots, bruised and bandaged, but they were always eager to face whatever the next day would bring. Although weapons training was not as entertaining for them, in time, they mastered every skill they were taught, and they encouraged the others in their group to do the same.

Luc was soon entrusted with the important role of section leader, reporting directly to the sergeant. Deep down, he felt Eli was more deserving of the promotion, but his friend had no desire to hold the title; Eli was far more comfortable being a follower.

One of their fellow recruits, Michael, was quite unhappy about Luc's advancement. He was openly resistant to it, and he was audibly disagreeable to any orders Luc gave. Michael's bad attitude, jealousy, and insubordination quickly became a detriment to Luc's effectiveness as section leader. Michael was thick-headed and liked to stir up trouble with others. He picked fights and caused harmful delays in training.

Knowing that Sergeant Bethor expected him to handle it, Luc arranged to speak with Michael alone, while the others were on assignment outside the barracks. "We have to talk," Luc said.

"Yeah? What do you want?" Michael said, petulant as ever.

A half-hour later, both soldiers donned a few battle wounds, some facial bruising and bloody lips, and a shiner between them, but some sort of understanding had been reached.

From that point on, Michael never openly defied Luc's orders, and he even began treating the others in his unit with their due respect. Fights ended, backtalk and sassing stopped, and his fellow recruits began to warm up to him. Truth be told, Michael seemed to enjoy being part of a team, a perk his previous attitude had kept him from experiencing.

With their newfound teamwork ethic, the section soon became a standout among their peers. Eli, Luc's right-hand man, had a gift for instilling confidence. All along, Luc had known Eli was a natural-born leader but sensed he'd been holding back. Leading his unit also came natural to Luc; he commanded respect, not only from the other recruits but also from his superiors.

When they were not training or practicing, they hung out together. Eli asked Luc everything about his past, his family, his friends, and his home world. When Luc asked Eli the same questions, however, Eli was not so forthcoming. Luc didn't think much about that and figured Eli had his reasons for not revealing much about himself. He was sure their friendship would survive anyway and that Eli would open up when he was ready.

Graduation from Division One meant two things: They had successfully completed basic training, and they would now officially be Tier One Angels. They beamed with hard-earned pride as they prepared for the day's events. The difficulty of what they had accomplished could only be known by other soldiers in the Lord's Army.

Rise of the Fallen

As recruits, they were obligated to attend all graduation ceremonies. Therefore, by the time they were ready for their own, they knew exactly what was expected of them. Something about this particular milestone was different though: Security detail was extensive, indicating that someone very important was scheduled to attend. Luc had never seen anything like it before. "Must be for my parents," he joked, looking around at all the eagle-eyed, stone-faced guards.

Luc's father and mother, Belial and Lamia, had traveled from halfway around the galaxy to get there. They glowed with pride as Luc and his section were praised as the best all-around unit in their class, and a wide smile stretched across his mother's face at the mention of Luc's accomplishments. They could not believe how he had changed since they last saw him. In only a few short months, he had grown taller and packed on thirty pounds of solid muscle.

After the ceremony, Belial and Lamia invited Luc and his friend Eli out to dinner to celebrate. They took an instant liking to Eli and very much enjoyed his stories about the healthy competition between the boys. After eating, laughing, and talking, they bid their farewells. As sad as they were to leave, and as much as they wanted to spend more time with their son, they had to return home in the morning.

His parents' quick departure tugged at Luc's heartstrings as well, but beneath that, way down inside him, there was a deeper sadness he could not quite explain or define. He suspected it had something to do with what he saw at the graduation ceremony, when he looked over and saw Eli peering into the crowd, as if looking for loved ones who just didn't show up.

Chapter 3

After graduation, they were finally allowed to leave the base and visit Araboth, a truly beautiful city. For the most part, all the soldiers stayed together, and Michael encouraged them to go with him. "Follow me," he cheerfully said. "I know a place with good music and plenty of good-looking girls. It's time to party, boys!"

There were, indeed, many girls there, many of them were recruits in the Angel core. It made the rest of the unit a little sick to see them hanging all over Michael. It also turned him back into the braggard he used to be, that annoying show-off they'd all grown weary of early in their training. It was apparent that Michael was a popular presence in the club, and Luc decided that was precisely why he had invited them all to go there.

In spite of Michael's jerkish ways, everyone had a great time. It sure beat sitting around the base. Two girls approached the table where Luc and Eli sat having a cold drink. Soon, they were on the dance floor, moving to the music. For the next two hours, everyone forgot about training.

All too quickly, the time came for them to return to base. After saying goodbye to the girls, with promises to see them soon, Luc and Eli rounded their unit up and left. For the entire twenty minutes of the commute, Michael graced the unit with tall tales, making sure everyone knew he was the shit when it came to the ladies. Everyone had to grudgingly admit he was in his element at the club, but that did not make him any less of an asshole.

For the newest set of Tier One Angels, the training quickly began in earnest. Although the physical part was mostly behind them, combat training was just as hard physically and mentally, if not harder. Luc and Eli continued to meet every challenge with the same enthusiasm as before.

A couple months later, during an afterhours pugil stick sparring practice session, Eli suddenly stopped. "There is something I need to tell you, Luc," he said sincerely, as if he were about to make a huge confession.

Luc smiled. "What? You're too scared to fight me anymore."

Eli tried to laugh but couldn't seem to manage. The serious look remained on his face as he answered, "No, really, I need to tell you something important."

Luc dropped his stick. "Okay. I'm listening. What is it, my friend?"

"A while back, you asked about my past, but I didn't want to talk about it. I appreciate you not pressing me on that, but I... Well, I do want you to know about my family."

"Eli, you know you can tell me anything, good or bad. I am your friend, no matter what," Luc assured him. He had tried to give Eli his space, but a niggling curiosity about Eli's family had been eating at him. *Is his dad a criminal or something? Is that why his parents weren't at the graduation?*

Eli looked around as if to make sure no one was listening, and he bit his bottom lip as if he were nervous.

"Go on, Eli," Luc coaxed.

"Okay. Well, for starters, my name is not really Eli. It's Elohim..." He paused for a second and just stared at Luc.

Luc wrinkled his brow as he looked back at his friend. He had heard the name before but could not place where.

"...and my father's name is Jehovah."

"Huh?" Luc stuttered. *Surely he's not talking about the*

galactic leader and ultimate ruler, about God, he thought. *That would make Eli a...prince.* He waited for Eli to punch him and say it was a joke, but somehow, he knew it was true. He sat back against a rough, wooden post, suddenly deep in thought. *No wonder there was so much security at our graduation. Eli was literally looking for Jehovah.*

"Please do not tell anyone, Luc," Eli said, jolting him from his thoughts. "I am to be trained like everyone else. No one is supposed to know, and if anybody finds it will ruin everything. Can I count on you to keep my secret? Most importantly, Luc, can we still be friends?"

Luc stood, picked up his pugil stick, and promptly knocked Eli upside the head with it. "Of course you can count on me. As for the rest of it, you are the best friend I've ever had. There is one thing though."

"What?"

"I guess we've never been properly introduced. My name is Lucifer Satanis, of Hell." With that, Luc stuck out his hand.

Eli grinned and reached for Luc's hand. "And I am Elohim El-Elyon, of Heaven."

With the formalities out of the way, Luc promptly popped Eli in the head with his stick again. Eli immediately returned the favor and managed a couple good shots himself. They groaned, then laughed, both knowing their friendship would last a lifetime.

Whenever they had opportunity, Eli and Luc sneaked into the palace through a secret entrance Eli had found as a young boy. The tunnel led to a large room that offered a view that was hard for two curious, young men to resist. Through the peepholes in the far wall, they could clearly see the female staff quarters. Perhaps in their adolescence, they would have stared in testosterone-driven awe and curiosity as scantily clad women relaxed and bustled about their private domiciles, but as the boys grew older, those urges were outweighed by the feeling that they're spying was wrong, not to mention a bit creepy.

They made it a point to avoid looking, striving to be men of honor. In fact, at their moment of shared epiphany, they settled on two rules to help guide them into their respective futures: "We will behave toward one and all with respect, until they prove themselves unworthy," they recited to one another, followed by, "We will behave toward one and all as we expect and desire them to behave toward us."

Just outside the palace, where security was still rather tight, there was a place where God and his family could truly enjoy nature without the threat of harm. Eli and Luc spent many hours fishing in the stream there and exploring the dense forest that made up God's private grounds. On one of those outings, while fishing in their favorite spot, something in the water caught Eli's eye. He reached in and pulled out a rock in the shape of a pentagon, and both friends marveled at the nearly perfect, five-sided shape.

"I give this pentagon to you, Luc, as a token of our friendship," Eli said, with a serious look on his face. "May it last forever."

Struggling to stifle a grin, Luc bowed and said, "I accept your gift as your humble servant, milord."

They both laughed, but Luc knew that from that moment on, he would never be without his most precious gift.

Chapter 4

While walking through the streets of Heaven near the base one day, Luc was ambushed by a group of thugs who quickly and easily overpowered him. Despite all his training and military prowess, he was sorely outnumbered, quickly bested, and rendered unconscious. When he awoke, he found himself strapped to a chair in a cold, ten-by-ten cinderblock room.

After Luc stared at the blank walls and dirty floor for a while, helpless to move or free himself, two masked men entered the room. The larger of the two spoke. "We want to ask you a few questions," he said. "If your answers are satisfactory, we will let you go unharmed."

"Let me go, you bastards!" Luc said with a growl.

In response, the smaller man produced a shock stick and held it against Luc's chest. Although he had been trained in resistance to that very weapon, Luc's body convulsed as pain tore through him. It was if his every nerve had burst into flames.

"Do we have your attention now?" the big man asked.

Other than a few groans, Luc remained silent.

For the next hour, they interrogated him and punished him for his continued silence. Early on, he noticed that many of their questions centered on someone in his unit, someone of prominence. At first, Luc thought they were talking about

Michael, that arrogant asshole, but it didn't take long for him to realize they were referring to Eli. He would not give them the satisfaction of any answers, no matter whom they wanted to know about, so he remained silent and revealed nothing. By the end of the first hour and into the second, he felt he was going to die. Then, as quickly as it had all begun, the pain and questions ended. The two men headed for the door.

"Is that all you've got?" Luc mumbled before he passed out.

Sometime later, Luc awoke and realized he had been moved into what appeared to be some sort of infirmary or hospital room. He tried to sit up, only to be stopped by a doctor.

"Be still, Private Satanis. You are safe here," the doctor said. "Just lie back and relax for a moment. You have been through quite an ordeal."

"Where... Where am I?" Luc managed.

"Someone will be in shortly to explain everything," the doctor assured him.

A short while after the doctor left the room, two men entered. They were not wearing masks like before, but, based on their physiques and the timbre of their voices, Luc was sure they were the same men who had worked him over. He tensed but knew he was in no shape to resist what was coming. The door opened again, and someone Luc recognized walked in.

"Sergeant? Sergeant Bethor?" Luc said as he managed a weak salute. "I-I do not understand, sir."

"You will in a moment, Soldier," the sergeant said, with an almost indiscernible hint of compassion in his voice. "There is someone here to see you."

The sight of Luc's next visitor sent a shockwave though him, almost as jarring as the jolts of those dreadful shock sticks.

"Hello, Private Satanis," said God Jehovah, Eli's father. "May I call you Luc?"

Luc sat up with a start and managed a slight nod, but

the look of confusion didn't leave his face. He nodded, wide-eyed, but said nothing.

Jehovah continued, "I am sorry for the suffering you have endured, and I am afraid to tell you it was at my request."

"Excuse me? You... At *your* request, sir?" Luc stammered.

"Yes, and I hope you will forgive me after I explain," Jehovah said. "Elohim, or Eli, is undergoing Angelic Corp training in preparation for his takeover of Heaven when I step down. The knowledge my son is now acquiring will help him better lead our people. We had to be sure you would not use what you know against him. It is vitally important that Eli complete his Angel training, for the future of us all." For the next hour, Jehovah outlined Luc's place in the years to come. "I ask two things of you, Luc," he finally said. "First, I want you to protect Elohim, with your life, if it comes to that. Second, all of what you have heard today must be kept between the two of us. I am afraid Elohim will never forgive me for my interference if he discovers I spoke to you about all this."

Luc nodded. "As for your first request, I would have done that without your asking

," he said. "Eli is my best friend. As for your second, I will not speak of this to Elohim or anyone else. You have my word. He is lucky to have you as a father."

Jehovah smiled, stood, shook Luc's hand, and left the room.

Before they followed God out, the two torturers offered Luc their apologies.

"I hardly felt a thing. Next time, do it like you mean it," Luc said, wincing as he shifted in bed. He managed a painful laugh, and the two left shaking their heads and chuckling.

Back at the base, Eli watched Luc enter the barracks. "What happened to you?" he asked, with obvious worry. "You look like crap."

"I was downtown, and some hoodlums jumped me, but believe me when I tell you they got the worst of it." It was the one and only lie Luc ever told Eli, and he made a promise to himself that it would be the last.

Chapter 5

It took a few days of recovery, but Luc was soon back to 100 percent. Had he not been, he still would not have missed the first day of antigravity training. For months, Luc and Eli had had watched with great envy as other soldiers pushed themselves high in the air, then moved to and fro with ease. There was no way they were going to miss their opportunity to fly.

Although personal antigravity units, AGUs, offered many practical applications, they were strictly forbidden outside use by the military and law enforcement. Balance was the most important aspect of the push. Many novice flyers found themselves headfirst on the ground, dumbstruck and wondering what happened. With practice and baby steps, though, each and every one soon mastered the push.

As was usually the case for Luc and Eli, they took to the training quickly. One day, they tried to show off a bit by performing a chest-bump in the air. Their efforts resulted in both of them being sprawled out on the ground, flat on their butts and red-faced.

Sergeant Bethor tried his best to hide a smile. "Until you have mastered the AGU, being cocky and screwing around can be very dangerous. One more stunt like that, and you will both be watching from the sidelines. Understood?"

"Yes, sir!" the embarrassed and chastened soldiers answered before they continued with their training.

Within a week, they had mastered balance and had moved on to maneuvering. They practiced winding through the shock maze, which gave an instant report of their proficiency and progress. No one was without pain during their first run, even those who tried to tiptoe at a slow pace. Once they mastered the run-through, an increase in speed was required for the next step. Then, after a soldier was proficient at navigating the maze in two-dimensional movements at an acceptable rate of speed, scaling up and down in three dimensions was required to successfully navigate the maze.

Finally, precision was added to the equation. Soldiers were required to successfully jump through hoops and slide under, over, around, and through moving obstacles at speeds that would save their lives in precarious real-life scenarios. At that stage, avoiding shocks and nonlethal projectiles was their key concern. Again, no one was immune from burns and painful bruises, and broken bones were not uncommon. A month and a half and several bandages later, everyone was AGU certified.

Another course they looked forward to was body shield training. For the next month, along with all their other duties, they learned every aspect of it. The potential to be protected from almost any attack was a dream come true for any soldier. Proper use of the shield controls was vital to a soldier's life in the heat of battle, and awareness of how much protection one required at any given time ensured having the power needed for a prolonged attack.

Shields could be calibrated to stop projectiles like bullets or even blasts from fairly large explosives. Of course, the latter required an extreme amount of power, only to be used when absolutely necessary. Every soldier had to take the force of medium-sized explosions during practice, just so they could experience the effects and learn to recover. In battle situations, shields were always calibrated to full, since the real drain on power would only occur in an actual explosion.

During one of their drills, Luc and his squad were advancing on a target building. Just as they were about to breach the perimeter, the structure exploded, knocking everyone about fifty feet back from where they started. Luc and his squad were a bit dazed and sore but still seemed battle ready. Only Private Ronobe, who had a momentary lack of concentration as the blast occurred, was knocked out cold; otherwise, he was fine, and he'd learned a valuable lesson: Concentration and preparation were the keys to using the shields properly. By the time the training was complete, every soldier could lean into a blast and avoid being thrown around.

Chapter 6

At the one-year mark, worthy soldiers were awarded the rank of Tier One Angel First Class and were granted one month of personal leave. Luc was proud everyone in his unit made the rank.

Although Luc was glad to be able to spend some time with his family, he was also excited about returning to base the following month. Then, they would be assigned to a one-year tour for field training, likely to fight along the borders of Empire space.

Luc landed in Hades spaceport, eager to be reunited with his loved ones. For the first time in a year, he actually cried; this time, it wasn't from exertion or pain but because he was the happiest man in the galaxy. That night, all his friends and family gathered at a party to welcome him home. His mother made all his favorite foods and could not seem to stop hugging him every time he was close. Luc, however, gladly welcomed every embrace.

"There is a girl I'd like you to meet," the soldier's mother told him, beaming. "She has a really great personality. She was going to be here tonight, but she could not get away."

Luc rolled his eyes. "No, thanks, Mom. No offense, but your matchmaking efforts haven't turned out too well for me. Besides, you're the only girl I need."

"Aw," she said, then pinched his cheek and hugged him

yet again.

Luc's father was absolutely bursting with pride. He had never been as affectionate as his wife, but he still took every opportunity to put his arm around Luc or pat him on the shoulder and brag to others about his boy's accomplishments.

His brothers also wanted to spend as much time as they could with him. After dinner, Luc and his brothers, along with a few friends, found time to toss the ball around in the yard. For Luc, it was a great day, full of happy memories and lots of laughter.

The next day, Luc got up early to exercise and run laps in the nearby park. He knew it was not wise to use his temporary leave as an excuse to fall out of shape. Besides, it felt good to push himself to his limits. After his jog, he cleaned up and spent the rest of the day enjoying his family. He even helped his mother cook that night. That was shocking to her, especially because he seemed to actually enjoy learning one of her recipes. She was shocked even more when he volunteered to help with the dishes. Truth be told, he was glad to work around the house; during his time away, he had come to realize just how precious time spent with family could be.

That night, Luc went out with a few friends to some of the local hangouts. He was enjoying the music and reliving old times when he noticed a large, rough-looking man trying to force a girl to dance with him. After her repeated rebuffs, the brute grabbed her arm and attempted to jerk her onto the dance floor. Luc never would have dreamt of interfering before, but the confidence instilled in him by his first year in the military gave him courage.

"You need to let the lady go and move on," Luc said when he walked up to the guy, as his friends looked on, amazed at his newfound bravado. The bully had at least seventy-five pounds on him and was at least a head taller.

"Go away, little man. This does not concern you."

The man was so close Luc could smell his foul breath, but he stood his ground nonetheless. "Look, she's obviously not interested in you, so I'm warning you to move on," Luc said.

Without another word, the asshole threw his weight into Luc and knocked him to the floor. The low-IQ lump of muscle then turned back to the girl and grabbed her again.

Luc stood up and tapped the scumbag on the back. "I'll give you just one more chance, buddy. Move on."

Luc then easily avoided the oncoming swing and punched the monster in the stomach, which felt something like hitting a rock. The lump smiled and hit Luc square in the face, but even when he felt blood running down his face and dripping off his chin from his split lip, Luc did not go down. The savage moved toward Luc to finish what he'd started, but Luc kicked him in the knee, hyperextending it, and the ruffian collapsed to the floor, holding his aching leg.

"Now, please leave the lady alone," Luc said.

As he wiped the trickle of blood from his chin and looked up at the girl under the dim lights in the club, he recognized her as the girl of his dreams. Feeling the heat of his own blushing, he just stood there, staring at her. He tried to form words that might make sense, but none were forthcoming. What he failed to notice, so enamored as he was by Vepar, was that the cad had managed to amble to his feet and was now limping toward him.

Quickly, Vepar delivered a firm kick to the side of her harasser's face, and he went down for good. She then looked Luc straight in the eye. "I did not need your help. As you can see, I'm capable of taking care of myself."

Before Luc could stop himself, he said, "Oh, I wasn't looking out for you. I was trying to protect him, merely trying to stop him before you really hurt him."

That brought a smile to her pretty face, and they shared a laugh.

"I do not know if you remember me, but I am Lucifer Satanis. We went to Hades High together."

"I remember. You were in a few of my classes. Why didn't you ever ask me out? You seemed...interested enough."

Wowed by her words and her beauty and a bit unsure of

himself, he muttered, "I just... Well, I guess I never felt worthy. You are so beautiful, Vepar. I just did not figure you'd be interested in someone like me."

"Hmm. Well, do you think you're worthy now?"

"I have no idea," he said with a shrug. Am I?"

Smiling once again, she replied, "Maybe."

"Obviously, I couldn't prove my worth by rescuing you," Luc offered, and they both laughed again.

"Let's find a quiet table, so we can talk," she suggested, then led him away to a dark corner.

As they got to know one another better, Luc found her very interesting. She actually held dear many of the values he did. They spoke of their school days, talked about the happenings of the year that had flown by sense, and discussed their future plans. She was so easy to talk to that Luc had no problem telling her all about his training and his friend Eli, though he was careful to keep secrets to himself. The time passed quickly, he realized, when he glanced up at a clock on the wall.

"Whoa! It's way past my bedtime, and I need to rise early tomorrow." He looked into her big, green eyes. "I've had the most wonderful time tonight. I'd really enjoy doing it again sometime soon, if that is all right with you."

"I need to get home myself," Vepar said, but she was also saddened to see the evening come to an end. "Would you mind walking me home?"

Luc tried not to let his excitement turn him into a blubbering mess as he answered, "It would be my pleasure, fair maiden."

As they walked, Luc felt himself slipping into Dreamland. *She is the most beautiful girl in all the worlds. How is it that she's interested in me?* he silently questioned, awestruck. Words came easy to him now, and he felt he could tell her anything. He did not have to put on airs, as he had to with other girls he'd dated on Heaven; Vepar was too special, and she deserved his honesty.

They reached her home much too soon. They stood on

her porch and talked a little more.

"I am serious about seeing you again, if you're agreeable to it," Luc said, his voice dripping with anxious hope.

She smiled, leaned in, and gave him a quick kiss. "Oh, I *will* see you soon."

The way she said it made him wonder what she meant. The rest of Luc's walk home was filled with excitement and wonder. He had just enjoyed the most unforgettable evening of his life, and he hoped it was only the first of many. *What if it's a fluke though?* he asked himself as his doubts crept in. He quickly tossed those thoughts aside and just enjoyed the high with a silly grin on his face all the way home.

When he reached his house, he walked through the back door and found his father raiding the refrigerator.

His father looked up for only a second, then shoved his head back in the fridge. "Hi, Son," he said. "I take it you had a good evening, if you're out this late."

"Not bad, Dad, not bad at all," Luc said.

Belial studied his son's face. "Not bad? From that look on your face, I say you had a great time. Be warned, my boy. Your mother still wants you to meet that girl she was talking about at your party."

Luc frowned. "Damn! I hoped she'd forget about that."

"I know that woman can be pushy about such things, Luc, but remember. She loves you and means well."

"Yeah, I know. I'm going to bed, Father. Goodnight."

The next morning, Luc was up early for his morning ritual. After pushing himself twice as hard as usual in his workout, he headed for the park. Just as he rounded the corner to start his run, he stopped dead in his tracks when he saw a lovely creature stretching her gorgeous legs on a nearby bench, beautiful as ever in a light blue running outfit.

"It's about time," Vepar said. "What would your sergeant think of his soldiers oversleeping?"

Luc stood there with his mouth agape, trying to find the words to express his joy.

With a wink and a smirk, she took off running. "Catch me if you can!" she challenged.

He finally realized what was going on and took off after her. She did not make it easy; she was a strong runner. Before he knew it, they had trekked four miles, and she'd barely broken a sweat. Another thing Luc had failed to notice was that they'd reached his yard. Now, he was faced with a dilemma: *Should I invite her in or not?*

Ultimately, he decided it was appropriate to offer her a seat on their porch while he went in to get something for them to drink. He found his mother in the kitchen preparing breakfast when he walked in.

"Your father told me you probably met someone last night, but I do not want you to give up on that girl I know," she said. "She babysat your little brother while you were gone. Her name is—"

She was interrupted when the back door swung open and someone walked in.

"Oh! Vepar, dear, I was just talking about you," Luc's mother said. "So, you already know each other?" Lamia asked with a coy smile.

"Good morning, Mrs. Satanis. Yes, Luc and I went to school together, and I saw him again last night.

Luc was speechless once again, struggling to catch up and not doing a very good job.

From that moment on, Luc and Vepar spent almost every waking moment of his leave together. Although Luc was excited about his upcoming ship assignment, he now felt the sadness of his impending return to Heaven. The day he shipped out, his heart was heavy. He hugged his parents, then turned to Vepar.

With a tear running down her face, she looked into his eyes. "Listen, Tier One Angel First Class Lucifer Satanis, you are *my* soldier now. You *will* remember me, you *will* love me, and you *will* return to me. Do you hear me, Soldier?"

"Loud and clear, ma'am," Luc said, just before he took her in his arms and kissed her deeply. He hugged his parents once more, kissed the teary-eyed Vepar again, then reluctantly entered the ship.

Chapter 7

Two weeks later, as Luc and Eli and two others entered the Tier One dorm after a day of intensive flight training, they received their orders to report to the *Angelic Fleet Warship Barakiel,* at 7:00 the following morning. They would be under the command of Captain Karael, and the AFW *Barakiel* was a dream assignment; they would be serving on the command ship of Heaven's fleet.

When he was able to get Sergeant Bethor alone for a few minutes, Luc asked, "Was there some sort of, uh…push from above? Is that why we were given this assignment?"

Bethor assured Luc, "No, only our top graduates among the Tier Ones are even considered. You, Eli, Turel, and Saniel have earned and deserve placement on the *Barakiel*." He also made it very clear that no one who made the decision was aware of Eli's true identity.

It was comforting to note that Michael was not called to the *Barakiel*. Despite the comradery they'd managed to drum up, Luc was relieved to know he no longer had to deal with him. While Michael and all the others in the unit did receive choice assignments, neither Michael's prowess with the ladies nor his family connections could push him to the top of the list. In fact, he was the last in his unit to be called. His displeasure with his placement hung in the air like a thick fog; while the young man was usually a loudmouth, now, his silent glare was the only communication he offered the others in his unit.

When Sergeant Bethor saw his men off, Luc was the last to enter the shuttle. Before he did, he leaned in and whispered, "Thanks for everything, you old bastard..." Luc quickly saluted, then finished with a smile and a loud, "...sir!"

Bethor returned the salute and a slight smile of his own, clapped Luc on the back, and said, "Get your ass on that shuttle before I kick it back to basic training, Soldier." The sergeant then leaned close and quietly reminded Luc about his promise to protect his friend.

"With my life, sir."

They shook hands, and Luc headed for the ship.

As the soldiers entered the shuttle, none of them spoke. All were occupied with deep thoughts about what was to come. After they moved beyond Heaven's atmosphere, they saw the AFW *Barakiel* through the windows. Luc had never seen a ship so massive. The closer they got, the more his awe grew.

The feeling ended when the shuttle docked inside the *Barakiel* and they prepared to undergo orientation. The new recruits were lined up and informed of their assignments. Luc and Eli would be trained as fighter pilots, while Turel would be a navigator, and Saniel would be an engineer. Any elation they felt was short-lived when they were informed of their work detail during the trip. Luc and Eli were none too thrilled to hear they'd be put on KP duty, tasked with washing dishes and serving food to the rest of the ship.

After being knocked down from their fighter pilot high, they headed for the next step in their orientation, meeting with second-year pilots and receiving their first assignments. They were instructed to paint a room a peculiar shade of pink. Even though they found it an odd color choice, Luc and his best friend tackled their first assignment with enthusiasm.

They had just finished the first coat when their training sergeant entered the room, in a rage. "What in damnation are you doing to my office?" he shouted at the top of his lungs.

Luc and Eli snapped to attention with quick salutes, and Luc was the first to find his voice. "Painting the room, sir."

At that point, the second-year pilots heard the shouting and piled into the office, some of them stifling laughs and smirks.

"Who told you to paint my office?" Sergeant Sidriel screamed.

Luc looked past the sergeant and into the eyes of the smiling second-year pilots who had so nicely set them up. "Well, we, uh... We were walking past your office, saw the paint, and thought it needed painting, sir."

Sergeant Sidriel moved closer to Luc's face, so close the tips of their noses almost touched. "Tell me who told you to do this, and tell me right now!" he said with a growl.

Eli followed Luc's lead. "It was our idea. We were just trying to help, sir."

Sweat began to bead on their faces as the Sergeant glared at them.

At that moment, just as the sweat began to bead on their faces under the heat of the sergeant's glare, Sergeant Sidriel burst out laughing. So did everyone else in the room, except for Luc and Eli, who just looked around in confusion, with smears of pink paint on their faces.

"Welcome to the *Barakiel*, boys. This is the one and only kind of new recruit hazing we condone on our ship. Do not be too mad at the guys. Every one of them went through the same thing," Sergeant Sidriel explained.

Luc and Eli slowly finally managed half-smiles when they realized they'd been had. They felt much better when all the guys moved in to greet them.

"Oh, yeah, just so you know, these are *your* quarters. I hope you enjoy the color," the sergeant said. He continued laughing as he exited the room, followed by the rest of the group.

Luc and Eli settled into their new quarters, laughing and shaking their heads every time they looked at their pink walls.

The next day came early. They arrived in the cafeteria at promptly 5 a.m. Luc started on the dishes, and Eli bused the tables. At 9:00, they reported to the flight room. There was a lot to learn; the specification and operational manuals were thick and packed with required information.

It was a month before Luc and Eli had time to repaint their room in the standard gray. It didn't take long for them to settle into their new routine, and they tackled their studies and KP duty with the same enthusiasm they had in basic training. They also exercised every evening, not willing to lose the physical fitness they'd manage to gain during basic.

Chapter 8

The boys were excited whenever they had the rare opportunity to test any new technology. The latest was a mind-enhancement device meant to send thoughts and knowledge into the brain without the need for real-life experience. In this way, information gleaned from the experiences of other pilots could be preloaded into the brain before a new pilot even set foot in a fighter. At first, it was a bit tricky to focus the device without causing memory flooding. In fact, on Luc's first few attempts, memories of his past raced into his brain in a mishmash of scattered thoughts. He was overwhelmed by vivid images of birthdays, his parents, and, of course, Vepar, who pretty much crowded out everything else as soon as she came to mind. There were also some images best left alone, specifically regarding Eli.

In the first section of training with the new device, they had to learn to control the flow of information. They were coached, "Try to look into your past while focusing only on major events." Then, as they progressed, they targeted more minor events, learning to hone their control.

Since the device provided such clarity, it was almost like actually being in the past. Luc relived more of his life each day, but the memories were not all pleasant. He made mental notes of times when he felt he had inadvertently hurt someone's feelings and made a pact with himself to try to apologize for each and every such incident. Because of his parents' teachings and fine examples, those indiscretions were far less numerous than they could have been.

The last fifteen minutes of every session belonged to sweet Vepar. Luc gladly relived the moment when she first came into his life, on her first day of high school. While trying to locate one of his classes, he passed her in the hall, and she smiled at him. He actually looked over his shoulder then, doing a double-take to be sure the beautiful smile was for him. As a result, he collided with Mr. Haggai, School Headmaster. As embarrassing as the memory was, any sting of humiliation was overshadowed by Vepar. So, the last fifteen minutes was always reserved for her.

It did not take him long to master the device, and knowledge poured into his eagerly awaiting brain. Within a week, he knew everything about fighters and was confident that, when tested in real-life situations, he would pass with flying colors.

At night, just before lights out, Luc and Eli compared notes on everything they had learned. Both wished they could use the devices during their off time, for personal reasons, but Illuminators, as they were known, were highly restricted instruments. The gadgets never left what Luc and Eli referred to as the Room of Memories, with good reason: If one of the training devices happened to fall into the wrong hands, it could severely undermine fleet security. They were glad to learn that there were future plans to make modified Illuminators available as learning tools for civilian applications, once the devices were fully tested and capabilities and dangers were fully known.

Soon, test day arrived. Luc entered the simulator with confidence. He did well on the knowledge section, but there were also concerns about physical response to real-life, traumatic situations. Muscle control and muscle memory were factors they had to contend with, and that required more training and practice.

Humbled by their need to improve, both Luc and Eli, did what they always did; they practiced. Before long, they were ready to take their fighters into space for formation drills.

Only a week later, they were trusted with combat situations. What they had learned in a mere few weeks took their predecessors almost a year. Within a month, the two were impressively combat ready.

Benjamin Oneal

Chapter 9

Nine months after they arrived on the *Barakiel*, word came down that there was trouble: The Dumah had attacked several outposts along the Empire border. The *Barakiel* and four other fleet ships were ordered to check it out. En route, Luc studied everything he could on the Dumah, though there was not much intel available.

What he did discover was that the Dumah were a race of intelligent beings, evolved from insects. They were roughly ant like, around four feet tall on average, with very hard exoskeletons. They were bi-pedal and stood upright on two thick legs and had four upper appendages that functioned much like human arms. The Dumah were predominantly female; only a few males existed to fertilize their queen. They were also divided via a strictly defined caste system. The queen, truly the mother of all who served her, ruled all fertilizing males, workers, and warriors who protected the colony at all cost. The Dumah were efficient, both on their home planet and in conquering other worlds as they spread throughout their surrounding star systems.

Once the Dumah moved past the boundaries of their system, they colonized every world capable of sustaining their needs, whether the indigenous species of those worlds agreed or not. When they made landfall in those locations, they left a queen, a few males, a multitude of workers, and enough warriors behind, as many as necessary to protect them until the resident queens produced enough offspring to control each new world. Since Dumah queens could lay an average of 1,500 eggs a day, it didn't take long for them to overtake whatever worlds they wished to inhabit.

The Dumah saw no value in non-Dumah life, except as possible food sources. That fact alone made them very dangerous, enemies to all. Any attempt to reason with them was met with swift rejection in the form of violent attacks. What they lacked in fighting skills, they made up for in sheer numbers. Because their opponents were always sorely outnumbered, it was impossible to weaken the onslaught in battle. No matter how many were struck down or killed, they just kept coming in swarms.

A half-hour before they were scheduled to enter normal space around the border Planet Tagas, Luc and every soldier on the *Barakiel*, readied for battle. Luc wished Eli luck, pulled him into a brotherly hug, then climbed into his fighter. He strapped in and brought the vessel to life. As the controls buzzed around him, he felt every inch of it, as if the vehicle was an extension of his own body.

As they departed deviant space, the five Angelic ships were immediately confronted by seven massive Dumah warships. Fighters from both sides poured from their battleships, and the Dumah outnumbered the Angelic fighters at least ten to one. Luc soon realized that what he had learned was true: the Dumah's best defense was their immense number.

The Dumah were easy to take down, but while Luc destroyed or disabled ship after ship, they just kept coming. The enemies were somewhat inept and failed to dodge most of his strikes, but as soon as one fighter went down in a flaming fireball, one or more was quick to take its place. After an hour of continuous battle, Luc was exhausted. *Damn. There are just too many of them,* he thought. Unimaginable numbers of Dumah bodies floated among the wreckage, mangled and hitting the sides of ships.

To make matters worse, Luc and the rest of the Angelic fleet soon realized that the Dumah floating in space were not dead at all: Their exoskeletons and minimal life support requirements allowed them to survive for long periods of time in outer space. They clung to almost every Angelic vessel, hanging on tightly with any appendages they had left. There were so many of them, clogging up the vents and propellers, wings and mechanical elements, that it was hard for the fighters to remain in flight. Eli cleared the stubbornly clutching insects from Luc's fighter with well-placed energy blasts, and Luc did the same for Eli, but no sooner did they clear them away, the fighters were again blanketed with more. Many fighters either exploded as the attackers breached the fuel cells or experienced explosive decompression, leaving the pilots to face unimaginable and painful fates as the Dumah made their way into the cockpits. Even the battleships could not escape the swarms.

Eli called to Luc, "Look! The *Barakiel*!"

Luc turned and saw the *Barakiel* covered with Dumah, who were using their own energy weapons to tear away at the shields. At one point, there were so many Dumah covering the outside of the ship that the *Barakiel* looked as if it were undulating. With so many concentrated points of attack, the shields would soon be breached, and the battle cruiser would fall. Luc and the other fighters cleared away as many as they could but could not keep up with the number of enemies.

In the midst of the chaos, as the Dumah on the outside of Luc's ship continued to tear away at the shields, making it almost impossible to maneuver, Luc's mind suddenly traveled back to his childhood. He recalled riding in the back seat of his father's antigravity land cruiser, when he noticed an insect on the window. As his father began to move forward, the wind started pushing against the insect. Luc marveled as the insect mightily held on to the glass, even as the rushing wind pushed the struggling creature against it. Finally, the wind resistance became too much, and the bug, vibrating, finally flew off to an uncertain future. With that on is mind, Luc called out to his friend, "Eli, this may sound crazy, but I have an idea. Signal the *Barakiel*."

Luc headed for nearby Tagas and entered the atmosphere there. Almost immediately, the Dumah clinging to his fighter began to glow, as the heat of the Tagas atmosphere and the friction from reentry pushed against them. He could see the tiny barbs on the ends of their limbs digging in deeper as they clung valiantly to the ship. The temperature inside the fighter increased as Luc flew deeper into the atmosphere. At last, the friction burned away the uninvited guests from his fighter. Even those who released early were moving much too fast to escape death.

As the Dumah breached the outer hulls of many of the ships in the Angelic fleet, they followed Luc's lead and moved into the Tagas atmosphere, burning off the parasitic enemies. Once the Angelic fleet had cleared the Dumah from their ships, using the clever tactic some had already dubbed Lucifer's Breath, they avoided the clouds of floating Dumah and instead turned their attack on the Dumah warships.

Once the enemy battle cruisers were rendered non-threatening, sans power or weapons, thousands of displaced Dumah poured into space, desperate to cling to any vessel they could. Since the Dumahs were too stubborn or too foolish to retreat, complete annihilation was the only option. When the last enemy cruiser was destroyed, the fleet took up the task of cleaning up the battlefield. What seemed like a million of the insectoids floated like landmines, just waiting for any chance to continue their mission. Since the Angelic fleet had never battled the Dumah before, they were unaware of just how long the creatures could survive in the vacuum of space. Within an hour, though, the Angelic fighters had cleared the space around the battlefield, and the Lucifer's Breath maneuver had removed the last of their uninvited guests.

In all, 217 Angelic soldiers were lost in the battle, and the *Hasmal*, an Angelic battle cruiser, had to be sent back for repair after significant damage. However, all but three of those soldiers and the majority of the ship damage happened before Luc's tactic was employed, something that did not go unnoticed by those in command.

Of course, the Angelic fleet would have preferred to let the Dumah retreat, but that was not the Dumah way. They did, however, capture twenty-six Dumah, and they hoped those captives would cooperate and help them better understand and learn anything that might help them during their next battle.

Once the extent of the damage and the number of casualties was known, a message came across from the fleet commander: "All in the Angelic fleet, I thank you for your courage. Our victory here today is marred only by the lost lives. Remember the fallen, for they will forever be heroes who sacrificed all..." His speech of gratitude went on for a while longer, giving all who listened praise, a reason to mourn, and a reason to be proud.

A few days after the battle, Luc and Eli went to see the prisoners of war in their cells. The first Dumah they met was easily two feet shorter than them. It didn't pay much attention to them but continued to explore every inch of the cell, presumably searching for any means of escape. Although the creature was much smaller in stature than either Eli or Luc, its exoskeleton made it far stronger than its size indicated.

In the second cell was one they could only guess was a soldier. It stood about seven feet high and continued to viciously slam against the forcefields that held it in. Its huge mandibles had already cut the metal bed into little pieces. Luc and Eli had no doubt that if that Dumah escaped, those menacing jawbones would cut through them as easily as a hot knife through butter.

Based on feedback from Planet Tagas, the Dumah were very effective ground fighters. They could lift ten times their own weight, and their front mandibles were sharp and very dangerous, capable of ripping limbs off or bodies in half with little effort. Needless to say, the people of Tagas were struggling to survive. Luc and Eli volunteered air support to the Tagas troops. Within three days, the Dumah were defeated, and Angelic ground forces even managed to capture a queen.

Chapter 10

The Angelic fleet continued to patrol the border of Dumah space for some time after the battle, knowing it was very likely the Dumah would continue to try to expand their territory. It was just in their nature. Jehovah ordered the commanders to do their best to prevent any future Dumah invasions in Heavenly space.

The Angelic fleet managed to board and study the remaining Dumah battle cruisers, and some Dumah still lurked in the walls. A lot of soldiers were killed or injured during those recon missions. Horrific tales began to surface, stories of Dumah grotesquely feeding on the Angelic soldiers, or their own fallen comrades. The only tool they had against the hiding Dumah was the insecticide fog that filled the ships before any Angelic soldiers or scientists stepped inside. It was not 100 percent effective, but it drastically cut down on Angelic casualties.

After months of study, they had learned much about Dumah technology and ship design. Scientists analyzed every piece of tech aboard the Dumah ships, including weapons, navigation, and communications devices. Meanwhile, Luc and Eli, along with a team of engineers and pilots, examined the fighters. Once Luc and Eli were able to understand the controls, they assessed the ships in open space to gain more practical knowledge of their weapons.

Even the Illuminators proved somewhat valuable when the mind patterns of the Dumah were tested. They were effective in the deciphering of the Dumah language. The biggest leap came from the captured queen. Once the fleet knew how to communicate with the Dumah, they broadcasted a message in Dumah space, on a continuous loop: "Make no further attempts to invade Heavenly space. Any attempt to do so will be met with immediate force. Any attacks on any planet or system protected by the Empire will be considered an act of war, and we will stop at nothing in our mission to destroy any and all Dumah if any attack occurs."

They continued to patrol the border for the next six months before a changing of the guard took place. Much to the relief of every soldier in the fleet, there was no further attempt by the Dumah to enter Heavenly space.

Chapter 11

As a result of his heroic efforts during the Dumah conflict, Luc was commended for his insight and bravery by Captain Karael. His tactic of moving into the atmosphere, the Lucifer's Breath method, became a well-known, routine battle maneuver, and he was awarded a field promotion to the rank of Tier Two Angel First Class and granted command of his own unit. Though Luc felt odd about Eli having to report to him, his friend was quick to assure Luc that he deserved the promotion and the commendation, and he was thrilled to be Luc's second-in-command when he was also promoted to Tier Two Angel Second Class.

Of course, they had to learn more ways to remove the Dumah from their ships, since they could not count on there always being a nearby planet with a substantial atmosphere. While patrolling the border for that six months, Luc and Eli used their time wisely, exploring new tactics for fighting such a savage foe.

Since dear Vepar was always on his mind, Luc also found time to write to her, to tell her the good news about his promotion and all he could about his mission along the border:

"Dear Vepar... I miss you dearly and think of you almost every waking moment. I wish I could see your face and hold you in my arms, but I am restricted to the written word until we return from this mission. We can take no chances, for fear the Dumah could intercept any messages that we send..."

He continued telling Vepar of the things he was allowed to reveal and finally concluded,

"I hope to be back on Heaven in two months. My only regret is that I cannot come home to see you, to hold you, to kiss you deeply. By then, though, I will hopefully be able to send a video message. At least that way, I can see your smile, a memory that brightens my every day. Please tell my family I love and miss them very much, and I will write to them soon... Forever yours, Luc."

The next few months eked by slowly, since there were no further attempts by the Dumah to enter Heavenly space. From Planet Tagas, they heard reports of attacks by the last remnants of Dumah. Four battle cruisers, led by the AFW *Simiel* relieved the tired soldiers along the border.

Luc and Eli could not wait to be back on Heaven, even if only for a short while. Everyone prepared to debark as they pulled into the space dock. Luc longed to walk in the open air, to feel the breeze and the warmth of the sun, and to enjoy the sensation of cool grass under his feet. Rank had its privileges, though, so Luc and Eli were forced to wait nearly three hours for their superiors to be situated before they could enter their shuttle.

Chapter 12

A week's leave was not enough time to travel back home, but it felt good to be away from the daily routines and the fray for a few days. In his quarters, Luc prepared to take a run in the park outside the base. He jogged the quarter-mile to the park, enjoying the wind in his face. As he turned onto the running path in the park, he thought to himself, *nothing in the world can top this.*

Suddenly, he heard the pounding of feet quickly coming up behind him, but he was in too good a mood to let that bother him. Feeling a little cocky, Luc said over his shoulder as he pushed his legs even harder, "If you think you're gonna pass me, you have another thing coming."

The footfalls surprisingly matched his speed, so Luc ran at his top speed. When he reached the place where the path followed the edge of the lake, he marveled as his unseen opponent breezed past him. It was a girl, and she was effectively kicking his ass.

When she was about six feet ahead of him, she looked over her shoulder and teased, "What's the matter, Soldier? Can't keep up?"

The voice was familiar. *Vepar?* he silently questioned. In an instant, his mind performed a few unplanned somersaults, and is body followed suit. Everything seemed to go wrong at once. He tripped over his own feet, lost his balance, and ran straight into the lake. As he broke the surface of the water, he did not see her but heard her laughing.

He wiped the water from his eyes and spied her rolling on the ground, about ten feet up the path. Dripping, he sloshed over to where she lay, holding her stomach and chuckling loudly. "What's so funny?" he asked.

She did not answer but just pointed at his soaked hair and laughed even harder.

Luc plopped down beside her and began laughing with her.

He was still laughing when she pushed him to the ground and kissed him deeply. At once, he was lost in the moment; there was no other place in the universe he wanted to be. The world around him slipped away, and time had no meaning.

Some indeterminable amount of time later, the mood was broken as Vepar broke into laughter once again. They both lay back and laughed some more. He could not bear to let go of her, for he feared she was only a dream and might vanish if he did.

Once his mind was able to command his mouth to form words again, he rolled toward her, propped himself up on his elbow, and released a torrent of questions: "Are you really here? When did you get here? How long can you stay? How did you know I would be here?"

She smiled. "Yes, yesterday, and that depends on you and Eli. Did I get them all?"

"I-I think so."

"Good. Now relax, Soldier, and let us start over." She kissed him again, then said, "You can thank Eli for me being here. He arranged everything. I don't know how he did it on such short notice, but here I am."

Luc knew exactly how Eli managed it, and it was a wonderful thing, but he had no idea how to repay his friend.

Vepar went on to tell him of plans to meet Eli and his date for an evening on the town, but they decided to go ahead and finish their run. "Besides, it will help you dry off, soggy boy," she taunted, flicking a bead of lake water off his cheek.

By the time they got back to her place, Luc was covered in sweat. He kissed her once more, then returned to his quarters to shower and get ready for their evening together. When he walked in, he found Eli sitting there, wearing the biggest shit-eating grin he had never seen.

"You look...happy. Did something happen today?" Eli asked, as if he didn't already know the answer. "Why are you in such a good mood?"

Luc said nothing at first and simply walked over to give his friend the biggest hug he could muster, lifting him right out of his seat. He then backed away a bit and looked Eli straight in the eye. "I fear there is nothing I can do to repay you for the gift you have given me. You are a true and excellent friend, Eli, and I am forever in your debt."

"Damn right you are, *sir*," Eli said with a salute and smirk.

Luc winced; he wasn't sure he would ever get used to the Son of God calling him that.

The night was a dream all its own. The four of them danced, laughed, and enjoyed every second of being together. Every night of his week of leave, Luc and Vepar ended their evenings with kisses at her door.

On the last night before Luc was to report back to the *Barakiel*, Vepar took his hand in hers and looked deeply into his eyes. "Please don't go. Stay with me tonight."

Helpless to protest, Luc allowed her to pull him into her room. They spent the night holding each other, kissing, and talking of the future. Although their bodies ached terribly to be one with each other, they knew the time was not right for such passion. They both agreed they should first tell their parents of their plans and ask for their blessings before they could move their relationship forward.

The next day, as Luc and Vepar stood just outside the restricted launch area, he suddenly went down on one knee, took her hand, and looked up into her eyes. "Vepar Gomory, will you be my one, true love from this day forward, to always love me as much as I love you, and promise to stand beside me as we walk into the future?"

With a tear rolling down her cheek, Vepar smiled. "Of course! I am yours forever, Luc, even more so than the day we met. Listen, Soldier. You are mine, and you mustn't ever forget it."

As if on cue, a chorus of whistles and catcalls came from Luc's shipmates, led by Eli. Luc stood, a little embarrassed, kissed her again, and quickly headed for the shuttle. Just as he was about to step onto the vessel, Vepar yelled after him, "I love you, sweetie pie!"

Luc cringed as the crowd howled. He turned and saw her laughing but just shrugged and offered an I-owe-you smile and smirk, then blew her one last kiss that she promptly caught, clutched in her fist, and held close to her heart.

Chapter 13

Almost as soon as they stowed their gear, the fleet moved out, again heading to the Empire-Dumah border. Although the Dumah had made no attempts to enter Empire space, their neighbors on both sides were not so lucky. Reports from the Dumah's galactic neighbors made it clear that they were indeed under an all-out attack. Without the power to defend themselves, the Hagith and the Scox, who had trade agreements with the Empire, asked for help in fighting the Dumah off.

Four battle cruisers continued to monitor the border, four moved into Hagith space, and four from Luc's group moved into Scox space. They were ready to implement new tactics, in the hope of repelling enemy swarms. All fighters were equipped with short heat blasts that mimicked the heat and force of atmospheric friction, an ode to the Lucifer's Breath method that had proven so successful before.

Hopes were high as they moved into normal space. The pilots were ready to launch at their captains' commands. Dumah warships quickly moved to intercept the fleet. As before, fighters from both sides poured from their ships, and space was soon illuminated by colorful energy beams from every direction; it might have been a beautiful, cosmic spectacle if it were not an act of war. Keeping as much distance between themselves and their fighters, the warships fired upon the Dumah battle cruisers. Energy beams tore away at enemy hulls, and, as expected, tens of thousands of Dumah warriors poured into space from resulting openings. Fighters from both sides exploded as the battle commenced.

As before, the Dumah offense was all about their shocking numbers. They attacked as if they had never encountered the Empire in battle. The only difference from their previous strategy, as far as anyone could tell, was the number of battle cruisers they brought to the fight. Again, it was very difficult to manage the overwhelming masses of Dumah fighters.

Luc and his unit soon found themselves in the thick of the struggle. They had no time for anything but the fight. As minutes turned into hours, fatigue began to set in, something that wasn't lost on Luc. "Fight, men!" he encouraged. "Not only are we battling for the Empire but also for all those we have already lost to these buggy bastards!"

The pep talk seemed to work, and his men pulled it together and pushed even harder against the enemy. At Eli's suggestion, eleven of the thirteen fighters in Luc's unit met the enemy straight on, while two stayed a short distance behind to clear the Dumah warriors from the skins of their fighters. Luc shared that tactic with the command ship; in turn, they sent an order to all fighter leaders to do the same.

Not so quick to give up, the Dumah used their fighters to taxi their swarming warriors toward the Empire battle cruisers. The Dumah moved into a cloud of warriors and came out with as many Dumah as they could carry. It was not unusual to see long strings of them clinging together, in chains that sometime stretch thirty meters in length. Special ships called Cloud Killers kept their distance while they burned away at groups of enemies. Even though the Cloud Killers accomplished ridding space of thousands of Dumah per pass, they barely held their own as the clouds continued to grow.

Word came that the Dumah swarm had overwhelmed the AFW *Ardoustus* and were threatening to bring the warship down. Luc looked toward the *Ardoustus* and saw it undulating, just as the *Barakiel* had during their first encounter. There was really nothing Luc could do but watch helplessly as the skin of the mighty warship ruptured. Every available fighter moved to rescue the *Ardoustus*, but it was too little, too late; the damage was already done. Anywhere the Dumah created a hole in the skin of the ship, thousands of the creatures entered. The areas once surging with Dumah were only clear for a moment, because every Dumah in the vicinity of the breach hurried to enter at any vulnerable point. The grim word soon came from Captain Otheos that the enemy had reached every level of the Ardoustus. "My men are fighting bravely, but I'm afraid there are just too many of them," he sadly announced.

Luc decided it was time to try something he and Eli had been working on since their first Dumah confrontation. Dumah swarms could not be avoided, so their only recourse was to eliminate them entirely. They assumed strategic placement of explosives would eradicate the problem at its core. After something akin to the flip of a coin, it was decided that Luc would deliver the bombs. Of course, Luc cheated to ensure that Eli would not be placed in danger. It wasn't that he needed to be the hero, and he certainly wasn't a glory-grabber, but he had made a promise to Jehovah, and he intended to keep it. The time had come for a test of his loyalty and his word, and that was a test he would pass.

"Captain Karael," Luc said, "I need you to order all Angelic craft to pull back from the swarm. I have an idea, but I need that airspace cleared."

Bravely, knowing the experiment could quite possibly result in his demise, Luc waited for the Angelic fleet to move away, then headed for the swarm at attack speed. He flew right into the body of it, with his forward guns blazing away, hoping to clear a path through the cloud of solid bodies. The weapons helped a little, but the path of beings was thick, and their bodies smacked violently against his fighter. Some managed to cling to his ship, and even as he released the last explosive, the clinging Dumah nearly brought his fighter to a standstill.

It wasn't characteristic for Luc, but he soon began to feel a great deal of despair. His hope slipped away in quick order; with the number of Dumah he was carrying, he could not fathom being able to move away from the bombs swiftly enough to avoid being exploded right along with them.

Just as Luc was ready to signal a farewell message, his team burned through the Dumah, took Luc's fighter in tow, and pulled him clear before the thermal explosives detonated. The four simultaneous ignitions, invisible at first due to the thickness of the Dumah, quickly reached the outer layer of the swarm with a cleansing burn. Luc's plan eliminated over 80 percent of them, and it did not take long for the Cloud Killers to clear away the rest. Thanks to that brilliant little maneuver, Luc was given a new moniker, Swarm Slayer. He was not exactly comfortable with the legendary nickname and shied away from it when he could.

With the swarm no longer a threat, the Angelic fleet turned their full attention toward the Dumah warships and defeated them in short order. It was strange though: even when the Dumah knew they had no chance of victory, they continued to advance, until every last one of them were decimated. Luc wished there were another way, one that did not involve complete destruction, but the Dumah left them no other choice. He could not imagine such a self-defeating, aggressive mindset, but he realized the Dumah probably thought the very same about the Angelic soldiers.

Chapter 14

Of the 1,100 crew members of the *AWF Ardoustus*, 396 were lost in the conflict. Another seventy-eight lives were sacrificed from the rest of the fleet. There were no victory celebrations to be had, for the sting of the deaths of comrades and friends was too overwhelming. The losses in the Hagith battle on the other side of Dumah space were quite a bit higher. Since they were not alerted to the efficacy of Luc's cloud maneuver till much later, they said goodbye to nearly 600 souls.

Captain Karael said over the com-link, "We have defeated the enemy and made our galaxy a safer place to live. Nevertheless, we should not rejoice in having to take the lives of any species. The Dumah gave us no other choice. We, too, lost many brave soldiers today. Everyone fought with courage and honor. Those who have stepped out of this life today will be remembered for all time, and we must honor their memory by continuing to fight any and all who threaten freedom and peace in the galaxy."

A few days later, Luc was ordered to report to Captain Karael's office. With a little apprehension, he entered the captain's office and quickly stood at attention, awaiting whatever was in store for him. His anxiousness only grew when the captain took a moment to look up from his paperwork.

"At ease, Lieutenant," the captain finally said, "or should

I call you Swarm Slayer…or maybe Sweetie Pie?"

Luc felt his face flush as it was painted bright red with his embarrassment. When he regained his voice, he answered, "I am not really comfortable with either, sir."

With a hint of a smile on his face, the captain continued, "Lieutenant Satanis, you have gone above and beyond your duty in two encounters with the Dumah. No doubt, you have saved the lives of thousands with your quick thinking and bravery."

"Permission to speak freely, sir?" Luc asked.

"Go ahead."

"I cannot take full credit for Lucifer's Breath or the cloud maneuver," Luc confessed. "Both were mutual efforts on the parts of Tier Two Angel First Class Eli Adonai and me. He deserves as much acclaim as I do, sir."

"That is not new to me." Captain Karael said. "I have spoken to TTAFC Adonai already, and it has been noted in his record, as well as communicated to all ships in the fleet and on his home world. His preliminary design that would allow our ships to maneuver safely through swarms is being considered. Now, as for Swarm Slayer, you must wear that handle with honor, Lieutenant. It brings strength to every soldier in the fleet. Do not think of it as a symbol of death but a symbol of life. You saved many today, Soldier. As for Sweetie Pie… Well, you're on your own with that one. Dismissed, Lieutenant."

Luc stood at attention and saluted, and he could steel feel the heat of a slight blush on his cheeks as he said, "Yes, sir! Thank you, sir!"

When Luc entered his room, Eli was busy drawing up plans for the new vessel, aptly to be named *Swarm Slayer*. Luc marveled at the beauty of its design and the skill Eli possessed. The skin of the craft would be as close to frictionless as possible, with no chinks in the armor where Dumah could grasp when the ship plunged into the swarm. The powerful forward guns would effectively cut a path, even through thick chains of bodies, allowing the vessel to easily penetrate into the heart of the swarm, drop off its payload, and emerge safely on the other side.

Once again, Luc and Eli were recognized for their actions during combat. Both were given field promotions to the rank of lieutenant. It was bittersweet for Luc, as he now had to fill in for Lieutenant Poiel, who lost his life during the battle. Now, he would serve as the daily operations leader of the *Barakiel* fighter squadron. In a move that surprised Luc and Eli, Eli was moved out of the fighter squadron and into a position on the bridge. As a tactical officer, he would also be in charge of new weapons development.

"I'm not sure I like this," Eli confided in Luc.

"Why? You're one of our brightest engineers, Eli. It only makes sense that they have you working in development."

Eli sighed. "No, it isn't that. It's just... Well, truth be told, I fear they are only coddling me by moving me to the bridge. They know who I am, who I belong to, and they won't let me risk my life on the front lines. That's why they're confining me to the bridge."

Internally, Luc knew his friend was probably right, but he assured him, "Eli, the *Barakiel* will be best served with you in the new assignment. It's a good fit for you."

"I guess."

Luc smiled and gave his friend a pat on the shoulder. "Besides, I'm tired of saving your ass every time we go into battle."

Eli bristled a little at the dig and was about to remind Luc who pulled him safely out of the swarm, but he looked at Luc's chuffed grin and just laughed.

Chapter 15

Almost two months to the day of the beginning of the Scox battle, the Dumah attacked for the last time with a merciless and unprovoked invasion of Scox space. Since a few Empire ships were still there to assist with cleanup and reparations, word of the attack reached the fleet quickly, and the response was swift.

The fleet had learned much in their previous battles, so the Heavenly warriors achieved a swift victory. Keeping their distance and using Eli's *Swarm Slayer* proved most effective. Within six hours, the space around Scox was free of Dumah.

The fleet chased the remaining ships to their home world and destroyed any battle cruiser they found, disabling any vessels that could hope to reach past their own star system. Unless there were others lurking undetected in some dark corner of deviant space, they were confident that Dumah attack capabilities had been severely crippled. They even destroyed the five space docks that orbited the planet.

Another message was quickly sent to the Dumah, in an effort to put an end to their aggression and vengeance once and for all. Using much of what they had learned from the Dumah queen, with quality of inflection, proper phrasing of the Empire threat, and the subtle nuances of Dumah speech, they created a comprehendible, clear, stern message to the Dumah. What sounded to Luc like a series of hisses, clicks, and other gibberish and noises loosely translated to the following: "Take no further action against anyone. Failure to comply will result in the destruction of the Dumah home world. The Empire will continue to patrol the Dumah border and to monitor your compliance. This is your last warning."

After placing monitoring sensors in strategic locations around the Dumah home world, all but two battle cruisers of the Empire fleet moved away. Their retreat was slow and methodical, as they did not want to give the temperamental Dumah any indication that they feared them. Alas, no one but another Dumah really understood the Dumah mindset and needs, but everyone was hopeful that the species understood that they had surpassed all levels of tolerance, and no further patience would be granted if they chose to go on the offensive again.

Benjamin Oneal

Chapter 16

Fortunately, it seemed the Dumah got the message that any violation would result in extermination. For over a year, things were quiet, and they remained within their allotted space. There were no reports of aggressive activity from any of the sentries placed strategically around Dumah space. The Scox, grateful for the backup and the protection, were adopted into the Empire at their request, but the Hagith chose to remain independent, happy with their trade relationship.

During that year, the *Barakiel* patrolled the borders of Empire space. Since there was little else to do, Luc and Eli made good use of their time by refining battle techniques and dreaming up new weapons to use in a wide range of possible scenarios. Eli was a creative thinker with a tremendous ability to bring life to any design they dreamt up. Luc, far more hands-on, preferred to work with a team of other engineers to construct many of Eli's prototypes. Their efforts did not go unnoticed by the captain. He saw the great potential his soldiers possessed and encouraged their endeavors.

Even though the two kept busy, their thoughts often drifted to home and their loved ones. Both longed to see their families, and Luc had the added incentive of reuniting with Vepar. A few females on the *Barakiel* kept Eli company now and then, but Luc was not interested in anyone except the young lady waiting for him back home. When the day finally came for the captain to announce their return to Heaven, a collective cheer echoed throughout the ship.

Communications had relaxed some during their year on patrol. For only the second time since he had left Vepar, Luc found himself face to face with the most beautiful girl in his world, or at least as face to face as they could be when they were countless miles apart. He was very glad the video rooms were private. A happy tear coursed down his face as a vision of her filled the screen. For a moment, they just looked at one another, utterly speechless, as if each were admiring a heart-touching work of art. She was just as he remembered, with brown hair that had a habit of falling in her face and dainty, soft, but busy hands that pushed it back.

Luc was the first to break their mesmerized silence with a simple, "I love you."

Vepar began to cry. "I love you, Luc, and I miss you so much."

Luc could not bear to see her in tears, and he found it difficult to speak. "You have occupied my every thought, when my thoughts were not mine to have. Not a day goes by when I don't wish I could hold you in my arms, look into your eyes, and kiss you deeply."

Vepar's tears burned as she felt the sting of her desire to be in the arms of the one, she so desperately loved. Through the tears, and as she wiped them out of her eyes, she shakily said, "I-I don't know how much longer I can survive without you, Luc. Every night, my dreams find you, but my heart aches every morning when I wake and realize it wasn't real."

They continued to speak for a few minutes, recounting how much they missed one another and going on and on about how they couldn't wait to see each other again. Vepar spoke of her plans for when he returned, excitedly promising picnics, hikes, movies, and lunch at a new restaurant she had found. She had his next visit planned down to the most minute detail. As she relayed it all to him, her eyes brightened, and she smiled, albeit with a touch of sorrow behind it.

Luc did his best to maintain a forlorn expression as he said, "I have some bad news, my love."

"What is it, Luc? Are you hurt or sick?" she asked, truly worried.

"No. I just…" Then, unable to contain his joy any longer, he allowed the broad smile to stretch across his face. "Vepar, this tour is over, and we are returning at this very moment. I will be home in five days."

"What!?" She seemed to vibrate in her chair as the tears of happiness washed away the tears of heartbreak. "Really!?" she screamed, jumping up and down in her seat.

At that happy moment, Luc looked past Vepar and saw his mom walking into the room. Luc cried tears of his own as he watched Vepar and his mother hugging and jumping up and down on the screen before him. He talked to his mom for a while and thanked her again for finding him the perfect girl. Then, he spent the last few moments of the call with Vepar.

Chapter 17

Back home once more, Luc had the privilege of enjoying is mother's cooking. Along with his favorite meals, his mom and Vepar made sure he had his fill of love and kisses. All too soon, his mother had to return to Hell, but he couldn't be too heartbroken about that; being alone with Vepar was equally wonderful.

The remaining few days of Luc's leave would belong to Vepar alone. Although they planned to make their union official in the near future, they already ached for one another in the worst way. Now that they had the blessings of their parents, they decided there was no harm in satisfying their most primal needs.

While she was attending her last classes for the week at the local university, Luc prepared a surprise for his love, just the beginning of three days of discovery. He wanted everything to be perfect, but his attempt to cook for her was a disaster. He barely had time to clean and pay the delivery man for the food from Zadar's, one of the best restaurants in town, before Vepar came home.

She breezed in the door an inhaled deeply, taking in the succulent aroma that gently filled the room. "Mmm. What *is* that smell?"

"Not nearly as delicious as you are, my love." Luc appeared at the kitchen door and quickly crossed the room to welcome her with a kiss. He escorted her to the dining room, furnished with a table he had found in the hall closet. He pulled the chair out or her, then lit the candles once she was seated. He sat her down and lit the candles. "Wait right here, and I will delight you with my world-famous cooking skills," he said before he headed for the kitchen.

A few minutes later, he returned with two salads, which he had scooped out of the carry-out boxes and into some nicer serving dishes he'd found in her cabinets. After they talked for a while about the events of the day, it was time for the main course. Luc again went to the kitchen, and this time, he returned with two thick steaks that made their mouths water. He watched as Vepar closed her eyes, took her first bite, and let the taste melt into her senses. Finally, he ended the meal with a desert that was pure ecstasy.

"Well? What did you think?" he asked, wearing a big grin.

Vepar looked into Luc's eyes. "I think you are an amazing cook. Everything was wonderful. I don't think it could have been any better if you'd had it delivered from Zadar's."

Luc hung his head, fully aware that he was busted. "What gave me away?"

"Well, maybe it was the delivery man who was leaving as I came up the street," she offered.

"Damn! Look, I really *can* cook, you know—maybe not as good as Zadar's or my mom, but I can. I'll tell you what. Why don't you go relax while I clean up this mess and look for my pride," he suggested, hoping to make up for his fib. He pushed her through the door and got busy. Just a few minutes later, he was putting the last dish in the cabinet and rushing out to find her.

As Vepar stood looking out of her apartment window, Luc came up from behind and pulled her close to him. They both felt the deep desire that burned within them, and, for the next few hours, they allowed themselves to explore those long-postponed desires, introducing themselves to every inch of one another's bodies. Somewhere in the middle of the night, with their lust sated for the second time, they lay happily exhausted.

Vepar snuggled in Luc's arms, with her head on his chest. "I could never have imagined how wonderful this would be," she cooed.

"I love you, Vepar," was all he could say as he lay there, smiling.

Vepar hugged him tightly. Then, for some time longer, they talked of their future together. They spoke of marriage and children.

As Vepar whispered sweet nothings to her lover, her hand moved across his belly, then traveled lower. "Any chance you are up for thirds?" Vepar said teasingly.

Luc said nothing but just rolled over and kissed her deeply. Once again, they became one. As they would later think upon that night, they would both agree that the third time was a charm. The first was spawned by raw lust, the second just a continuation of the first, but the third was deliberate, slower, and emotionally intense. They found their rhythm, finished together, and held each other for a while longer until exhaustion lulled them to sleep.

Chapter 18

The next morning, Luc slipped out of bed while Vepar continued to sleep. He decided to shower before his morning run.

As he began to wash, the door opened, and Vepar joined him. "Trying to sneak out on me, Soldier?" she lovingly admonished.

"No, ma'am. I just figured you needed a little more rest after last night. Besides, I was going to get you some breakfast," he replied with a mock salute.

"Listen to me, Soldier, and listen to me good. We have only a short time together, so I want to be with you every moment. You follow me?" she continued in her best ranking officer voice.

They held each other as the hot water washed away the night before. They almost went for a fourth go, but both realized if they gave in to those wants, they would never leave her apartment. Instead, they washed each other thoroughly and prepared for their run.

Once Luc tied his shoes, he stood, took her in his arms, and kissed her once again. "Well, try to keep up," he taunted as he ran for the door.

She followed, right on his heels, laughing.

They ran in the morning sun, building up a good sweat, still warm with the glow of their interludes the night before.

Rise of the Fallen

Every time Luc looked at her, a sheepish smile overtook his face. There was no doubt in his mind that he would love her till the day he died. He knew no other woman would ever hold his heart as she did.

They decided to cook the evening meal together. Luc cut the vegetables as she prepared the pasta. Talking, laughing, and sometimes dancing to the music in their hearts, both now truly understood the wonderful, powerful meaning of having a soulmate.

The three days whooshed by all too soon, and Vepar once again found herself hugging Luc tightly at the north gate of the base. Luc unashamedly let a tear creep down his face. He was truly sad to leave her. As he looked into her eyes, he watched Vepar's tears travel past her nose and touch the pink of her lips. He moved to catch the next one with a kiss, then followed the course of the previous tears to engulf her lips with his own. He was lost in the moment and could have stayed there forever if not for a familiar voice behind them.

"Hey, you two," Eli said, "if you don't stop, you're gonna make me cry."

Luc and Vepar pulled apart a bit but still held each other close.

Vepar smiled through her tears. "You're just jealous that he likes me more than he likes you. Mark my words, Soldier," she said. "While you are gone, you better keep your hands off my man, or I will kick your ass."

Eli raised his hands in faux surrender to her threat.

She broke away from Luc and hugged Eli, then whispered in his ear, "Please keep Luc safe." She kissed his cheek and moved back to Luc.

Luc kissed her once more and soundlessly mouthed, "I love you," then headed through the gate. Just before he lost sight of the north gate, he turned to wave. Even as his shipmates murmured, "Sweetie Pie," to mock him, Luc missed her already.

Chapter 19

For the next few years, all remained calm in the Empire. Luc and Eli continued to be recognized for their many technological advancements and leadership. After the sudden illness of Lieutenant Commander Nariel, Eli's direct superior and the tactical and security officer, Eli was promoted into that void, a very prestigious and well-deserved position for him.

The calm, like all things, would not last forever. One day, there came word of a new threat to a region of space, the Titan system, mostly unknown to Luc. *The Barakiel* and the *Hayyoth* were ordered to move at once to the area, to contend with an influx of pirates. Almost nothing was known about the invading criminal element, and Luc found only vague references to them in his research through the archives. One thing they did know was their origin: They were outcasts from many worlds, even Heaven itself, so their home bases varied and were unknown, as were their numbers. Their attacks were known to be vicious, and they were quick to kill anyone who got in their way or refused to join them. The Titans were a different story.

Although Luc had learned in passing about the Titans during his history class in basic, he was not aware of the real threat they imposed. Not of that world, he was unaware of what every child on Heaven learned in their studies. As the *Barakiel* and *Hayyoth* departed on their three-day trip to Titan space, Luc learned everything he could about their newest adversary.

After having breakfast with Eli, Luc settled into his favorite chair, donned the Illuminator, and opened his mind to Heaven's past. Since his first use of device, it had evolved into a wonderful tool for learning. He had been warned beforehand that the first part of his learning would include reenactments, rather than real memories. The room melted away, and the far distant past of Heaven unfolded in his mind, a Heaven before technology, when nature held sway over man and the only roads that cut through nature were well-traveled paths, worn by use. The luscious greens of the forests and fields were sparingly peppered here and there by little villages, whose residents toiled laboriously about their days. Stone castles rose here and there, as if giving the finger to the forces of nature.

Wildlife was abundant and feared nothing but the natural ebb and flow of extinction. Balance was palpable among all living things, and the villagers took only the resources they required for survival. They were still able to hide their good fortune from the lords of the land.

Change became evident as the scenes in Luc's mind jumped from the luscious greens to a terrifying, bloody red. The pleasure he'd sensed at the outstart was soon replaced by sickening grief as he watched people being slaughtered for bringing meat to their tables or trying to protect the lands, they called home. There was much vile suffering at the hand of brutal soldiers, and helpless villagers were forced into servitude for daring to hold on to the crops they grew and the livestock they raised. They were left with barely any life-sustaining fruits of their back-breaking labor, prevented from providing ample sustenance for their families. It soon became clear that the mayhem and turmoil were due to a tyrant, who wasted more food in one day than the commonfolk had for an entire year.

The Hyperions, as the Titans were known at that time, ruled over much of Heaven. Chaos, the leader of the Hyperions, lusted for ultimate power. His was a cruel, self-serving reign, and his place in history was marked by fear and bloody villages and battlefields. In his eyes, people were merely livestock, no more valuable than the beasts of the field. The Hyperions viewed their subjects as means to an end. They expected the people to toil from dawn to dusk, with only a pittance as compensation. Then, they taxed that pittance to fill their own coffers. With those tax moneys and the sweat and backbreaking work of the common folk, the Hyperions built their great castles.

The stone structures they called home consisted of three walls. Around the outside lived the people who tended the fields and kept the animals for their ruler. Within the first wall, merchants sold wares, and blacksmiths supplied the common need.

Inside the second wall were the nobles, families who had somehow earned their lord's favor. Most were of Hyperion blood. Also within that wall were the blacksmiths tasked with producing and repairing weapons and armor for the Hyperion Army. It was not prudent to allow commonfolk access to anything they might use to form a mutiny or a coup.

The third wall was thick and impenetrable and curved out at the top to keep outsiders from scaling the surface. This wall protected and contained the castle proper. No one could pass through that gate without permission from the lord.

It sickened Luc to watch as the Hyperions took possession of the most desirable, young females to use as sex slaves. Many were impregnated against their will, and they were expected to give birth to female children; most male infants were killed immediately. When those bastard daughters grew up, they faced the same cruel fate as their mothers. The Hyperions reasoned that a male child might grow up to become a threat to the kingdom, and they couldn't be used for sexual pleasure or breeding either.

This was also why any family who tried to resist the law was met with the killing of their male children. Parents tried to hide the births by secretly moving their newborn sons to presumably safe places. It was heartbreaking for them to lose their children that way, but it was the only way they had to save their lives.

The cruelty was not only reserved for men. Many Hyperion women excelled at debauchery and torture. All Hyperions, male and female alike, looked down on anyone outside their bloodline and believed the townsfolk were no better than the animals, to be used and slaughtered for their pleasure.

The evil was also not kept among their own inferiors. The Hyperions gladly waged war on any neighboring kingdoms who refused to bow to their rule. Out of fear, many agreed to be assimilated, only to find their arrangements broken by the Hyperions. Ruling families were murdered, and Hyperions claimed the bloodied thrones. Their homicidal, greedy expansion continued through the years, until they ruled much of Heaven.

Chapter 20

"Luc?"

Luc was jolted back to the present moment by the sound of a knock on his door. He reluctantly set the Illuminator aside and rubbed his eyes. His whole body was tense, his head ached, and his insides were twisting after experiencing such horror. He could not believe anyone could be so cruel. He looked at the time and discovered he'd been delving around in those implanted thoughts for over three hours. He rose from his chair and opened the door, then quickly expelled every gory detail to Eli.

Since Eli's knowledge of the Hyperion Empire came exclusively from history books, he longed to see what Luc had seen, to learn why his friend was suddenly so upset and passionate about it. Luc's anxious feelings about the evil he had witnessed made him tense with anger, and while he wanted nothing more than to continue his research right away, he agreed to let Eli catch up before he resumed.

After they ate lunch, the two headed straight for Luc's quarters. As Luc donned the Illuminator, Eli linked in, right where Luc had left off. There was a distinct change from the night before, a feeling of hope as the Illuminator focused on areas of Heaven that not only resisted but actually managed to halt the Hyperion advance. One such kingdom, Araboth, rose up to be a real threat to the domination. As it turned

Rise of the Fallen

out, many of the male children who were rescued from the Hyperion's, found a home in Araboth. Most joined the army of Araboth when they came of age, wanting nothing more than to fight for what was left of their families, their loved ones who were still suffering under the Hyperion tyranny.

Abba El-Elyon, the leader of Araboth, was a truly just king. His subjects adored him, and he felt the same about them. He and his royal court grew ever more wary of the evil that threatened them, and the grim tales of oppression and violence that came from his spies and the male refugees tore at his heart. Unable to turn a blind eye any longer, and ashamed that he had waited so long to strike back, he contacted the leaders of the seven kingdoms who were not under Hyperion rule and declared, "It is now time to act!" The seven kingdoms had been preparing to defend their lands; now, they would prepare for war.

With Abba El-Elyon at the helm, they attacked on multiple fronts. Although the Hyperion Army outnumbered them ten to one, the fighting took its toll on all. As the weeks stretched into months, the seven kingdoms continued to push the Empire back. The Hyperions were prideful and refused to withdraw without butchering any and every villager they could find. It wasn't for any reason beyond a childish need to destroy and lay claim. What the Hyperions did not realize was that every killing only solidified the survivors' resolve to defeat them. The commoners were more determined than ever to stand against their oppressors, and they joined their saviors in a quest for revenge against the Hyperions.

Over the next year, The Seven, as they came to be known, achieved pushback on the Hyperions. The castle where Chaos now ruled his shrinking empire was in sight, evil on the outside and inside alike. The dark walls of the Hyperion castle were foreboding and reeked of death. Bodies of slain servants and villagers were scattered around the outer wall, and dead, hanged corpses dangled grotesquely from every opening in the parapet. More bodies were strung up as they watched. Upon closer inspection, they realized some were still alive, doomed to serve as living shields.

Benjamin Oneal

The evil ones' plan seemed to work, at least for a while, because Abba El-Elyon resisted using a catapult to hurl boulders at the castle wall. The first attempts to rescue the hanging people, who were much too high to reach, were met with heavy fire from above, but the hanged bravely and selflessly begged their saviors to carry on with their attack, more than willing to sacrifice themselves to bring down their evil lord. El-Elyon and his army were at a loss, however, with little idea how to destroy the Hyperions without harming the people along the walls.

As fate would have it, an unexpected occurrence remedied that problem for them when the living shields began to plummet to the round, one by one. Unbeknownst to their captors or their heroes, they had hidden knives on their persons, which they used to saw away at the ropes, taking their destinies into their own hands. El-Elyon was horrified at the site of fallen but was unwilling to let their sacrifices be wasted, so he ordered his troops forward.

Upon El-Elyon's command, boulder after boulder, stone after stone battered the castle walls. Soon, there were breaches in the first two, and even bigger boulders pummeled the final barrier. Suddenly, white flags waved above the ramparts on every side, as well as one high above the castle keep. Abba El-Elyon ordered his army to cease their catapult blasts, and after a round of cheers from the attackers, all grew quiet for a moment.

In the midst of everyone's stunned silence, a messenger came from the castle and stood before El-Elyon. "Chaos is ready to surrender," the messenger said. "In good faith, he will free the rest of the hostages."

"If this is indeed true," El-Elyon said, "we will end our attack here and accept your terms of surrender. Set our people free"

As promised, the hostages were released and soon began to exit the castle. Some were worse for the wear, but they all eagerly climbed over the rubble and ran to their saviors.

El-Elyon wrinkled his forehead in confusion when he noticed one group of them, wearing hoods that covered their faces, moving in unison but not with the rest of the rescued. Suspicious, he ordered his men to stop them. Once the curious quintet was surrounded, El-Elyon commanded them to remove their hoods. When they resisted, his soldiers pulled the hoods down. Just as El-Elyon suspected, they had thwarted a bold yet cowardly escape attempt by Chaos and his sons. As the soldiers closed in around them, with bloodlust in their eyes, Chaos fell to his knees and begged for his life.

The crowd was not moved in the least. In fact, his pleas for sympathy would have been laughable if not for the depravity of the crimes he'd committed against those he was now begging for mercy. El-Elyon watched as the former captives closest to the five began to punch and kick the once powerful family, beating them beyond all recognition. Before they met their deaths, though, El-Elyon ordered his men to stop and demanded that they be brought before him. Chaos and his sons were forced to kneel before Abba El-Elyon as he raised his hand to quiet The Seven.

"People of the seven kingdoms, hear me," El-Elyon said. "On this pivotal day, we have put a well-deserved end to the Hyperion plague that has threatened our world for so long."

Once again, cheers arose from every direction and did not quiet down until El-Elyon held up his hand and continued, "The atrocities that were the hallmark of the Hyperion regime end here. Never again shall evil hold sway over the people of our world. Mark my words, dear citizens! Every person of Hyperion blood who has meted out evil against others shall be sought out, captured, and brought to justice."

The loud celebrations of the army of the seven kingdoms could no longer be silenced. El-Elyon stood before The Seven and joined them in their revelry, with much applause and merrymaking of his own. It was truly a glorious day.

Suddenly, though, El-Elyon's voice quivered, and his eyes grew wide. He looked down and saw the handle of a knife, jutting out of his side. He was quick to discover the thruster of the blade, and he swung his metal-gloved hand in response, so hard that he knocked Chaos to the ground when he connected with the side of his face. Chaos, already beaten and bruised by the people he'd tortured, was still barely alive but was unconscious and dead to the world around him.

Wincing in pain, El-Elyon said, "Take this Hyperion swine and his wretched spawn away and lock them in the dungeons they built. We will hold them there until justice can be served..."

Eli shook Luc, jolting him back to the present and away from the tales fed into his mind by the Illuminator. Eli looked as tired as Luc felt, but it was a good kind of fatigue, as if they had worked hard and were admiring a task well done.

Chapter 21

A relatively speedy trial was held for the Hyperions, and all were found guilty of crimes against their fellow men. Some were executed, some were condemned to live out the remainder of their days in prison, and many fled. The few who were not imprisoned or punished were outcasts and treated like the scourge of society; several were found dead in the months that followed. Those who could, went into hiding, in a part of Heaven where there was little chance they would be recognized. It was rumored that in that remote corner of Heaven, the survivors busily plotted to regain their dominance.

The seven kingdoms formed a unified government, a democracy, in the hope that evil would never again rise up against them. Under that new rule, their first elected leader was God, and he held that office until people saw fit to replace him. His tenure would last as long as God acted in a just and truly honorable manner, keeping in mind the best interest of the people of Heaven. Furthermore, when the term limit did come to its decided end, one of his children, properly trained and found to be worthy, would be elevated to the esteemed position.

That was the point in history when Heaven was named. By unanimous decision, Abba El-Elyon was elected as the leader, to henceforth be known as God. While it was not a position he sought, he found it impossible to refuse. He was beloved by the rest of Heaven, just as he had been in

Araboth. It was only fitting that Araboth became the capital city of Heaven.

El-Elyon, being very wise, knew he needed help to lead an entire world, so he assembled and appointed several trusted advisors, organized in three distinct groups. The first group consisted of the kings of the six other kingdoms. They were known as Seraphim, and they were the highest-ranking officials second only to God himself. The Cherubim, the second group, were worthy nobles from the seven kingdoms. Finally, the Thrones, were representatives of the commoners, and they came from every major region of the newly formed government. Their job was to help God rule wisely and to watch over the administrative duties of their world.

The Illuminator did not dwell on anything for long after the monarchy was established. It did teach Eli and Luc that the next 1,000 years was a time of great prosperity for Heaven. Many God-heads came and went and served their world with honor during what was known as the Millennium of Enlightenment. Near the end of that era, Heaven began exploring planets that shared their star, expanding their journeys farther and farther out over the next two centuries. They discovered many other planets, some inhabited by life in its primitive stages and others who were in the infancy of space travel. Alliances were formed, trade agreements were negotiated, and the Heavenly Empire began.

The Illuminator again slowed to offer more details about a time in the more recent past. Five hundred years before Luc and Eli's time, the young God Yahweh El-Elyon moved into service much earlier than expected, due to the untimely death of his father. With wisdom beyond his years, Yahweh proved to be a great leader, one of the most remarkable in Heaven's history. It was during his reign that the Angelic Corps and the Holy Ghosts were formed. He was also the first to bring women into the ranks of the Seraphim, Cherubim, and the Thrones, as he felt it immoral to exclude any group from Heavenly service, particularly one that represented close to half the population.

During the reign of Eli's great-great-grandfather when a

new Hyperion threat began to brew. The descendants of the Hyperions had once again become a very powerful presence on Heaven. Fearing the true name of their ancestry might label them as evil and subject them to violence or being ostracized, they renamed themselves as Titans.

It had been 1,200 years since Chaos and his ilk were punished, but his descendants had never lost their thirst for the power they once had. They dearly longed for their second coming. For years, the family led by Uranus, a direct descendant of Chaos, schemed and connived, growing impatient for the day when they could again slither into high government positions and take back what they believed to be theirs. They recruited politicians and high-ranking military leaders with the promise of money and honored places in the new regime, and many fell prey to their bribes and even threats.

Once the Hyperions felt they had their claws in enough key politicians and military power, they began their assault on God Yahweh. Prominent advisors of God's became victims of assassination attempts. Yahweh himself was the target of one such attack and barely survived the blast of an explosive placed near the palace. When the evil ones felt they had disoriented the government to a point of low weakness, the Titans struck. A rather large military force moved on the palace in a surprise attack, under the cover of the dark of night. The palace guards and Yahweh's loyal Angel military repelled the attack with minimal casualties, and the enemies who survived the failed coup were arrested and questioned.

Uranus was typically very strategic and careful, but one mistake he made was to believe those who allegedly backed them had even an ounce of real backbone. When word came of the failed hostile overtaking, all the families who had previously pledged their support turned cold shoulders and blind eyes to Uranus, as if they had never heard of him or his Titans.

The most detrimental error Uranus and his advisors made was their failure to realize the true reach of Yahweh's mighty Holy Ghosts, who infiltrated almost every layer of the Titan hierarchy. The attack plans, along with the names of many of the conspirators, were known well before the botched effort took place. Once the magnitude of the plot against the government was revealed, more than 2,000 people were detained. Even though the people responsible for the assassinations were brought to justice, there was no solid proof of the involvement of Uranus, except to say that he played some role in forming the coup.

Yahweh often wondered if it was right for Abba El-Elyon to spare Chaos, but he kept those thoughts to himself. Instead, he met with his advisors to discuss the matters at hand, rather than dwelling on history. After long deliberations, it was decided that the Titans and their followers would be given a choice: They could either be imprisoned for the majority of their lives, or they and their families would be exiled, forced to live off-world, on a planet of their own, with no hope of return.

The latter offered them a chance to form their own government and live in freedom, so it was the obvious option. Uranus and his followers were exiled to the Planet Titan, an uninhabited rock far enough from Heaven that they would likely not be a threat but close enough that they could still be monitored. In all, just fewer than 11,000 conspirators and their families made Titan their new home. They were generously given enough supplies and technology to give them a good start, but they were deprived of any means to leave their new planet. It would be years before they could build ships to carry them beyond their system. Not only that, but Angelic fleet ships were assigned to patrol the space around Titan, and the Holy Ghosts kept careful eyes on the activity on the ground. Heaven also maintained a trade relationship with Titan, on the condition that there was to be no further aggression against the Empire.

The next 500 years moved quickly through their minds as the Illuminator acted as their tour guide. It became apparent that, left to their own devises, the Hyperions were quick to name Uranus God and grant him rule as such. Unlike the government for the people on Heaven, on Planet Titan, Uranus' word was law. Any who dared to object was publicly and permanently relieved of life. Under the guidance of Uranus, society soon reverted to its old ways. Though they were far more advanced than the ancestry of the first Hyperion Empire, both socially and technologically, Uranus and his family who ruled under him carried out unspeakable atrocities against the people.

The Uranus line was once the inspiration behind many stories about the Titans, tales that were the stuff of childhood nightmares. His son, Cronus, even more vile, was said to have killed his father to take the throne. Cronus was also infamous for shamelessly sacrificing children, even his own; he undertook dark, taboo rituals in hopes of bringing his idea of order to the galaxy and to satisfy his bloodlust. Morbid fairytales about the Titans were told to children in the Heavenly Empire to frighten them into being good. It was even stated that Cronus ate his own children, because he feared they might somehow rise up against him. The people who needed to know realized he did not actually consume his progeny, but they also knew Planet Titan to be the seat of a very intelligent and dangerous foe to the Heavenly Empire.

Cronus was certain he would not see Hyperion revenge on Heaven come to fruition in his lifetime. Thus, he thought only of the future, a time when the galaxy would once again fear the might of the Hyperions. To that end, he made it law that every woman of childbearing years would be ordered to bear children. As one would imagine, Cronus did his part to populate Titan. Any woman who was not pregnant was expected to have an infant, as an example of her compliance with the law; those who had no young and were not expecting found themselves imprisoned, facing hard, physical labor, and still forced to procreate.

Cronus also made education a priority, as he aimed to free Planet Titan from its dependence on Heavenly technology as soon as possible. Every citizen of Titan, young and old, was commanded to be educated and work toward the betterment of Titan. Children and their parents took education seriously and ensured that all learned the sciences and any vital technology. Any child who did not achieve high marks was removed from school to work in the factories.

Over the next 500 years, the house of Cronus built Titan into a regional power. Due to their push to populate their planet, they numbered over four million. Although they still relied on the long-established trade agreement with Heaven, Titan was as technologically advanced as any planet in the Empire. The Empire still kept a close eye on the exiles, though, watching with interest and a little dread as Titan expanded to control the neighboring star systems.

Their lesson came to an end as Cronus VI became God in his twentieth year and revealed an even greater savagery than his namesake. Although cloning was in its infancy when they were cast off Heaven, it was believed that every God of Titan was one and the same. If photographic evidence could have been considered, all exhibited the same visage, right down to the shoulder-length blond hair and the fiery stare from almost crimson eyes. That was the so-called God the forces of Heaven were now sent to protect.

Then, just like that, the Illuminator released their minds, and the room around them was normal and quiet once more.

Chapter 22

Luc and Eli set the Illuminator aside, with the nightmarish face of Cronus VI still lingering in their minds. They were silent for a long moment, not sure what to say about what they had seen and heard. After about five minutes of introspection, they talked about it and discussed the possibilities of the days to come. They were both at a loss as to why they were being asked to offer help to a society that had such great animosity toward Heaven.

Their conversation was cut short by a ship-wide announcement from Captain Karael: "Attention! We are approaching Titan space. One hour to reentry to normal space. All hands, prepare for battle." The announcement repeated, but Luc and Eli were already out the door.

Within a half-hour, Luc was in his fighter and ready for action. Eli took his place on the bridge. No matter their personal opinions about the new mission and about Cronus in general, they were prepared to follow orders.

The transition to normal space was textbook and went smoothly, but such ease did not await them on the other side of it. The pirate attack on the Empire fleet as it came out of deviant space was entirely unexpected and vicious. At first, everything seemed chaotic, but it soon took on an air of sophisticated calculation. It was depressingly clear that the information from Titan had sorely underestimated the size and might of the pirate forces. Every fighter suffered from multiple blasts at their shields. Due to the nature of their trade, pirates were experts in sudden attacks, able to quickly disable their prey, then disappear into the darkness of space with their spoils.

At no time in the history of the pirates have they ever attacked an Angelic warship. It is unheard of, yet, here they are, Luc thought. His mind quickly focused on the enemy, and his training and experience kicked in. In the little time he had to observe the enemy ships he noticed something: Unlike the sleek fighters of the Angelic fleet, the pirate vessels seemed to be a patchwork of mechanics and metal. While they were built for speed and equipped with weapons as deadly as any Luc had encountered, their shields could not hold up to multiple direct hits.

As the battle waged on, Luc also realized that an unusually large group of pirates had concentrated around the *Barakiel*. The other warships and their fighters were busy fending them off, albeit not nearly to the same extent as his own ship. Luc signaled Captain Karael and quickly found that he was also aware of the situation. Unfortunately, before Luc had opportunity to intercept, four pirate fighters broke away and attacked the bridge area of the *Barakiel*.

The first concentrated blast from the pirate weapons weakened the shields, and the second tore away almost all that protected the bridge. At full speed, Luc destroyed first and the second pirate ships, then zeroed in on the third. In an instant the two remaining pirates opened up with what they had left, tearing at the skin of the *Barakiel*. Luc hastily eliminated the two impotent ships, but it was difficult to keep his mind steady, because his thoughts were on Eli. He did his best to remain positive and guard the weakened area of his beloved *Barakiel*.

Luc called for Captain Karael, but there was no response. He next requested an emergency response team (ERT) to move to the bridge right away. As he awaited a response, his thoughts traveled back to the hospital room, where he had made that fateful promise to Eli's father. *If Eli is already gone,*

I've not only broken a vow to the Lord God but also to myself, he grimly reasoned, *and I've lost the greatest of friends. I will never forgive myself.*

Much to his delight and relief, no further attacks came from the retreating pirates. They just vanished into the darkness of space as quickly as they appeared.

Benjamin Oneal

Chapter 23

Captain Karael shouted for the shields over the bridge to be strengthened to full force, but it was too late. The enemy fire was deafening. As the shields weakened, the bridge shook violently. Nevertheless, everyone courageously remained at his or her post, even as the last blast from the enemy ships tore the bridge apart. Everything collapsed around them. The bridge went dark and silent, except for an occasional spark from a broken control panel or the clatter of a broken piece of the bridge falling to the floor.

The rupture of the shields caused a momentary explosive decompression on the bridge. Two of the crew were sucked out into space, before the emergency atmospheric shield activated. Moaning from the survivors came as the remaining crew began to pull themselves from the rubble. The scene was more than disturbing.

It was even more eerie when the emergency lights came on, for that only illuminated the utter devastation they'd sustained. Eli was jolted to consciousness by the loud crackle of a spark, but he remained still as pain stormed through every fiber of his body. In a few moments, he forced himself up by sheer will. His puffy eyes scanned the bridge, and he saw the captain struggling to get up. Quickly, he made his way over and around the debris, only to find that his captain's injuries were very severe, if not life threatening. He called for help, but there was none to be had.

As soon as he heard the voices of the ERT on the bridge, Eli called for them to help the captain.

Karael painfully stretched his neck to look around the bridge. "I..." he said, then paused to groan. "Eli, you are the highest-ranking member of the crew left alive," the ailing captain said. "You are in charge now, Commander Adonai. Go to the alternate command center, the ACC, and take over command until further orders, and..." Then, before Eli could protest, Captain Karael's eyes fluttered shut.

After Luc received word from Eli, he positioned four fighters in front of the weakened area of the ship and quickly assessed the damage around the fleet, then headed into the *Barakiel*. Although he felt responsible for the devastation on the bridge, everyone knew it was not his fault. No one could have foreseen the pirate attack, and the intel they'd received from Titan was faulty at best, if not fraudulent altogether. They simply were not prepared.

A signal was sent to the Titan government to let them know the pirate threat had been neutralized, but the Angelic fleet would remain in close orbit there until further notice. Cronus himself thanked the fleet, wished them well, and expressed what seemed like genuine sorrow for the lives lost. As Luc watched the video screen, he couldn't help but notice a slight smile on the Titan's face as he mentioned the casualties. Perhaps it was just because of what he'd seen on the Illuminator about the vindictive nature of the Hyperions, but he just couldn't shake the feeling that Cronus was somehow involved. Sabotage and betrayal were strong in the Cronus family line, after all.

For the next few days, repairs were a priority. The damage to the bridge, however, would have to wait until they reached the home world. As the work continued, the fleet fighters patrolled the space around Titan, but there were no further signs of the pirates.

Chapter 24

Four days after the attack, Luc and Eli were summoned to Captain Karael's bedside in the infirmary.

The second they stepped into the room and the door shut behind them, Eli's father appeared on the screen. "My son," God said, "the implications of this attack are worrisome. We can only assume that whoever was behind it knows who you are. Not only that, but they were aware of your specific location aboard the *Barakiel*. I have spoken to Captain Karael, and he assured me that you are up for the task at hand. From this point on, you will take command of the *Barakiel*, with Luc at your right hand. You will return to Heaven at full speed." Then, just like that, Jehovah was gone.

Stunned, Eli looked at the captain. "With all due respect sir, I am not ready. *You* are the captain, not me."

"No one ever feels he's ready for command, son," Captain Karael said, offering a kind and encouraging smile. "You must take what you're given and do your best. I am in no condition to continue serving in a captain capacity. Although my injuries have not proven fatal, they do warrant that I relinquish command. Surely, there are spies aboard this ship. Since we are aware of it, we must take steps to ferret them out. Son, no matter what you feel at this moment, you have been given a great deal of responsibility, and you must make the best of it."

"I will do all I can," Eli said.

"Good." The captain then opened another ship-wide communication: "This is Captain Karael. Under General Order 17, Paragraph 3 of the Angelic Code, I hereby relinquish command of the *Barakiel* to Captain Eli Adonai. I expect each and every one of you serve under his command as you have served under mine, with loyalty, courage, and honor. Due to the loss of Ruax Sytry, Lucifer Satanis, along with his duties as operations leader of the *Barakiel* fighter squadron, will assume the position of second-in-command."

Luc and Eli left the infirmary, still reeling from their sudden promotions.

"Did that just happen?"

"Yes," Luc said, shaking his head.

"I am really not ready to command the *Barakiel*," Eli confessed.

The remark earned Eli a slap from Luc.

"Ow!" Eli squealed, reaching for the back of his head. "What did you do that for?

Luc shrugged. "You need to calm down and face the facts. You are now the captain, so you mustn't complain about it. Mostly, though, I did it because it might be my last chance, now that you are my fearless leader."

Eli punched Luc in the shoulder. "Well, you did not have to hit me so hard."

They both laughed as they made their way to the ACC.

Luc and Eli entered the smaller alternate bridge, and everyone came to attention.

"As you were," Eli said, struggling to keep the nervousness and feelings of inadequacy out of his voice. "Lieutenant Oranir, status report?"

"Repairs are underway, and the pirates seem to have vanished. Angelic casualties are 180, serious injuries at 142, sir," the lieutenant reported.

"Any enemies captured?" Eli quickly added.

"None, sir. All the pirate ships were destroyed before we

could get close enough to board them, Lieutenant Oranir said, shaking his head.

Smart! thought Luc. *They left no one behind to give us any information, to let us know the real motives behind the attack.* It did not make sense to him. *Wait. What if... Was it a direct attempt to assassinate Eli?* he wondered, looking worriedly at his friend. He knew the only one who would desire such a thing was Cronus, if only out of revenge for his exile. There was simply no reason the pirates would want Eli dead. Everything pointed to Cronus, but without proof, there was little he or anyone else could do about it.

The only thing they could do was what Karael had asked of them. They had to determine who the mole was, the spy, or spies, aboard the *Barakiel*. Luc was not even sure there were any, as it could have just as easily been someone back on their home world feeding information to the Titans. The investigative assignment brought little satisfaction, but it was at least somewhere to start, so he made a mental note to discuss it with Eli.

As Luc pondered all the possibilities, Eli gave his first ship-wide communique in his new role: "This is Captain Eli Adonai. The *Barakiel* will shelter in place until the *Setheus* arrives to relieve us. At that point, we will return to Heaven for the remainder of the necessary repairs. Until then, we will continue to protect Titan space and search for any further signs of pirate activity. It is an honor to lead this great crew. Captain out."

Chapter 25

The very next day, communication came from Titan that Cronus was requesting to board the *Barakiel,* under the guise that he wanted to thank his Heavenly saviors personally. Although Luc and Eli suspected it was a bad idea, arrangements were made for his arrival. Luc personally took charge of security, as he refused to leave anything to chance when it came to the life of his friend or the wellbeing of his ship.

Luc and Eli met Cronus as he entered the *Barakiel*. While they had seen him before on the Illuminator, they were taken aback when they met him in person; his crimson eyes, arrogant smile, and overwhelming confidence hit them like slaps in the face. On direct orders from Heaven, no one showed the slightest deference to his position. Everyone was courteous, but none made him feel special. He was, after all, the leader of an outcast conspiracy that had most likely murdered at least one loved one of everyone in the crew.

Cronus' cockiness did not waiver, even when he was forced to close the distance between himself and the unmoving Captain Eli. He took Eli's hand and offered a seemingly heartfelt thanks. "You have rid our system of those bothersome pirates. My sincerest condolences to the families of those who were lost in the little skirmish."

Little skirmish? Eli thought, ready to punch him in the face for so belittling and devaluing a battle that had cost so many lives. Nonetheless, he would not allow Cronus to bait him. Luc was a little unnerved as Cronus leaned in close and whispered something in Eli's ear, but Eli just said, "Follow me." Then he led Cronus to a room just off the dock, with Luc in tow.

"I hoped we could speak alone," Cronus said, peering over his shoulder at Luc as the door closed behind them.

"Anything you want to say to me can be said in the presence of my first officer," Eli said, without a smile.

"Very well then," Cronus continued. "I know who you really are. I would know the son of Jehovah anywhere. Your strong, handsome features give you away."

"Why are you really here, Cronus?" Eli said, without any pretense to mask his impatience.

Cronus smiled. "I would like you to tell your father that I hope to meet him, God to God, to discuss the future of our galaxy."

Eli smiled; he could not believe Cronus had the audacity to refer to the galaxy as his. "I am afraid we must cut this meeting short," he said. "The *Setheus* has arrived, and I must return to Heaven at once." With that, he confidently turned his back on Cronus and walked through the door.

Luc motioned toward the door and followed Cronus out of the room and to his ship. He felt like taking the self-proclaimed God by the neck and choking the pseudo–Supreme Being out of him for attempting to kill his friend, but he was sure Cronus probably had a clone lying in wait for just such an occasion. When it came down to it, he really did not want to touch the Hyperion pile of shit. He nearly chuckled aloud as he thought, *Gee. I might have to apologize to the metaphorical pile of shit for that little misplaced comparison.*

After Cronus was off the ship and en route back to Titan, Luc ordered his men to check everywhere Cronus and his men had been. "Let me know of anything suspicious, both inside the *Barakiel* and out," he advised. He was positive Cronus was behind it all, and he would leave no pebble unturned to prove it. He did not trust the arrogant bastard in the least.

Rise of the Fallen

He was glad the impromptu meeting was over, but he knew it was not the last time he would be in the presence of Cronus.

Chapter 26

Upon the return of the *Barakiel*, a meeting of the council was convened. Cronus had made it clear that he knew Eli's true identity, so it was time to reveal it to the rest of the galaxy. Before the Seraphim, the Cherubim, and the Thrones, Eli was formally promoted to captain of the *Barakiel*. At the same gathering, Luc was officially promoted, to be known thereafter as Commander Lucifer Satanis and to serve under and alongside his friend from that point on. Later, in a private meeting with Jehovah's most trusted advisors, and with the help of the Illuminator, Eli and Luc divulged the events of their mission to Titan space.

After the report concluded, Jehovah spoke first: "The only real strategy we have is to keep closer watch on Cronus. His orchestration of the events in Titan space is quite disturbing. There is a growing danger for the Empire, as well as Heaven itself. He is planting evil seeds of discontent, and we mustn't let those seeds grow."

Samael, a Seraphim who was head of the Holy Spirits, replied, "There are agents in key positions on Titan and the surrounding systems, but it is clear that we need a stronger presence. We may soon be able to break into the red-eyed beast's inner circle, but we must move cautiously. Our best course of action is to tread lightly here. We cannot allow the Hyperion ass to become suspicious of our interest in him."

Luc smirked. He very much liked Samael's coarse nature and his stern way of speaking, always raw and to the point. He looked toward Jehovah and saw that he, too, was amused by his friend's turn of phrase.

Another Seraphim, Nathanael, offered his own bit of advice: "I do not believe it would be wise to send Captain Elohim anywhere near Titan space. Cronus has already attempted to kill him once, and he will most assuredly try again. He has never been one to bow out and take no for an answer."

The meeting went on for another hour, and many more assemblies took place before the *Barakiel* set out for space again.

***

The only good thing that came of the mission to Titan was that it would take at least a month to repair the *Barakiel*. As soon as Luc was able to safely break away, he headed straight for the love of his life, desperately in need of her warmth and encouragement.

Vepar left her last class of the day at Araboth University and made her way to the library to finish some research. She had always been dedicated and studious, and she was a mere few months away from earning her master's degree in education science. As she sat at a table, poring over the books scattered in front of her, a piece of paper bounce between her arms and across the table. She looked up in disgust but saw no culprit. She went back to her studies, only to be assaulted by another paper wad. Really pissed now, she rose from her chair and stormed angrily over to the first stack of books near where the arsenal had been fired from.

When Vepar rounded the corner, ready to give the offender a piece of her mind, she found Luc, holding a single blue flower and smiling from ear to ear. Unable to stifle her subdued shriek of happiness, she jumped into his arms and kissed him deeply.

Before the kiss was finished, a librarian shuffled around the stacks and held her fingers to her lips. "Shh! If you cannot keep quiet, you two, you will have to leave." Then, when the bookish, mousy woman noticed that Vepar was in Luc's arms with her legs tightly wrapped around his waist, she further admonished them for their public display of affection.

Vepar slid down Luc and feigned embarrassment. "Sorry. It won't happen again."

The librarian left with a slight smile on her face, shaking her head as she disappeared into the nonfiction section.

Luc helped Vepar gather her research and writing utensils, and they headed out the door. As soon as they stepped outside, Vepar dropped her books and resumed the position in Luc's arms. They were both in a world of their own; nothing and no one else was part of their reality. They spent the rest of the evening getting reacquainted, from head to toe, several times over.

Early the next morning, Luc awoke with a raging appetite, as he had not eaten anything since lunch the day before. He stirred, thinking about heading for the kitchen, and she awoke. After one look at his sleepy princess, all thoughts of food were replaced with a desire much stronger. "Breakfast can wait," he whispered under his breath, before he gently fingered a wayward strand of hair out of her eyes and woke her up the rest of the way with a flurry of kisses.

A while later, they showered the well-quenched desire from their bodies, then decided to take a run. Anyone who saw the two grinning joggers might have thought they were crazy; they would have been right, for Luc and Vepar were absolutely, head-over-heels, crazy in love.

Chapter 27

In light of Luc's most recent promotion, they could afford a better place to live. Vepar had been dreaming of a new place for quite a while, their own little love nest. While her tiny apartment had served her needs so far, it was a bit crowded as Luc's possessions began piling in there, added to her own. Over the next few days, they visited several potential domiciles. Then, on the third day, they found a really nice apartment that was close to the university and not too far from the base.

Since the building was relatively new and the colors were agreeable, they were able the move in right away. A week later, it was their home. Luc trusted her excellent judgment, and he admitted to a deep-seated aversion to furniture shopping, so he left the decorating up to Vepar. To his great relief, she required little of him in that department; all she asked him to do was choose the electronics. Luc found himself in and, more literally, on Heaven, with the perfect job, the perfect woman, and, now, the perfect home.

One of the first evenings in their new place, Luc did his best to surprise Vepar with a home-cooked meal. Suddenly, she burst through the door, wearing a smile of excitement that made him drop the colander of vegetables he was draining. He watched in awe and joy as she danced around the living room. "Uh...good day?" he finally asked when she stilled and just stood there, smiling at him.

She ran into his arms. "Oh, yeah! You're never gonna guess what happened to me today."

Luc's curiosity got the best of him, so much so that he was unable to think of one of his trademark, smartass remarks. "What's up?" he asked.

"The university asked me to join a research team!" she squealed, beaming. "They want us to delve into the practical uses of a device known as the Illuminator."

He paused for a moment, then stuttered, "Really? That's... Well, it sounds wonderful. The Illuminator, you say?"

She mistakenly thought he didn't comprehend what the device was. "Yes. It's... Well, as I understand it so far, the Illuminator can reach into the mind and let you see even the deepest, oldest memories, in accurate, vivid detail."

"Wow. That sounds awesome," he said, doing his best to feign excitement.

"It is." She suddenly stopped, looked around, and sniffed the air. "Wait. Are you trying to cook again?"

Luc bowed and pointed toward the kitchen. "Yes, milady. I have prepared a feast for you," he said proudly.

She frowned and crinkled her nose. "Something is burning."

When they looked at the brown, scabby crust on top of his entrée after he pulled it from the oven, they both decided it was a good time to go out for dinner. For the rest of the evening, Vepar was like a child babbling about a birthday gift. She danced around some more, humming, singing, and peppering Luc with hugs and kisses, which he immensely enjoyed. He understood what she was feeling, because he felt the same way when he was given the opportunity to use the device.

***

A week went by, and the day came for Vepar to participate in her first Illuminator research team meeting. She was anxious but also excited as she sat in the conference room with her colleagues, awaiting the military representatives who

Rise of the Fallen

would bring and explain the wonderful device the team had only heard about. When the conference room opened, she was shocked to see a familiar face among them.

After the presentation, Vepar cornered Luc. "Why didn't you tell me you are part of this, Luc? Please tell me you didn't cherry-pick me for the opportunity," she said, a little miffed. "I'd like to think they chose me based on my own merits."

"Believe me, I had nothing to do with it. The university board of directors made that decision, with no input from any of us," Luc explained.

"But you acted like you've never heard of the Illuminator!" she scolded. "You just let me dance around like an oblivious idiot!"

"A cute idiot though," he said, wearing a coy smile that seemed to soften her anger. "Anyway, I couldn't say anything. We've been under strict orders to keep the existence of the Illuminator private. I didn't know about their plan to explore its educational potential, until you said something about it," Luc said.

"Why did they pick *you* to be here?" she asked.

"Probably because Eli and I used it extensively during our last deployment. It's a truly wonderful device, Vepar. I can't wait for you to try it."

Her wonder and excitement about testing the Illuminator far outweighed any anger she had regarding his deception. Besides, she knew everything Luc told her was the truth.

When they got home later, Luc surprised her by producing an Illuminator from the safe. She couldn't wait to put it on, but he was compelled to warn her about the dangers. "You must take it slow at first," he cautioned. "It is very powerful technology, and it can get away from you if you are not careful. The rush of memories might feel overwhelming, but in time, you will learn to control that. Now, sit down and try to relax your mind."

Vepar did as she was told. She took a deep breath and did her best to calm her mind and body, then nodded at Luc. "Ready," she said.

Gently, Luc placed the Illuminator on her head and activated the device. When he saw her shudder with the flood of memories that burst into her mind, his voice broke into thoughts: "Vepar, try to concentrate on a single memory, one that is extraordinarily strong." He watched as she made the effort. When he saw a smile dance across her face, he was pleased. "Now, just hold on to that thought, whatever it is," he coached. He gave her a chance to experience the memory before he removed the device.

Vepar looked at him and frowned, then laid her head back and laughed a little. She waited for a moment before she exclaimed, "Wow!"

"May I ask what memory you experienced?" Luc asked.

"I thought of the time when I saved your ass from that big guy in the bar. It was so clear," she said.

"Hmm. Maybe there's something wrong with the circuitry on this thing," he said, softly thumping the side of the Illuminator. "I seem to remember saving *you*," he teased.

"No, I think it's working just fine," she said.

He laughed. "Why *that* memory though?" he asked.

"Probably because that was the moment when I knew I'd always love you and that we would be together forever," she sweetly said.

He leaned down to kiss her. "I love you, Vepar," he said, before he pulled her into a tight hug.

"Okay, let's do it again," she said."

"Wait. Define 'it,'" he said with a naughty wink.

Vepar smiled and grabbed the Illuminator. "You know what I mean, Soldier!"

"Great. I think I've created a monster."

Chapter 28

Once the repairs on the *Barakiel* were complete, it was time for its maiden voyage under the command of Captain Elohim El-Elyon. While Eli said goodbye to his family, Luc spent his last few moments with Vepar.

They stood at the gate to the base, and she was crying. "It has been so wonderful having you home." She cooed and hugged him tightly. "How long will you be gone this time?"

"At least six months. I'm going to miss you, my love," Luc said.

"I will miss you too. I promise to have our home in order and beautiful by the time you return. I will make it a place you want to return to."

"Anywhere you are is home for me," Luc said, looking into her eyes. "I love you, Vepar."

"You stay safe out there. You hear me, Soldier?"

"Yes, ma'am," Luc said as he offered her a small salute. He gave her one last kiss, then headed for the transport. Just before he entered the shuttle, he turned, waved, and mouthed another, "I love you."

***

After their mission to Titan, the galaxy settled into a time of calm, with only a few minor border disputes and random pirate attacks to burden Heaven's fleet every once in a while.

The *Barakiel* was reassigned to a new mission: visiting other worlds to see if they had any interest in joining the Heavenly Empire. It was an easy sell on many counts, for there were obvious benefits to joining the citizenry of Heaven.

From day one, security for each star system was the responsibility of Heaven's fleet, in cooperation with local forces. Each system had access to all the knowledge and technology Heaven had to offer, as well as trade opportunities with all other Empire worlds. That, alone, was an incalculable perk, enabling planets that could once only trade with ten to twenty star systems to now trade with thousands. Each system retained its autonomy but also had to agree to adhere to the fundamental laws of the Empire.

By the end of their six-month tour of duty, the *Barakiel*, under the command of Captain Elohim El-Elyon, had expanded the Empire by nineteen star systems, and fifty-seven new worlds had agreed to join the Empire. The *Barakiel* returned to a heroes' welcome on Heaven, having accomplished a feat that was unheard of before.

Eli was humble and just saw the whole mission as part of his job, so he was reluctant to celebrate or to be celebrated. Luc, with help of Jehovah finally convinced his best friend that it was time to party.

"Look at all you've accomplished in such a short time! Why, it is just short of a miracle," Jehovah said, pulling Eli in for a hug. "Although you were only following orders and doing your duty to the best of your ability, you have achieved much. Enjoy yourself now, if not for your own glee, for that of the people of Heaven. They all see, as I do, that you have done a wonderful thing."

"Wait a minute! Why is *he* getting all the glory? *I* did all the hard stuff, like talking those worlds to join the Empire. Where's *my* hug?" Luc joked, smiling in an ornery way and pointing at his own chest with both thumbs.

"That's it. Take him out and have him shot," Jehovah ordered his guards.

"Whoa! Well, maybe he did help a little," Luc corrected as the guards approached.

Rise of the Fallen

The jest soon had everyone laughing, even the guards, who were usually stone-faced and obedient to a fault.

An announcement was sent out to let everyone know that a grand party would be held one week later, at the palace. One of the great halls was readied for the occasion, and preparations for the festive event were overseen by Anaita, Jehovah's wife.

It was a well-attended, grand affair, but Eli, the guest of honor, was more than a little self-conscious. He still felt that what he had done did not really warrant a celebration.

"Just forget about all that and enjoy yourself, would you?" Luc said, hoping his friend would loosen up.

"This party is for the young," Jehovah told Eli and Luc after a quick speech to the crowd. "We are going to retire for the evening."

Once Jehovah and Anaita made their quiet exit, Luc joined Vepar for a dance. Meanwhile, a girl walked into the room and immediately caught Eli's eye with her breathtaking beauty.

"Well, don't just stand there. Go get her, tiger," Luc said when he noticed a particular look in his best friend's eye. He gave Eli a slap on the back, then pushed him toward her.

"I...uh...I don't know," Eli mumbled.

"Go!" Luc pressed.

Eli walked up to the table where the girl was sitting. "Um, excuse me, but I... Would you like to dance?"

She looked up at him and smiled. "Sure," she said, with a giggle and a shrug.

Eli took her hand and led her to the dance floor. The song was soft and slow, and when he held one of her dainty hands in his and put his other arm around her waist, he found the courage to properly introduce himself. "I am Eli," he said. "What is your name?"

"Dilyla."

Dilyla, he thought to himself, liking the sound of it. There was something about her, and even though they'd just met, he knew he had never felt that way about any other woman in his life. There was an instant connection, a mutual attraction between them, and Eli spent the rest of the evening with her while Vepar and Luc side-eyed them through every dance.

Although Eli didn't know it at the time, Dilyla came from a very prominent family, one known to be at odds with Jehovah's reign as God. They would have loved nothing more than to move into the palace. Even if Eli did know of her kinfolks malintent, it would not have stopped him from pursuing her; he was hopelessly smitten with the woman in his arms. Much to the disappointment of all the other young ladies hoping to gain the attention of the son of God, Eli gave every dance and all his time to Dilyla. From that night on, he spent every waking moment he could with her, enraptured by the girl who had so quickly captured his heart.

Luc was a bit envious, as he was not able to spend as much time with his best friend as before, but he understood. After all, he felt the exact same way about Vepar. They double-dated as much as they could, but in time, something began to bother him. "What do you think of Dilyla?" he asked Vepar one night.

"She's fine. Why?" Vepar said.

"I don't know. I just sense something...a little off."

"Well, she does have a bit of a reputation, and she's definitely not a virgin. Of course, that's not necessarily a bad thing, but she *is* dating the son of God," Vepar said honestly. "I'm not sure she's right for him, to be honest."

"No, it's something else. She just seems a little...controlling," Luc observed. "I have a feeling she doesn't want us around."

"Hmm. Maybe. Then again, when I first met you, I wanted you all to myself. Maybe that's it," she offered.

"I can't put my finger on it, but I have a feeling she resents me. I can't think of anything I might have done to warrant that though," Luc said, frowning.

"Maybe she is jealous of you."

"Of me?" Luc said in disbelief, pointing to himself. "Why?"

"Well, you're really close to Eli. As a matter of fact, I'm even a little green under the collar when you two are together," Vepar admitted, with a little chuckle.

"What do you mean? He's just my best friend."

"You may not realize it, but it is abundantly clear that you and Eli are exceptionally close, almost like brothers. It doesn't bother me, but I can see how it might bother someone like Dilyla."

"Yeah, I guess," Luc finally conceded.

"Well, whatever it is, you had better figure out how to get along with her. I have a feeling she's going to be our queen someday," Vepar said before she kissed him on the forehead, then went to finish some work for the university.

Queen? Luc sighed, for it was a possibility he had not yet considered. He couldn't deny it, based on the way Eli acted when he was around Dilyla and the way his eyes lit up whenever he talked about her. "Queen Dilyla," he muttered under his breath, then sighed again.

Chapter 29

Before they knew it, they had to ship out again. As Eli said goodbye to Dilyla, Luc kissed Vepar as if it were their final farewell. It was no different than any of his previous departures; he always hated leaving the only woman in the universe he would ever love. He would only be gone for six months, but it felt like a lifetime apart.

Just before he headed for the shuttle, though, Luc had something to say. As he was walking away, he looked back at Vepar and put his hand up beside his mouth, as if trying to hide his conversation from everyone but her. "I've got him all to myself for six months now," he said, in a whisper meant to be louder than a whisper, loud enough for Dilyla to hear. Then, he performed a little jump for joy.

"Shh!" Vepar admonished, unable to stifle her smile.

"Love you, now and forever," Luc said as he waved and gave her a naughty grin and a wink.

***

The new mission entailed visiting a world Jehovah had approached fifty years prior, Planet Eden. At that time, the elders of Eden and their leader, Lornash, declined to join the Empire but found it agreeable to be visited again in the future.

As the *Barakiel* approached, they opened communication with Eden. Once they were given permission to land, Eli and

Rise of the Fallen

Luc navigated the shuttle to the planet. Upon their arrival, they were greeted politely and escorted to the dwelling of Chief Elder Lornash, the same man Eli's father had spoken to a half-century earlier. Luc and Eli had experienced the first meeting, through the Illuminator, and were surprised to see that Lornash hadn't seemed to aged a day.

Once official introductions were made, Lornash asked, "And how is your father?"

"Doing well. He specifically requested that we call on you if we could. He speaks very highly of you, sir."

"Thank you, and likewise. I found your father to be a very honorable man. To be honest, I liked him the moment we met," the chief elder offered.

"Thank you, sir. I can only hope you see the same character in me."

After Eli and Luc relayed the reason for their visit, Lornash sat back in his big, wooden chair, tented the tips of his fingers together under his chin, and contemplated what they had laid out before him. He wore an unreadable expression as he pondered it; Eli and Luc couldn't fathom what the elder of Eden would say next.

"To be honest, we do not seek the knowledge you have, nor do we desire the technology you possess. We are comfortable and content with Eden as it is. At this point, I can't think of anything we need by way of trade," Lornash began.

Eli and Luc looked at one another in disgruntlement, both fearing it could be another fifty years before they could return to make the same offer. Suddenly, the ornate, wooden chairs they were sitting in weren't nearly as comfortable as before, and they squirmed a bit.

"However, we do have one pressing problem," Lornash stated.

"And that is?" Luc asked.

"Pirates. In our dealings and exchanges with the planets we have trade agreements with, we have lost many shipments while traveling to and from those worlds. To that end, your offer of security is intriguing. If you can agree to give me some time to talk to our council, I will give you an answer. Please join us for dinner tonight."

"It would be our pleasure. Thank you."

Later that evening, as they dined on an elaborate feast, they spoke of many things, but there was something pressing on Luc's mind, and he simply had to bring it up. "Forgive me for any impropriety or offense, sir," he started, "but the Lord God Jehovah shared his memories of your meeting through a device known as the Illuminator. I must say, you look as young as you did 30 years ago."

Lornash laughed. "I appreciate the compliment, but that is a conversation for later. First, you must know that we have agreed to discuss a trade agreement with the Empire."

"That's wonderful!" Eli said.

"In the council meeting tomorrow, we will discuss the terms. Will you sleep here tonight or on your ship?" Lornash asked.

"It has been a long day, so if you don't mind, we'd like to lodge here."

"Glorious! It is an honor to have you as our guests. When we finish our meal, Dranon will show you to your rooms."

"Actually," Luc interrupted, "I have a call to make on our ship, so I'll bunk there for tonight."

"Very well," Lornash said.

"I will be back in time for breakfast," Luc said with a smile and a pat of his belly, "especially if it will be as delightful as this very generous meal!"

Lornash grinned and nodded at him. "We are blessed with culinary geniuses here, I do believe. We will see you in the morning then."

As Eli settled into bed in the room provided by the Edenites, Luc made his way back to the ship and counted the moments until he could see his beautiful lady.

"I miss you so much!" Luc said when he finally opened the secure line to talk to her.

"I don't want to hear it," Vepar growled, wearing a slight

hint of a smile.

"What?" Luc asked, taken aback.

"You are a real shit, Luc. Do you know that?" she continued.

"Huh? What did I do?" he asked, confused and genuinely concerned.

"You bragged about having Eli to yourself for six months, that's what," she explained. "Because of that, I had to drive Dilyla home. She was a little pissed, to say the least."

In an instant, Luc went from concerned to laughing uncontrollably. He laughed even harder when Vepar tried to feign her anger and failed, giggling along with him.

After they talked for a half-hour or so, and he told her all about Chief Elder Lornash and Planet Eden, with its lush vegetation and delicious food, they both decided it was time to get some sleep.

"It's beautiful here, but not as beautiful as you. I love you, Vepar," Luc sleepily said, trying to hide a yawn.

"I love you, too, even if you are a shit," Vepar said, and they both laughed again as their images faded away.

Chapter 30

Dawn gave way to another magnificent day on Eden. Eli woke up feeling invigorated and better than he had in a long time. He wasn't sure if it was because of the bed he slept in or the atmosphere on Eden itself, but it had been quite a while since he had felt so well rested. When Luc arrived a short time later, he relayed the same feeling.

"I don't know about you, but I woke up feeling great today. I mean, *really* great," Eli said.

"Yeah, me too. I feel like I could take the universe on all by myself," Luc agreed.

"Hmm. I guess it wasn't the bed then, since you slept on the ship last night. Maybe there was something in the food they gave us."

"Are you saying they put tranquilizers in the food?"

"Who knows?" Eli said with a shrug.

"Well, whatever it was, I want more," Luc admitted.

"Me too. Me too," Eli affirmed.

Dranon soon came to escort them to breakfast. It was as incredible as the meal they'd enjoyed the night before. After they ate, they were led into a great hall, where Chief Elder Lornash was seated in an exquisite, wooden chair, flanked on both sides by his councilmembers. Eli and Luc sat in the front row, surrounded by a full room of Edenites.

Rise of the Fallen

The excitement was palpable. News of their visit had traveled fast, and everyone was eager to meet the off-worlders. The stares and whispers made Eli and Luc a bit uncomfortable, and they began to worry that they might be the main course at the evening meal.

Right on cue, Lornash rapped his cane hard against the wooden floor. The room quieted, but the anxious looks continued as the chief elder got right down to business.

"As I told you last night," Lornash said to Eli and Luc, "there is little we need by way of trade. Eden and our suppliers provide everything we need to relish healthy, wonderful lives here. In other words, we are not in need of material goods. We also have no need of your technology, and while we admire the accumulated knowledge of the Empire, it is simply unnecessary here. Gentlemen, we are a solitary world, and we prefer not to be visited by others."

Again, Luc and Eli found themselves squirming in their seats, but they listened intently as the chief elder went on.

"We are interested, however, in the security you have to offer. We need the Empire to protect the trade we currently have with a few select worlds. Pirate attacks have increased in frequency and intensity, and our ships and the ships of those who trade with us have been victimized. We have already communicated with the other worlds, and they are willing to undertake their own trade agreements with the Empire, on their own terms.

"Planet Eden wishes to be left alone, but we do understand the need to facilitate trade with off-worlders. This will be strictly limited to a minimum number of individuals, only those who are crucial to fulfilling our arrangement, and all off-worlders will only be permitted access to restricted areas, as designated by us. I am sure there are questions, so please ask them now," Lornash finished.

"I mean no disrespect, sir, but what do you have to offer in exchange for the protection you seek?" Eli asked.

"Ah, a very good question indeed. Last night, Luc mentioned that my appearance has not changed in fifty years."

Luc looked at Eli and shook his head.

"There is a very good reason for this. There is a tree native to Planet Eden. This tree grows fruit that provides... extended longevity. It gives us the ability to live extremely long lives."

Eli and Luc did their best to tense their facial expressions, so they would not disrespect the chief elder with their disbelief.

"Look around you. No one in this room, other than you, is younger than 5,000 years," Lornash offered.

As requested, Eli and Luc looked at the Edenites, wondering if it could really be possible.

"I know this may sound ludicrous and might be difficult for you to believe, but we would like to invite the Empire to send a team of scientists to validate our claim. You ate the fruit last evening, and I am sure you have already felt its effects."

Suddenly, Luc and Eli were struck with a realization: Their invigorated feeling that morning had nothing to do with sleep at all. It was real, and it was because they had eaten the Eden fruit. In fact, they were still experiencing the energetic, healthy feeling even as they sat in the great hall.

While he wanted to believe the story about the magic fruit, Luc was not one for fairytales. He was a bit skeptical, and questions began to stir in his head: *Did they drug us, just to make us feel good so we will sign their agreement? Surely there is not any fruit that could offer near immortality. Or is there?* After a moment, he looked up at the chief elder and asked, "If you have something so wonderful, why would you risk letting the galaxy in on the secret? Aren't you afraid this revelation might lead to the end of your way of life?" Luc asked.

"That is a good question. For a very long time, we feared we were being selfish. Is it wrong to keep the miracle to ourselves? Perhaps. Many believe we should share it with the galaxy, but I have my doubts. I worry we may not be able to protect ourselves if the secret gets out. We may have no choice though. Others, like those with whom we trade, have begun to take notice. They wonder why we do not seem to age, even as their people continue to grow old and die. It may only be a matter of time before the fruit becomes common knowledge. When that time comes, we will need protection. The Empire can help us stave off any invading forces, once your scientists confirm what we already know. In exchange for this protection and security, we will supply you with fruit from the Tree of life. In addition to that, we ask for only one other thing."

"And what is that?" Eli asked.

"You mustn't reveal the location of your supply."

Eli nodded. "Very well, Chief Elder. If your claims about the fruit are determined to be truthful, it is wise to keep it hidden, for as long as you can. I will travel back to Heaven and meet with my father and his council to discuss your terms. I'd rather not send a transmission, for fear that it might be intercepted. In the meantime, I will call for two of our warships to patrol Eden space. Our fighters will also be on the lookout for the pirates you spoke of."

"But we have no signed agreement yet. Why are you willing to protect us already?" Lornash asked, sounding pleasantly surprised but also a bit suspicious.

"My father believes you are an honorable, good man. We will watch over your planet whether you sign an agreement or not."

"Thank you."

"I would like to stay on Eden one more night and leave in the morning. It would be helpful if you could provide us with some samples to begin our research."

"All of this serious talk has stirred my appetite again. Let us eat, and you can tell me more about your father and Heaven," Lornash suggested.

"Wonderful, and I would love to hear more about the history of Planet Eden."

The next morning, once again very rested and refreshed, Luc and Eli prepared to leave. As promised, samples of the fruit were brought to their shuttle.

"Wow. This is a lot," Eli said, as the Edenites loaded the samples. "Do we really require this much for research?"

"No, of course not," Lornash said. He then handed Eli a small box, one he could easily carry under his arm. "*This* is all your scientists need."

"Then why are you sending us back with so many crates?" Eli asked, looking at six large containers.

"That is for you, Luc, and your families, enough to sustain you until you return. I prefer the fruit served raw, but cooking does not diminish its effects. Please encourage your dear father to eat plenty upon your return. You will be surprised by the results, I'm sure."

Chapter 31

It didn't take long for the Heaven scientists to discover the benefits of the fruit of the Tree of Life. The test subjects, who ranged in age from 17 to 70 years, showed remarkable improvement. Although it was harder to tell in the teenagers, the older test subjects exhibited obvious reversal in age-related problems. While they could not yet verify that life expectancy was extended, it was clear that the fruit provided astounding health benefits to all who ate it.

In short order, arrangements were made for the signing of the trade agreement. Of course, Jehovah would have gladly offered assistance to his friend Lornash, with the trade agreement for the fruit or without. He had only spent a few short weeks with him fifty years earlier, but he had fond memories of the time they spent together.

The scientists, curious by nature, inquired about the origins of the fruit, but that information was deemed top secret. Those orders came straight from God Jehovah. Only a select few knew about Eden, and even fewer knew about the fruit from the Tree of Life.

As it turned out, during the three months while Luc and Eli were away, twelve pirate ships had been captured or destroyed. Eden's six trading partners were now free to do business, without fear of lost shipments.

While the researchers had isolated the antiaging agent

within the fruit, they could not duplicate the effect; they needed more fruit. They calculated the amount that would be necessary to service the entire population of Heaven, and it was astronomical. Jehovah was desperate to share the wonderful miracle with everyone, but he was not sure Eden could supply the entire Empire.

When the Barakiel returned to Eden again, Dranon met Eli and Luc at the shuttle. Quickly, he escorted his guests to council chambers, where Lornash and the elders awaited them.

Before they were invited to speak, Lornash announced, "I must thank you for removing the threat of the pirates, especially since you did so even before the agreement was signed. Our trade with the six planets is very valuable, for it is how we take care of our own. You may not be aware of it, but those planets are colonies. Many years ago, some of our bravest, most selfless brothers and sisters chose to move to those other worlds, not only to help control the population here but also in search of other climates where the Tree of Life could spring up."

"And have they found any?" Eli asked.

"As of yet, we have found no other planet capable of producing the fruit. The trees grow in several locations, but their fruit is sterile, devoid of life-giving properties. Those who inhabited the colonies have grown comfortable on their new worlds and have chosen to remain. This is why it is so important to keep the trade routes open, so we can safely deliver the potent fruit to our people."

Eli smiled. "You have my personal guarantee that those six worlds will remain protected under the agreement we sign here today. There is just one concern."

"And that is?" Lornash asked.

"Just as we do," Eli said, nodding toward Luc, "my father, Jehovah, believes that such a gift of longevity should be shared throughout the galaxy. He feels it is sinful to give it only to the people of Heaven and a few select star systems, excluding others from the blessing."

"Jehovah is indeed a good, wise man. We, too, have had these thoughts and concerns. It is a sin to keep this wonderful fruit to ourselves. We have done our own calculations and have determined that we should be able to grow enough to supply the Empire. It will take some time to increase our harvest capabilities and packing facilities, but it is doable."

A great celebration was planned for the following day, to mark the signing of the trade agreement between the Empire and Eden. Since Lornash was not comfortable traveling to Heaven, the signing and the celebration would be held on Eden. Although festivities were handled much differently on Eden, far more subdued, they were just as meaningful.

Lord God Jehovah surprised everyone by attending the signing. Luc and Eli watched with intense pride as Lornash and Jehovah stood in the great hall, affixed their signatures to the agreement, and shook hands. Everyone raised a glass of a wonderfully tasty, wildly intoxicating brew, made from the very fruit that would soon change the galaxy.

Chapter 32

Until they could ensure the absolute security of Eden, any hint of where the fruit was grown had to be kept confidential. The production and distribution centers for the Factor, as it came to be known, were designed and built with great discretion; none of the engineers or architects were made aware of the true purpose of the facilities they were constructing. Even long after the facilities were built and fully operational, most were completely clueless.

One thing Jehovah and his counsel were keenly aware of was that the Factor would have an adverse effect on the economy of Heaven. When sickness was no longer a concern, the healthcare industry would face a devastating blow, as would businesses who dealt in death. While this did give some pause, the pros of the Factor far outweighed the cons.

While Lord Jehovah and his councilmembers struggled to find answers to the problems the Factor created, Luc had something else on his mind. One morning, while out on a run with Vepar, he stopped at the place where she had once surprised him and caused him to run into the lake.

It took Vepar a second to realize he had stopped. When she did, she backtracked to him and asked, "What's going on? Are you okay?"

"I'm fine." He took her in his arms and kissed her. "Do you remember this place?"

"Yeah, of course. This is where you almost drowned. You looked so funny and confused when your head popped up out of the water," she reminisced with a laugh.

"I guess I probably did look a little stupid, but you surprised the shit out of me. Now, I have a surprise for you." With that, Luc went down on one knee and held up a ring. "Vepar Muriel Gomory, will you marry me?"

Vepar's eyes widened, and an accidental, little gasp escaped her lips. She just stood there for a moment, waiting for her mind to catch up with the question he had just asked. Her hand lifted up to her mouth, and tears moistened her eyes. "Yes! Of course, Luc. Yes, yes, yes! I *will* marry you."

That was all she could manage before her happy tears and joyous sobbing took over. Suddenly, as he stood, she jumped into his arms, wrapped her legs around his body, and kissed him, harder and deeper than ever before.

The bride-to-be composed herself, and the two sat down where they had once curled over in laughter after his fall into the lake. They held each other for several moments.

After another especially passionate kiss, she looked at Luc and asked, "Can we call my parents and tell them the news?"

"I was kinda hoping we could tell them in person," Luc said.

"Really!?" she squealed, hoping he was serious.

"Really. In fact, I have two weeks off, and I have made arrangements for us to travel to Hell in three days, if that is all right with you."

"That will be wonderful! Oh, Luc, I love you so much."

***

When they landed on Hell, Luc and Vepar headed straight for her parents' house. They were thrilled to hear the news, and there were hugs and pats on the backs all around before they left to drop in on Luc's parents.

After discussing it with their mothers and fathers, Luc and Vepar decided it was best not to wait. They wanted to be married on their home Planet Hell, so they opted to hold the ceremony before they had to return to Heaven.

On their wedding day, Vepar was pleasantly surprised to see Eli, accompanied by a couple of her friends from the university. She wasn't sure why Dilyla could not attend, but her absence really came as no surprise; Dilyla craved all of Eli's attention, and she resented them for taking him away from her, even for a little while. Truth be told, they did not like her any more than they trusted her, and that wasn't much at all.

After the simple but beautiful ceremony, it was time to leave again. It was a bittersweet gathering at the shuttle that would take them to the *Barakiel*. Their stay on Hell was a happy one, but it never seemed long enough, and they hated telling their loved ones goodbye.

Eli was not at all surprised that he saw no sign of Luc or Vepar during the entire trip back to Heaven. *They're probably just sleeping,* he told himself, then smiled at the thought.

Chapter 33

Something must have been in the air, because just a month after their return from Eden, Eli made a shocking announcement of his own: He would soon wed Dilyla. Luc and Vepar had their reservations, but since they had no solid proof that she was up to anything sketchy, they kept it to themselves.

Jehovah, however, was not one to hold his tongue. "Son, I know you think you love this woman, but are you sure?" he asked. "Her family has nothing but disdain for me. They have had their eyes on my palace and my throne for a very long time. So, I ask you again, are you sure?"

"Yes, Father. She and I have discussed it at length, and Dilyla does not believe as her family does. I have never known anyone like her. When I am with her, I just... Well, I can't imagine being with anyone else," Eli assured him.

"Very well, my son. If this is your wish, I am happy for you. I only have one request."

"What is it, Father?"

"Before you officially announce your upcoming nuptials, will you please bring Dilyla and her family here to meet your mother and me?"

So, sometime later, it was announced that the son of God would be married. Jehovah was a beloved leader, so everyone in the Empire looked forward to the happy occasion.

The wedding was a spectacular affair, full of pomp and circumstance. No expense was spared. Luc, of course, proudly served as Eli's best man and stood beside his friend, beaming with pride. When the clergyman said, "Two are now one," cheers rose throughout the Empire.

With the placement of Eli's ring on her finger, Dilyla was elevated to a position she'd only dreamt about. She took full advantage of the power she now possessed. Her arrogance and contempt were obvious to everyone except for her groom. In Elohim's eyes, she could do no wrong. Although her presence and her attitude failed to meet up to the grace of her new mother-in-law, she was now undeniably one of the most important persons in the galaxy.

After a honeymoon on Utopia, a paradise planet not far from Heaven, Eli and Dilyla returned home to settle into their new lives. Unfortunately, Eli was set to ship out soon after. The night before they shipped out, Luc and Vepar joined Eli and Dilyla at the palace for some socializing. Although Dilyla seemed happy and acted as if she were enjoying herself, she could not hide her air of superiority. Everything she said or did seemed condescending, and she would not even give Eli his due.

Early the next morning, Eli and Luc prepared to board the shuttle. Luc gave Vepar one last kiss, gave the thumbs-up to Eli, and headed for their ride. One glaring absence was Dilyla. Even though Eli made excuses, claiming she was just tired from the night before, Luc was sure his friend's new wife would continue to humiliate and dismiss him from that point forward.

**

The *Barakiel* had been in space for three months when news came that Dilyla was with child. Eli was beside himself, the happiest man in the galaxy. Luc knew in his heart that Eli would be a great father, and, for the following three months, it was all Eli could talk about. When their six-month tour was finally over, Eli could not contain his excitement.

The moment the shuttle touched down, Eli ran to catch a ride home, forcing Luc to kick it up a notch to catch up. Luc drove, sensing his friend's desire to get home as quickly as possible might result in an accident. As soon as the car lifted into the air, Luc punched the accelerator. Eli's door was open before Luc touched the ground. He laughed as he watched Eli sprint into the palace, wearing a broad, silly grin on his face.

Inside, Eli grabbed the round-bellied Dilyla and twirled her around. They were both happy and laughing. Nevertheless, when Dilyla saw Luc walk in the door, she frowned.

Despite the icy reaction, Luc did his best to remain positive, if only for the sake of his best friend. "Congratulations, Dilyla," he said, almost choking on his words. "I know you will make a great mother."

"Uh...thank you, but would you mind leaving us alone to celebrate?" she asked, with as much venom as she could display, while still not alarming her better half.

"I need to see Vepar anyway. Congratulations again," Luc said before he backed out the door. He was glad to know that his use of flattery had caused her to falter just a little before her claws came out.

The welcome-home tryst between Luc and his missus was a powerful event. Just three months after that night, around the time when Dilyla gave birth to a son of her own, Vepar broke the news to Luc that he would soon be a father too.

One week after the birth of his grandson, Jehovah stood before the masses with Queen Anaita, Dilyla, and Elohim, holding the baby. Jehovah looked a little fatigued and weary, but he was smiling just the same. "Today, I am proud to present to the Empire my new grandson." He paused for effect, then finished, "Please welcome Jesus Adonai El-Elyon."

Cheers and adoration erupted all over the Empire, and all admired the beautiful, precious baby as he cooed in the very proud Elohim's arms. Luc and Vepar were quick to notice that Dilyla was not smiling as brightly as everyone else; she was miffed about the whole observance. She thought it was her place to hold her baby, for all the galaxy to see, but that was not the custom.

Six months later, and with far less fanfare, Vepar gave

birth to her own bouncing bundle of joy. They named him Sandel Belial Satanis.

Elohim seemed just as happy about the birth of young Sandel as Luc was. "Our boys will grow up together, be the best of friends, and have many wonderful adventures." Elohim raised his glass. "Lucifer, you are my dearest friend. You have saved my life more times than I can count, often at the risk of your own. My only hope is that our sons will know that kind of friendship, that kind of brotherhood. Congratulations, my friend."

As always, Dilyla was quick to show her distaste for anything that took the attention off her and baby Jesus. At no time did she even express a desire to hold the newborn Sandel, and she rarely let anyone outside her family get close to Jesus. Luc and Vepar could almost feel the heat of Dilyla's stare when Eli handed Jesus to one of them. Although she said nothing verbally, her body language spoke volumes.

Luc often wondered why Dilyla was so obsessed with Jesus. It was natural for a mother to be protective of her child, of course, but there was something different about her. From the bits and pieces of the stories Eli relayed to him, he knew her actions were odd and disconcerting. For instance, the only other person who was allowed to tend to Jesus was Dilyla's servant, Tubiel. She also refused to let her child be seen in the same outfit more than once. One of Tubiel's duties was to clean or destroy anything that came into contact with the child.

Chapter 34

Sadly, during one of Eli's six-month missions, word came that his father had collapsed and was not expected to live long. Within days, the *Barakiel* returned to Heaven. Eli rushed to his father's bedside, and he was horrified to find him looking so frail. The sight of his father in that condition crushed him more than anything in his life.

The doctors could not explain the cause of his decline. Even though the Factor had rejuvenated Jehovah in the years since its discovery, something beyond the scope of the best medical professionals in the Empire seemed to be eating away at his life, little by little. Just two days later, Jehovah, Lord God of Heaven, was gone.

Word of Jehovah's death quickly spread throughout the Empire, and a great sadness blanketed the world. He had always been known as a powerful but good and decent man, beloved by all. The nearly debilitating heartache of his loss darkened the lives of Elohim, Anaita, and Lucifer. Although Luc was not his blood relative, Jehovah had treated him like a son, and the pain and grief were almost unbearable.

Almost immediately, Elohim, the son of God, ascended to his place as God. At his ascension ceremony, Luc stood by his side as he addressed the Empire: "I cannot, in good conscience, stand here and tell you I will be as great a man or leader as my father was during his reign as God. What I can promise is that I will aspire to be the best I can be, that I will do my best to follow the example Jehovah set for us all. I vow to continue the work my father began and to implement the dreams he held for the Empire. Jehovah believed the Empire belongs to all of us, and I will endeavor to do what is best for all. It is my hope that I can live up to my father's example, but I cannot achieve this goal without the help of every citizen of the Empire."

A few days later, a funeral was held for the beloved God, Jehovah. Although Eli and Luc struggled to stay strong for everyone, they could not fight back tears. Luc's mind wandered back to his first meeting with Jehovah, just after God ordered his men to kick the shit out of him, to see if he would inform on Elohim, when he was incognito during Angel training. As he stood there with bitter rivers streaming down his face, he reaffirmed his promise to Jehovah: *I will always, always protect Elohim, even at the risk of my own life.*

As Luc surveyed the mourners, his eyes fixed on Dilyla. She had not shed a tear. In fact, she seemed rather bored, annoyed, and detached from all the sadness around her. Luc wasn't sure, but he thought he detected a hint of a smile. He decided it was probably just another of her many strange quirks, but he couldn't help being a bit perturbed at the wife of his best friend.

Chapter 35

When Elohim stepped into his lofty position of Lord God of the Empire, Luc was promoted to head of security and commander of the Angelic fleet. The part of his job that pleased him the most was protecting Elohim and his family. Not only that, but he suddenly found himself serving as primary advisor to God. That placed him at a higher standing than even the Seraphim advisor, second only to God himself. Lucifer Satanis was truly the right hand of God.

Most days, even though he worked out of his palace office, Elohim spent more time with Luc than he did with his family. That did not sit well with Dilyla, who was still rampantly jealous of the unbreakable, almost brotherly closeness between Elohim and Lucifer. To top it off, because of her family's animosity toward the El-Elyon rule, she was excluded from almost all galactic affairs of state. Although Eli loved her dearly, he had promised the people of the Empire that he would be the best ruler he could, and that sometimes meant sacrificing time with his wife.

Dilyla, however, was quick to blame Luc for her exclusion, even though such an accusation couldn't have been further from the truth. It was Elim Seraphiel, Eli's Seraphim One, who had advised God to keep her at bay. Seraphiel had served under Jehovah, and his wise counsel was trusted above all others. Dilyla felt a deep yearning to be her husband's foremost confidant and advisor, but that was not to be. She did not like that one bit, but although she made her feelings well known throughout the upper echelons of Heaven, she dared not publicly voice her underlying disdain toward the will of God.

Elohim was not naïve to Dilyla's indiscretions. It was commonplace for his queen to be seen talking, in hushed tones, to anyone who would listen, bashing Lucifer and gossiping about his hold on her husband. Many nights, Elohim entered their living quarters, intent on discussing the problem with his beloved, only to forgo those thoughts when he was hopelessly drawn into the intoxicating allure of holding her in his arms.

Luc and Dilyla had mutual misgivings regarding one another, but he felt some pity for Eli's dilemma. His friend was hopelessly in love with her, and he understood because his feelings for Vepar were every bit as powerful. What he didn't understand was Dilyla's intense animosity toward him. Luc had never done anything to warrant such feelings, at least not that he was aware of. He eventually came to recognize that she was just jealous of his close friendship with her husband. Although Luc neither trusted nor particularly liked Dilyla, he couldn't help but sense some sympathy for her. *How it must eat at her soul to be excluded, to not be her husband's best friend and most trusted ally, as my Vepar is to me,* he pondered.

***

As the years passed, Dilyla shamelessly did everything in her power to keep Jesus and Sandel apart. Nonetheless, the boys spent much time around their fathers, and they grew up together and felt the same strong bonds of friendship. Whenever Elohim and Luc had free time, the two youngsters sat in rapt attention as their fathers told them of their adventures throughout the Empire.

They were most intrigued by the tales of Planet Eden, a wondrous world green with vegetation and vast blue oceans, and they longed to visit the place that seemingly held the secret to everlasting life. Stories of the Dumah War and the nearly hopeless fight against the overwhelming number of insect-like creatures, covering the Empire fleet, both scared and captivated their young minds. The story of their encounter with Cronus, the eater of children, scared them but also filled them with pride, knowing their brave fathers had prevailed.

Even though they were best friends, Jesus often displayed a sense of superiority over Sandel, no doubt under the influence of his prideful and controlling mother. Once, when they had reached the age of the pseudo-independence of young adulthood, Dilyla tried to stop Jesus from being with Sandel, only to find that her son was quick to rebel.

"He is my best friend, Mother, and nothing in the universe can break our bond," Jesus responded.

Try as she did, that proved true for poor Dilyla, who could simply not put a wedge between them as she wanted to. However, Jesus was not quite correct in his assumptions that no one could get in the way of their friendship. Ultimately, Dilyla was not the woman who came between Jesus and Sandel; no, that was one of their classmates. Both young men were infatuated with her, but she could belong to only one.

Jesus found himself using his position and wealth to woo the fare Lilith. Sandel certainly felt the pressure of his lack of what he brought to the table, in his quest for her attention. It was something that he shared with his parents.

"Sandel, you are my son, and I can tell that you

have strong feelings for this girl." Lucifer looked toward Vepar, and reached over and took her hand in his. "I think that your mom would agree with the only advice that I can give you. Just be yourself. There's no amount of money or power, that can match the person you are."

Sandel started to protest, but his mother interrupted. "Your father is right. If this girl is everything you say she is, she will see through all the power and the presents. Just be the man that we raised, and if it's meant to be...well time will tell."

Although Jesus and Sandel made an agreement that the loser would happily concede, Jesus couldn't bring himself to accept or understand why Lilith ultimately chose Sandel. Instead of living up to their agreement, Jesus was crushed and humiliated, and was visibly bitter. *I am the son of God,* he thought. *How dare she not grant me her affections?*

That jealousy sparked something foul in Jesus, and for the first time since his birth, Dilyla's insidious influence seemed to grow exponentially. Her words were suddenly powerful in the ears of her son. She had noticed the rift forming between them, and she knew just what to say to deepen it. "What magic did he use to make her choose him over you? You are the son of God. Now that he is with her, he will spend less time with you. Sandel is only a man, dear one. One day, you will be God," Dilyla said, feeding into the confusion of his mind and the fragility of his heart.

As Dilyla suggested, it did come to pass that Sandel began spending much time with the female and far less time with his so-called best friend. As Jesus brooded, Dilyla continued to fill his mind with thoughts of Sandel's betrayal. Soon, the chasm between them grew to the point where Jesus altogether refused to see Sandel. When their paths crossed, the son of God was arrogant and deemed himself superior to the unworthy son of Lucifer.

Rise of the Fallen

After a few years, the two came of age, and Jesus and Sandel were included in all but the most secret council meetings. In his arrogance, Jesus often offered childish, shortsighted solutions, usually even before he was asked to contribute. During these times, Elohim found it hard to mask his embarrassment. He felt as though everyone in the room saw it as a direct result of his lack of parental teaching. Although he could not know it, everyone in the room suspected, that Dilyla was the true reason.

Lucifer was more than proud as Sandel sat quietly, listening and pondering, just as his wise father had instructed him to do. What Sandel learned in the meetings would serve him well in the future that stood before him. On the other hand, Sandel was proud, as he watched his father commanded the respect of everyone in the room. He did not say much, but what he did say, was always concise and to the point.

Jesus bristled as his father listened to Lucifer's advice. He particularly hated it when Luc countered his ideas, and he felt Luc was trying to make a fool of him. "Father just sat there and let Lucifer contradict my words," he whined to his mother. "He made me look like an idiot, right there in front of everyone."

Such ranting became the essence of most of Jesus' and Dilyla's conversations. Soon, Jesus and his scandalous mother found themselves attending clandestine meetings with her family, the sole purpose of which was to teach the son of God the skills he would need to be taken seriously in the future. They stroked his ego and made him feel important. Since he was much too immature and easily manipulated, he also became an unwitting spy for Dilyla's family.

Using the skills he learned in those covert conferences, he began to make worthy contributions to the council meetings he attended. Soon, he gained reluctant respect from Eli's councilmembers. Even Lucifer began to confide in Elohim, and all hoped Jesus was finally becoming the man and the God he was meant to be.

While Jesus still felt the sting of rejection from the young Lilith, he soon found love in the arms of a beautiful girl named Sarah, who just so happened to be Lucifer's niece. They were soon married. She brought stability into his life. With her by his side, he began to reject the ungodly counsel of his mother and saw the wisdom in the teachings of his father.

It was during this time that Jesus rekindled his friendship with Sandel. They began to spend more and more time together. Unfortunately, on their first anniversary, Sarah died of an apparent suicide. Her demise tore at Jesus' fragile mind. Once again, Dilyla took the opportunity to push her distraught son in directions that would benefit the goals of her family.

It wasn't long before Jesus found love again. This time, Dilyla introduced him to the daughter of a family who had strong political ties to hers. Like Dilyla, Magdalene had been groomed to be the wife of God, and the two women in Jesus' life began to push them into a future of their choosing, eager to see their own agendas fulfilled.

Unfortunately, the death of Sarah, signaled the death of Sandel's friendship with Jesus. Sandel couldn't understand, what had changed, but it hurt him deeply.

Chapter 36

Over the next twenty years, Jesus was given more say in Empire affairs. Unfortunately, he never truly took the knowledge or wisdom of his father and Luc to heart. His motivation was still deeply imbedded in jealousy, hatred, and inflated self-worth. He truly believed his father was weak, just a puppet controlled by Lucifer and the rest of the council.

Sadly, as it was with Jehovah, Elohim's health began to fail. The healers and physicians were at a loss as to why. The only explanation they had was that it had something to do with his genetics, that it was a hereditary flaw handed down by Jehovah, some sort of biological resistance to the Factor. Sooner than anyone would've wished it, Jesus became God.

Immediately, Jesus removed Elim Seraphiel from his appointment as Seraphim One and replaced him with Nithael, who came with high recommendations from Dilyla. Before long, many councilmembers were similarly replaced. Although Lucifer remained head of Empire security, he was suddenly excluded from any and all council decisions. "You will do as you are told and nothing more," Jesus said. Outwardly, Luc complied, but in the shadows and with great caution and care, he continued to work against the increasingly erratic behavior of the new Lord God Jesus.

Elohim, as ill as he was, was still ceremoniously displayed whenever Jesus gave a speech to the Empire. He sat behind Jesus, gaunt and looking as if he were unsure why he was there. Lucifer feared someone was drugging his friend, but he had no way to bring those very valid concerns to anyone's ears.

The people of Heaven soon realized Jesus had no intention of ruling as his grandfather or father did. In every speech he gave, he made it clear that the citizens of the Empire were there to serve him and not the other way around.

Year after year, as his power grew, Jesus' rulings became increasingly bizarre. Anyone who dared to oppose him in any way died under suspicious circumstances. Luc was sure that Holy Ghosts had some hand in that. While they were once honorable spies, intelligence gatherers, and messengers who worked for the good of the galactic government, they had degenerated into a dark, unseen cache of criminals, blackmailers, and assassins. They answered only to Jesus, and Ghosts who would not conform were killed or forced to run for their lives, forever exiled.

Soon, it was rumored that Dilyla's family, believing they already had great power over Jesus, rose up to publicly challenge him and secretly plotted against him. Within one bloody day, 174 of the rebels lost their lives under mysterious circumstances, leaving Dilyla and Magdalene as orphans. It was rumored that this massacre was the work of the Holy Ghosts, under Jesus' orders. His goal was to strike fear into anyone who tried to stand against him, even if it meant destroying his own kin.

When Jesus learned that his mother was instrumental in the failed coup, he opted to spare her life. Since he never again wanted to hear her voice, he ordered her tongue to be cut out. He also decreed that she could no longer be in his presence unless under heavy guard. Magdalene somehow convinced Jesus that she was happy her family was dead, claiming her parents had forced her to betray him, and she swore her obedience and allegiance to him forever.

Chapter 37

Lucifer watched the rise of Jesus with growing concern. He felt helpless and hopeless as the Empire he had loved and served his entire life morphed into something sinister, sinful, and evil. Jesus was a dictator, and he shamelessly chose to rule under the fist of fear. Not since before the reign of Abba El-Elyon, the first God of Heaven, when Heaven was ruled by the evil despot Chaos, had the world known such malevolence.

Lucifer's first thought was to step down as head of security, but he thought it over and decided he might better serve the Empire by working from within. Alongside him, a few who were still loyal to Elohim and believed in his way of government secretly did whatever they could to disrupt Jesus' reign and his self-serving plans. Knowing the Holy Ghosts had their fingers in almost every part of the Empire, Lucifer quietly sought those who were also displeased with Jesus' misguided commands.

Many members of the resistance found excuses to visit their home worlds, where they could prepare them for the impending battle. They were relieved that their loved ones had left Heaven. Once Lucifer was sure Vepar and Sandel had safely arrived on Planet Hell, a great weight was lifted from his shoulders. That burden was quickly replaced, however, and he was not happy about what he had to do next.

Many looked up to Lucifer as their leader and guide, and he felt a great weight of responsibility. It was a heavy burden to bear. Mostly, he felt alone. He knew his time on Heaven would soon reach its end. Angels and the Holy Ghosts who were loyal to Jesus were beginning to suspect dissension in the Angel ranks.

Some captains of Heaven warships began to disobey orders to kill innocent beings. Those whose only crime was to choose freewill above Heavenly domination were executed for their disobedience. Loyalty and respect had been earned by Elohim, but Jesus, who was nothing like his father, forced it upon the citizens of the galaxy, through fear and intimidation.

Lucifer knew he could no longer safely remain on Heaven, but he longed to see his old friend Elohim. Carefully placed and trusted spies in the palace informed him that Eli was still alive, albeit barely, and under heavy sedation. They also told him where he could find Elohim. Using the secret entrance, the two boys had discovered in their youth, Lucifer sneaked into the palace. What he saw brought him to tears. Eli was feeble, a fraction of the man he had once known. Even worse, his mind was deluded; it was evident to Luc that Jesus had convinced Eli that Lucifer had turned against him and the Empire, because the first thing Eli asked was, "Are you here to kill me?"

"No, my friend! I am here because I've missed you."

It took a while for Lucifer to convince the intoxicated and weak Eli of the truth, but he managed to regain his trust again and even garnered a crooked, pained smile from him.

"I have missed you also," Eli confessed, wrinkling his brow as he fought with his deranged, chemically altered mid.

Before he left, Lucifer promised to return and free Eli. To seal his promise, he gave him a rock in the shape of a pentagon, a relic they'd found together during their first year of Angel training. He wrapped his arms around Eli once more and sniffled. His once powerful friend was now reduced to a withered, frail fraction of his former self, but he loved him all the same.

Chapter 38

Somehow, Luc's visit with Eli was detected by one of Jesus' loyal followers, but Lucifer was thankful that one of his spies gave him a heads-up. "They are coming for you...now," the spy warned. Quickly, Luc destroyed all evidence of the resistance. His portable disintegration unit would leave no trace of anything, not a shred of proof the evil Empire could use against them.

He soon received word that Angelic soldiers were swarming in through every entrance of the security building. The lower floors were soon flooded with them. Lucifer had already instructed everyone to show no defiance, for he did not want to see anyone injured or murdered. "Even if it means my capture, protect yourselves," he told them. He had long anticipated a need to escape the clutches of the ever more demented Lord Jesus, and he had planned for as many worst-case scenarios as he could think of. At least 100 soldiers had breached the security building, with the sole purpose of taking him prisoner, of capturing him, dead or alive. Lucifer knew Jesus would have preferred to make an example of him and make him suffer, but putting him to death would save a lot of time.

Lucifer had never run from anything, but that time had come. He was not scared, at least not on his own behalf. His only fear emanated from his desire to be with his family and his longing to put a stop to the reign of the evil despot Jesus.

Having served as Empire head of security did provide him some advantages. For one thing, he'd had opportunity to put the right people in the right places to facilitate his escape, even though it would be no easy feat to get to them. He sealed off his office. The outer walls were made of impervisium, a relatively newly discovered metal. When combined with aluminum, it was almost indestructible, and that barricade provided Luc with some extra time he desperately needed.

Just as the soldiers finally managed to break into his office, he climbed into a hidden chamber. They shot at him just as the door shut behind him; their energy pulses cut deeply into the walls. The soldiers ran to the place in the wall where he had disappeared, staring at it in awe. Suddenly, there was a loud roar, and the hidden door blew open, killing half the men in the room. A one-man shuttle burst through the roof of the security building, heading up and away from Araboth. The soldiers were furious that they had failed to capture Lucifer in the building, but they were certain their fighters would stop him before he was able to land. If not, they could always just shoot him down.

No matter how fast the shuttle went, the fighters were faster. They quickly closed the gap, knowing he had nowhere to hide. Rapidly, the fighters overtook the shuttle, locked on to it, and forced it to the ground. They ordered Lucifer to open the shuttle and surrender, but he did not comply. Finally, the soldiers used a plasma cutter to slice through the door. To their surprise, the shuttle was empty.

When the shuttle took off from the security building, Lucifer had cleverly slid down through a tube that dumped him out in an underground chamber. There, he changed into a disguise and walked, entirely unnoticed, among the growing crowd on the street. As he made haste to get away, he looked back and smiled. By the time they discovered that the shuttle was vacant, he would already be well on his way to deviant space.

While the sneaky escape had bought Luc some time, he knew he had only one chance to escape Heaven before they shut space travel down. The trade ship left Araboth space port just moments before the hatch of the one-man shuttle was cut away. Once he was safely in space above Heaven, Lucifer sent a signal to the resistance: "The time is now! To save the Empire, we must leave Heaven."

Nearly 40 percent of the Angelic fleet followed him. Many rebels had already left Heaven in the weeks and months prior, in preparation for that very day. Of course, some courageous volunteers had remained behind, to gather information and take more active roles in the uprising, daring individuals who served at all levels of Heaven government, including the Seraphim, Cherubim, and Thrones. There were also many within the organization of the Holy Ghosts and quite a few within the ranks of the Angels.

Lucifer was their reluctant leader, and Hell was now the base headquarters of the resistance. In all, 666 worlds joined in the fight against the evil Empire. Because of their core beliefs, they were known as the Freewill Alliance, and the battle for the Empire had truly begun.

Benjamin Oneal

Chapter 39

"We are now at war against the traitors to the Empire. Lucifer, once the right hand of my blessed father, has betrayed us all," Jesus stated in his latest transmission to the Empire. "I am sorry to share this grim news, but this harsh treachery by my father's dearest friend was too much for Elohim to bear. Last night, he breathed his last." While Jesus pretended to be stricken, there was a hint of a smile on his face.

The outcry of grief echoed through the palace and in all parts of Heaven as soon as the transmission was broadcast. Lucifer openly cried as he watched the evil spawn of his best friend deliver the news; he knew Jesus had killed his own father. The final insult was the familiar object in Jesus' hand, the pentagonal rock, a souvenir of Luc's and Eli's childhoods. By holding that stone so visibly during the announcement, Jesus made it clear to Lucifer that he knew about their meeting and that it was Lucifer's fault that Elohim was now dead.

What Lucifer did not know was that Jesus would not allow Elohim to die. He wanted his father to live forever, to be always haunted by the knowledge that he, Jesus, was now God of the Empire. To that end, Jesus ordered his men to extradite Elohim to Nod, a prison planet that circled a lonely star in the Limbus sector of the galaxy.

"When you arrive, you will quickly recover from the drug

that has torn away at your health. You will be given the Factor, to ensure that you will live indefinitely, but you will never see Heaven again. You will spend eternity knowing that I have taken everything from you—your Empire, your freedom, and your life. On Nod, you will be forced to watch everyone around you grow old and die, year after year, century after century, millennium after millennium," Jesus cruelly said.

"I know you must wonder why I won't just kill you and get it over with. The answer is simple, dear Father. I want you to suffer. I want you to pay for all the years you chose that demon from Hell over me. I am your son, for Heaven's sake. You should have confided in me, not in Lucifer." As Jesus spoke the name, he growled.

"When you are safely stowed away on Nod, I will kill everyone you have ever considered a friend. I have already removed all the councilmembers who were so foolishly loyal to you, and I've rooted out the turncoats among the Angels. Know this, Elohim. Someday, I will visit you on that lonely planet and bring you the heads of Lucifer, his wife, and Sandel. Then, you will know how truly alone you are in the galaxy."

That disgusting thought made Jesus smile. He hoped Elohim comprehended all he said, even in his drug-addled mind.

"I must go now, Father, for I have your funeral to plan."

***

The memorial service for Elohim was monumental, and no one was the wiser to the fact that Elohim was still alive. The ruse went off without a hitch; all it required was a body about the same build as his father's, with a little facial reconstruction. The imposter corpse, a fallen Angel spy they had captured and killed, was encased in glass for all to view.

The Empire mourned the death of their beloved God and feared for their future. Not only did they have to bid farewell to a good God they loved but also to an era of peace and prosperity. Their world had changed significantly already under Jesus' iron-handed rule, and many began to silently pray that he would quickly follow his father to the grave.

Chapter 40

    Jesus quite enjoyed his life as the supreme being of the Empire, and he was too arrogant to believe it would ever come to an end. Jahoel, Seraphim Two, advised Jesus that it would be wise to protect Eden at all costs. Although Seraphim Two was thinking of himself and his possible succession to the throne, he knew his Lord would take this advice to heart.

    As much as Jesus wanted to believe he was immortal and invincible, he knew better. The fear of death became real to him as he watched many of the elderly die off, even those who were given the Factor. To that end, he was willing to break a promise his grandfather, Jehovah, had made to the Edenites so many years ago, when he offered them his protection but also promised to give them their privacy. Jesus, having no honor, ordered the takeover of Eden, and within just a few short weeks, he controlled production of the Factor.

    "We must protect Eden at all costs," he said, as if it were his idea.

    "Yes, milord. You are indeed wise," Jahoel brown-nosed, stroking God's ego. "I shall send ten ships immediately."

    "Only ten? You must send fifty!" Jesus ordered. "The Alliance can never control the immortality I deserve."

    "Once again, holy God, you see possible futures we mortals can only dream about." Jahoel resisted the urge to roll his eyes. He had intentionally suggested a low number of ships so Jesus could correct him.

That pivotal moment marked the beginning of the most terrible era in Eden's history. Jesus was determined to take control the production of the Trees of Life. He and the scientists he controlled began to tamper with the natural growth of the miraculous arbors, even though that went against everything the Edenites believed in; very early in their evolution, they had decided to be one with nature. The self-serving researchers put so much emphasis on the Trees of Life that the ecosystem that had created the tree was now at risk.

Another thing Jahoel suggested was to limit the amount of Edenites, for security reasons. Great vessels called arks arrived in the space above Eden, and soldiers forced hundreds of thousands of Edenites into shuttles that escorted them there. Some were taken to faraway star systems and left to fend for themselves. They also planted Tree of Life seeds on those planets and thousands of others, hoping to grow more fruit to produce the Factor. Jesus longed to be immortal and believed that was his right. The trees grew, but none bore the life-giving fruit. It was a grand experiment that could ultimately destroy the Factor itself.

Unfortunately, Jahoel was an evil muse. He whispered in his Lord's ear, telling him lascivious things. "Even though the arks carried an untold number of Edenites from their world to inhabit new planets, there are still far too many for us to control them," he said. Thus, Jesus ordered his soldiers to herd almost a quarter of the remaining Edenites and exile them as well. Since there were no inhabitable planets nearby, the soldiers were told to dispose of the unwanted Edenites any way they saw fit. Ultimately, the heartless Angels dropped them off on a barren planet and left them to die.

Jahoel was quite full of himself, and his newfound confidence coerced him into secretly fulfilling the sadistically lurid, sexual needs of Magdalene. Jesus had lost all desire for her after he had her entire family killed. He kept her as his queen, but she was not much more than a possession that he paraded around at his whim. Even though Jesus wanted nothing to do with her sexually, he would not tolerate his own Seraphim Two using her in that way. He was quite aware of her deviant sexual encounters with servants, many of whom lost their lives during the experience. That didn't bother him in the least, but Seraphim Two's indiscretion would be the ultimate betrayal, and result in an unspeakable punishment.

Jahoel had a wakeup call one day when Jesus took exception to Seraphim One, Nithael, who openly disagreed with his Lord's orders. Jesus beat him to death in front of the entire council. Jahoel knew his ascension to the rank of Seraphim One was a dangerous move, but with his ambition and Magdalene's pushing, he was ready to take the job.

Unfortunately for Jahoel, one of Nithael's relatives attempted to kill Jesus. While Jahoel cowered nearby, a Throne by the name of Zabkiel tackled the knife-wielding attacker, saving Jesus and receiving a life-threatening wound in the process. Jesus was so impressed by the heroic effort that he named Zabkiel Seraphim One, just before he was taken to the hospital. Jahoel wanted to argue with his Lord's decision, but he thought of the plight of Nithael and reluctantly accepted his life behind Zabkiel.

Zabkiel quickly became something of a friend to Jesus. As Seraphim One, he was able to temper down some of Jesus' insane commands. He helped Jesus realize that the disturbance of the natural processes on Eden could eventually lead to the end of the Factor. As a result, the forced evacuation ended, and the remaining Edenites were once again responsible for care of the trees. Zabkiel was also given the task of making the Factor available to even the enemies of the Empire, to prevent any jealous acts of destruction of the most valuable planet. Most importantly, he learned the skill of always making Jesus believe it was his idea.

Chapter 41

The war between the Empire and the Freewill Alliance waged on for thousands of years. Many Edenites who were taken from their home world and left to survive elsewhere forgot about their ancestral roots and their true origin. Stories of faraway places and travel among the stars soon became part of their mythology, the stuff of legends and nothing more. Most worlds that had not yet reached for the stars were unaware that war was happening all around them. They continued on with their lives, albeit much shorter due to the loss of the factor, in ignorant bliss.

Their obliviousness to the galactic war did not mean they were immune from other problems. Nearly all the planets who had reached out for others in their star systems were involved in conflicts, the same conflicts that had plagued millions of other worlds throughout the history of the galaxy. Some had won their own battles and were able to shine their lights brighter than the star that gave them life. Others lost and they faded into the darkness of obscurity. The battle they fought was between awareness and the Trinity of Evil: ignorance, apathy, and arrogance. Whether it was the killing of their planet through environmental devastation or violent wars in the name of power, the planets that could not intellectually grow past these ultimately destructive phases simply died.

One such planet was Earth. In galactic terms, the world

was very similar to Eden. In fact, many Earth inhabitants had once lived there. During the thousands of years since the Edenites were placed on Earth, and as the effect of the Factor began to wear off, the Earthlings started to live severely stunted lives. The oldest ones, like Methuselah, Jared, and Lamesh told stories of Eden, with its lush vegetation and beauty and the wondrous Tree of Life. However, as the ancients began to die off, they took the truth of their origin with time. Somewhere within that time, there were also stories told by the Romans and the Greeks of many gods. In time, the stories of God's or of where they came from were reduced to folklore, myths, and some were dismissed as fairytales.

About 2,000 years in, Jesus initiated his campaign to control the inhabitants of Earth through fear of an unseen God. To that end, he tasked his best storytellers to pen a book. The Bible, as it was known to the people of Earth, filled in the backstory of their origins and even included a tale about the Garden of Eden, where there was planted a Tree of Life.

That part rang true, as it echoed what the ancestors had said. As something of a joke, Jesus asked his writers to mention another tree in the garden, the Tree of Knowledge of Good and Evil. Since God supposedly guarded it with flaming swords, no one would ever know the truth. Of course, the flaming swords were symbolic of the battleships of the Empire fleet, and the truth was that the being who held their lives in his hand was not omniscient, omnipotent, or omnipresent.

To keep up the lie, Jesus also instructed his Angels to display the powers of this unseen God to the displaced Edenites. Angels donned magnificent wings and flew high in the air with the help of antigravity belts. Some, who were made in the image of Jesus himself, healed the sick with advanced medical techniques, proclaiming miracles. Most importantly were the weapons that blazed with the intensity of the sun. Those demonstrations brought the desired fear and awe they needed to control the masses.

Jesus ordered that versions of the Bible be placed on

thousands of worlds. Periodically, he sent Angels to reinforce the words that were written. With the introduction of the Bible, he provided a carefully tailored origin story, complete with his ascension to a supreme being.

For thousands of years, the Edenites spread throughout Earth, mingling with every race, until every human on the planet was a mutt, a mix of indigenous and Edenite. Any inclination to be one with nature was shoved aside, in the search for wealth and power.

During those centuries, great civilizations rose and fell. When Jesus first began his propaganda campaign, the Roman Empire dominated the world. His introduction was so instrumental that it actually changed the way the people of Earth described the passage of time. The Bible dated Jesus' birth at 4 BC (before Christ), and the start of the new era was AD (*anno domini*, the year of the Lord).

The Bible told the story of Jesus' life, the virgin birth, and miracles. When the powers of that time felt threatened, they put him on trial. Governor Marcus Pontius Pilatus, under the authority of Emperor Tiberius, gave the order for Jesus to be crucified. Some questioned why Jesus wanted his storytellers to mention his death, but it was only because it led to the opportunity to brag about his resurrection. At that point, he could no longer be thought of as a man. He would be known to all as the conqueror of death, a supreme being, a God to rule over everything.

From that point on, no one would ever see any part of God. They had to accept him on faith. That faith demanded that they gave their lives to an unseen God; otherwise, they would suffer eternal damnation, an eternity to burn in the depths of Hell. That fearmongering was very handy, as it allowed the powers-that-were and the Angels in key positions to control the mindless masses like stupid sheep being led to the slaughter.

Because of the great distances between the peoples of Earth, the world was soon divided into a multitude of nations and empires. Each kingdom held its own beliefs. God was known by many names: God, Allah, Buddha, Zeus, and Jesus Christ. Some societies worshiped many gods. It wasn't of great concern to Jesus, as long as they believed in something.

In time, the only reference to Eden was the biblical origin story. A growing number of people gave up believing in an all-powerful God and thought of the Garden of Eden as nonsense. As time passed, true believers were fewer and fewer. Since the Angels could no longer perform miracles, they had to work hard to perpetuate religious beliefs. The main goal of giving the Bible to the people of Earth was to make them more inclined to join Heaven when the galactic war hit their shores, and Jesus was fairly certain a majority of humans would do just that.

Chapter 42

No matter what the Earthlings believed in, what God they served, or where they lived, they thrived. As the Earth population grew, so did their need for land. Even though it required the clearing of trees and pushing many species of animals out of their natural habitats, Earth did its best to keep up. Along with the natural processes, nature was forced to contend with the consequences of mankind's behavior, but it did a miraculous job.

A time known as the Industrial Revolution started innocently enough, in 1712, with the invention of the first practical steam engine, the brainchild of an Earthling named Thomas Newcomen. From that time on, the people of Earth found a path of great technological innovation and growth in industry.

New kings took power positions as well. While they were not necessarily leaders of nations, through their wealth, a new underground power appeared. Because of the Industrial Revolution, environmental pollution increased exponentially. Factories spewed toxic chemicals into the air and water, all in the name of progress. Though many government officials saw the devastation, the people behind the people in charge knew profits would decline if the advancements ceased, so they made sure any votes went their way.

While the inhabitants of Earth seemed callous in regard to the natural world that surrounded them, they did show some forward thinking. They began to explore the planets around their star. They did not travel too far or look very far beyond, though, and they were still unaware of the galaxy that engulfed them, a galaxy teeming with life. Some were so shortsighted and arrogant that they believed Earth was home to the only intelligent life in the universe.

The Angels on Earth were in charge of watching the humans, but they really didn't care what happened as the inhabitants reached for other planets. They were also not concerned with the environment. Their sole mission was to make sure the planet would supply soldiers, the Empire, and the Angelic Army with its natural resources.

Chapter 43

One day, something totally unexpected happened. Two Angels sat in a windowless cinderblock building in the El Yunque Rainforest, some twenty-five miles southeast of San Juan, Puerto Rico. One was a soldier and the other a scientist. The fact that there was a structure there at all was odd; there were no other signs of civilization anywhere close. So, when the scientist released a scream of joy, it was not heard by human ears. It did silence the myriad of forest life for a moment, but the chorus of nature soon resumed.

Just one more test, and then I can send Heaven the news, he thought. The Trees of life, planted in the clearing in El Yunque, bore the fruit. The only question now was whether or not it contained the Factor. That evening, a second scream of joy silenced the orchestra in the nighttime foliage. Within minutes, though, nature's musical reached its previous crescendo.

"Are you sure, Gadreel?" the soldier asked.

"I am. It is a fact, Pravuil," the scientist answered, smiling broadly. "Earth is the only planet beyond Eden that is able to grow the Factor. I have run the test three times. This will change everything! Prepare to be famous, my friend."

"I will contact Heaven and tell them of your findings," Pravuil said, with a seriousness that didn't fit the occasion.

Gadreel looked at him strangely. "You do not sound so

happy about it. This is cause for celebration."

"I'm sorry," Pravuil said as he pointed his energy weapon at Gadreel and ended his life. He did not want to do it, but he was a soldier, and he had orders to follow.

Once he was certain the scientist was dead, Pravuil opened a secure line to Archangel Gabriel. "Sir, this is Sergeant Pravuil. The test was positive."

"Lock down the building and bring me Gadreel's research, along with some samples. We must get them to Heaven as soon as possible," Gabriel ordered.

***

Seraphim One, Zabkiel, watched as Gabriel and Michael, the two Archangels entered his Lord's private office and shut the door. Even though Jesus counted Zabkiel as a friend and confidant, there were things his Lord kept secret, even from him. He was beyond curious when he heard a joyous scream from Jesus; that only added to the questions Seraphim One would never ask his Lord. Over the years, he had learned that it was dangerous to question Jesus. Nevertheless, he knew that proper stroking of his Lord's ego would entice him to reveal his secrets eventually.

As Michael and Gabriel prepared to take their leave, Zabkiel heard something very curious: "I want four ships of the Angelic fleet sent there immediately. They are to know nothing about the true nature of their mission. They will be under your direct command, Michael. Only the three of us may know the truth," Jesus said, looking around as if to make sure no one was within earshot.

"What about Sergeant Pravuil, milord?" Gabriel asked.

"Can we trust him?" Jesus asked.

"He is one of my most trusted soldiers. He answers only to me," Gabriel offered.

"Very well then. Let him live…for now," Jesus said, with a smile in his voice.

Chapter 44

While Jesus dispatched four of his battleships to patrol Earth, the Freewill Alliance was already planning their next assault on the Empire. The Purgatorian sector of the galaxy bordered Alliance space. Although that sector was controlled by the Empire, they had done surprisingly little to develop it, so it was the least guarded by the Angelic fleet.

Many worlds within the Purgatorian sector had reached out to the Alliance for help. The Alliance did what they could, but the Empire still held dominion. Lucifer and his council decided it was best to send scouts, so they could nail down the locations of the Angelic fleet and gauge what they were up against. Two of Lucifer's own sons, Saleos and Sandel, were the first to volunteer for the dangerous mission.

The three scouts dropped out of deviant space near uninhabited Planet R-1474 in the Dachus star system, not completely cloaked but traveling in stealth mode. They were all but invisible and would not be spotted unless someone was actually looking for them and knew precisely where to look. They parked in space above the third moon of R-1474, well hidden from any prying eyes.

There was one inhabitable planet in the Dachus system. Corsa was still a few years away from exploring their solar system, so there was no reason for the Empire to leave a ship nearby. It was merely a starting point, and once that mission was complete, it would return; from that location, they could enter deviant space undetected.

For the next three months, three scout ships were strategically situated to document the Empire's strengths and weaknesses throughout Purgatorian space. Sandel finished his assignment early and waited in a safe place adjacent to the moon where it all began. Two days later, his brother Saleos joined him, and the two immediately shared the important data they'd collected. It was crucial that the intel was passed on to the Freewill Alliance right away, and both were made aware of all information, in case only one of the scouts made it home.

Ishim, the third scout had not yet returned, and this was a bit worrisome, since he was two days late.

"Saleos, have you heard from Ishim?" Sandel asked.

"No, and that's a little troubling. His was the smallest sector," Saleos said, the concern thick in his voice.

"Hmm. Let's give him one more day. If he doesn't turn up by then, I want you to head back home with the intel we've gathered," Sandel advised.

"I really don't think it's safe to leave you—" Saleos started, only to be interrupted by a frantic Ishim.

"They're right on my tail! We have to move…now! Go! Go! Go!" Ishim shouted, as he dropped out of deviant space.

Saleos and Sandel wasted no time in ignoring his warning and heading straight into the fray to defend him. Within seconds, they had caught up to the third scout ship.

Sandel's scanners picked up five Angelic battleships dropping out of deviant space and moving toward them in a hurry. "Data download!" he shouted.

While doing their best to avoid energy blasts from the battle cruisers, they began downloading. The battle cruisers were closing the distance rapidly, but they could not afford to jump to deviant space until the download was complete. Not only that, but neither Sandel nor Saleos could bear to desert Ishim. Their shields would help for a while, but they were no match for the firepower of the battleships.

Rise of the Fallen

Finally, the download completed, and the three scouts prepared to enter deviant space.

"Jump now!" Sandel shouted.

With the other two in tow, Sandel led the way. They knew they could not possibly outrun the battle cruisers, but if they could make it to their next jump point, there was a good chance of escape. Also working in their favor was that it was nearly impossible to track and fire weapons accurately in deviant space.

Unfortunately, a wayward energy blast clipped Ishim's scout ship. As they entered normal space, Sandel tried to get a read on the location of the enemy ships, but before he could, their forward guns ripped white-hot lines of destructive force through the star-studded blanket of the cosmos before them.

The scouts' only chance of survival was to avoid irreparable damage before they could make the next jump. Because they were much smaller than the battle cruisers, the scout ships were much faster and more maneuverable. That said, they were also outsized, outgunned, outmanned, and outnumbered. With five battle cruisers on their tails, it was close to impossible to avoid taking on damage.

"My shields are failing, and I can't—"

That was the last message Sandel and Saleos heard from poor Ishim before a brutal energy blast sliced through his ship.

"Ishim!" Sandel screamed.

"He's gone, Sandel. We need to jump...now," Saleos sadly stated.

"I'm hit, too, Saleos," Sandel confessed. "It will be a moment before I can make the jump. You go ahead and get that data back to the Alliance, no matter what!"

"No way, big Brother. I will not leave you," Saleos said with conviction.

"The battle cruisers are locked on to me. Go, for the sake of the mission," Sandel implored.

"Just...try to play dead. I love you, Sandel." With that

and a small sob, Saleos skillfully maneuvered his scout ship between Sandel and the ion-charged particle beam.

Sandel watched in horror as his younger brother boiled away in space, reduced very quickly to a glowing fizzle. When the indicator for the jump engine suddenly flashed, he knew he had no time to mourn the loss. If he was to complete his mission and prevent the deaths of Ishim and Saleos from being meaningless, he had to deliver the surveillance they had gathered in the Purgatorian.

Sandel's crippled vessel was certainly not functioning at 100 percent, but it made the jump. Cascading failures in almost every part of the ship forced him back into normal space, and the battle cruisers followed, firing their arsenal. Sandel remembered what his brother had told him, but he had to act fast. As the scout ship buffeted from force of the energy beams against his failing shields, he rigged a small explosion and rode the wave of the blast. He floated there, allowing no indication of life. When the space around him settled down and all seemed quiet, he donned his helmet and released the atmosphere from the ship. The rush of air caused his scout vessel to slowly spin. He wasn't sure they would notice, but to sell the playing-dead scheme, he had to go all the way.

As dizzy and nauseous as he was, Sandel made no attempt to control the ship in any way. Instead, he allowed himself to drift aimlessly through the zero gravity of space. He was grateful for his training, which had taught him to slow his breathing and other bodily functions. He only hoped that the five battle cruisers would soon move back into deviant space, believing the scout ship was now nothing more than useless space debris.

For the next two hours, he continued the fiction. With the enemies parked nearby, there was nothing he could do but wait and think. The good news was that he was still alive, but his thoughts often traveled to the gut-wrenching loss of his friend Ishim and his older brother Saleos. *They died saving my life,* he struggled to fathom. It was the longest 120 minutes he'd ever spent, and he worried the whole time that one of those cruisers would ultimately decide they had a civic duty to clean up after themselves and obliterate him completely.

His worst fear came true when a blast tore through the space in front of him. A second blast hit his front end, causing his vessel to spin even faster. He braced for a third blow, but it never came. Soon after, the quintet of battle cruisers disappeared into the void.

Sandel stopped the scout ship from spinning and took a second to shake off the dizziness. "How dare they use me for target practice!" he mumbled to himself as his head continued to spin. He knew he desperately needed to figure out where he was, because his ship would likely not make it all the way back to Alliance space after sustaining such damage. His main objective was to find somewhere to land, so he could make the necessary repairs.

His instruments indicated that he was near Star T-75513. *If I only use the required systems, I might just reach an inhabitable planet in one piece,* he told himself. It took almost a day to find a place, and he detected Angelic battle cruisers nearby, but he had no other choice but to land. Otherwise, he would be doomed to die in the vacuum of space, with his tattered scout vessel for a tomb.

The dark side of the planet satellite was his best option. Luckily, the moon was not beholden to any natural rotation, so the dark side stayed that way. He set the ship down in one of the deeper craters and began making adjustments he hoped would keep his ship in usable condition until he returned. He had no way of knowing if he could find the necessary supplies there, but he had to try. Even more frightening, since he had had to use some of the oxygen in his suit while he played dead, he was not certain if enough remained, but it was his only chance to repair his ship and get back to Hell.

Once he shut down all nonessential systems, Sandel again donned his helmet and his antigravity belt and disembarked. Pushing against the moon, he soon was high enough to see the curve of the horizon. He pushed harder, and his speed increased. As he left the dark side, the beautiful, blue-green planet came into view, so reminiscent of Hell that it made him homesick.

Chapter 45

Sandel pushed hard against the moon, and his speed increased. If his calculations were correct, he would reach T-75513 within three galactic days. He would have to hibernate for most of it, to save as much oxygen as he could. Once he was at an optimal speed, he took one last look at the swirling aquamarine orb, and then activated the hibernation sequence.

As he went into hibernation, in a kind of waking sleep, his heart slowed, and his breathing was at the bare minimum. The dreams began immediately. First, grim visions of his brother flashed in his mind, specifically the fatal energy beam and the resulting explosion that killed him. The terror of that moment tore at his soul. Next, thoughts of his father, his mission, and his duty laid heavily on him. Finally, he thought of his wife Lilith and his children, Naberius and Deumos. Even though it was only something of a waking dream, the uncertainty of whether or not he would ever see them again made his tears flow. Unfortunately, the nightmarish visions seemed to cycle around, taunting him again and again.

The torture of his dreams seemed to go on forever, so he was quite relieved when he heard the distant sound of his alarm. The hibernation sequence was ending, but something was wrong. He couldn't seem to catch a full breath.

Benjamin Oneal

He needed to concentrate to slow his descent into the exosphere of the planet that loomed large before him, for it would have been nothing short of disaster to enter the atmosphere at his present speed. He pushed, then slowed. He pushed again, knowing that the next and final push would put him at optimum speed to approach the planet.

His breathing continued to be problematic, especially since he had to focus on controlling his plummet to the planet. He hoped the air would be breathable once he reached the surface, but it would be a while before he was at that point. As the moved through the exosphere, friction caused his body shield to glow. Although the atmosphere burned hot all around him, Sandel was still quite comfortable.

Once the friction subsided and he slowed his descent, he was able to see clearly again. It was truly a beautiful world, he surmised. He still had some trouble concentrating, but he could see that it was a truly beautiful world. He shook his head, hoping to clear the growing fog. It was imperative that he remained focused, but at that altitude, the air was still too thin to breathe. He began to lose consciousness, and his next push against the planet became erratic. Sandel was still too high when he passed out completely.

Precisely then, a professor of religious studies walked through the woods in Kentucky, thinking about the son and wife he'd recently lost to a tragic accident. He watched in growing horror as a figure dropped from the sky and hit the ground not far from where he stood. *An Angel?* he wondered; sure he had seen a halo. With that strange thought on his mind, Justin Grant ran in the direction of the fallen Angel, not knowing what he would find, but somehow knowing his life was about to change...

Made in the USA
Middletown, DE
04 January 2025